WHATEVER YOU SAY, SAY NOTHING

WHATEVER YOU SAY, SAY NOTHING

Julian Bell

ISBN-13: 9781518824463

For Jean and Alice

CHAPTER ONE

On the morning when Aisling came Harry Lovegrove woke knowing he couldn't stand any more. The bedroom stank of the stale breath of his sleeping wife, because she never left her bed and she would not let him open the window. The bitter stench of her urine rose up from under the bed. She could never get as far as the lavatory; it was as much as she could do to drag herself out of bed and squat over the chamberpot. Sometimes he had to help her even with that. He looked across at her. A great weight seemed to press her down, and her eyes were filled with tears. The skin on her face was stretched as if there was not enough to go round. On a plate by her bed a dollop of cold scrambled egg, burnt a little at the edges because last night Harry had left it too long in the pan, lay abandoned on a limp slice of toast. She's twenty-five, he thought, and she looks seventy. My wife is dying by her own hand, and I don't love her any more. I can't go on like this.

'Don't leave me, Harry,' she said, as soon as she saw he was awake.

The dust rose chokingly up from the floorboards and the fetid air in the house hung as heavy as Harry's thoughts.

It had been like this all week. He half wished it would rain, even though it was a rare and remarkable day in Dublin when it didn't rain, never mind a week. It was all clear to him now. Emily would never get better. He could not look after her. His marriage was a sham. Time for action. He thought of the pamphlet locked in his desk that he had read many times late at night, secretly and urgently, like a dirty book. *St Mary's House, Kingstown. Discreet, attentive care for women with nervous complaints. Our staff of dedicated nurses and highly trained doctors ensure that patients receive an irreproachable level of treatment. Sea air and supervised walks on the beach assist recovery. Visiting hours every Saturday from two till four pm. Discounted payment for long term residents.* She would be properly looked after. It was the kindest thing to do. He would place a telephone call from his office in the Castle that morning, make arrangements. Then he would move into a room in a boarding house and live as a bachelor. He couldn't afford the rent for the house at the same time as the fees for the home; he would only just have enough left over for the boarding house. But he felt relieved to have made the decision at last.

'I'm not going to leave you, Emily,' he said, squeezing her wrist as her arm lay flopped like a dead fish across the bedsheets. He sat up. Outside the birds were singing, and through the window he saw a young girl in a white dress on the other side of the street, arm in arm with a soldier. He could see her laughing at something the soldier was telling her, but because the window was closed, he could not hear her. Sometimes Harry felt he could hardly breathe and he longed to fling the window open, especially when he woke sweating with nightmares of France, of limbless men screaming at him out of faces covered with blood, but Emily would never let him.

'I worry about you, Harry,' she said.

'I know you do. But don't. I know how to look after myself. I survived France. I'll survive this.'

'Those Irishmen. They all want to kill us. They all have guns. I hear them. I heard a man being shot in the street.' That was when she had made him put a lock on the window.

'It was six weeks ago.'

'It happens most days. I read about the shootings in your newspaper.'

'You shouldn't read the *Irish Times*. It only upsets you.'

'How else will I know what's going on? I never go out, and you never tell me anything. It's all there. It's horrible. Every day, men are being shot in the street, murdered in front of their wives and children. We're at war.'

'The war finished a year and a half ago.'

'The war with the Germans, maybe. Not the one with the Irish.'

'Dublin isn't France.'

'How do you know they won't just walk through that door and kill you and me in our bed?'

He stroked her face.

'That won't happen, I promise. Emily, dearest, you should have eaten some of the egg last night, or at least the toast, you need to –'

'No. No. I can't. You can't make me.'

He sighed impatiently, and got out of bed. The floor was covered with piles of his filthy laundry, shirts, underpants, socks. He rifled through one pile, tossing things over his shoulder, until he found a clean pair of underpants. Christ, this house was a tip. It was a disgrace for a soldier to live like this. Normally, he was almost obsessively neat and tidy; his office at the Castle was famously precise. But somehow Emily sucked all the energy out of the room, out of the whole house, just by being there, and there was none left for him to keep it in order.

'Dearest, I have to go to the Castle now,' he said as he retrieved a shirt from a second pile, and began rummaging in a third for trousers. I will see you tonight.'

'You'll be shot on the way.'

'I won't. I have a pistol, and I know how to use it.'

'They can shoot you in the back, before you know it.'

'I will be careful. Dearest, while I am out –'

There was a knock at the door, downstairs. Who? Tradesmen never came in the week. The grocer and the baker delivered on Saturday mornings.

'Who's that?' said Emily. 'Is it a gunman, come to kill us?'

'It'll be the baker's boy.'

He finished dressing quickly. He was glad to get out of the overheated stench of the bedroom. It would be women begging for money for one of their missions. He would tell them he was a Protestant and send them away. He couldn't afford to be generous in his soon to be changed circumstances.

He opened the door. There was a woman standing on the doorstep. His first thought was that she was nothing like Emily; that she was the very opposite of his wife in every respect. It was a thought that he would come back to often in the weeks ahead, weeks when she would occupy his thoughts like an invading army that could not be got rid of, that had to be accommodated. She stood straight and strong, and she looked him directly in the eye, with none of the suspicion and evasion he had grown used to since he had come to Ireland. She had thick, generous auburn hair down to her shoulders where Emily's was thin and tentative. Emily barely looked at him these days, but this woman had a determined face, one that would shoulder difficulties out of the way. She was carrying a small suitcase, holding onto it tight as if she was sure he would try to take it off her. When she spoke, she seemed to be accusing him of something.

'Major Lovegrove?' she said.

'Yes. Can I help you?'

'I've come about the job.'

'What job?'

'Housemaid.'

'Yes. Of course. But the advertisement's been running since March, and - '

'So you have a maid now?'

'No. No, I don't.'

'Can I come in?'

'Yes, please do.'

She stepped past him into the house. She seemed to assume the job was hers.

He took her into the kitchen, steering her through the three months' copies of the *Irish Times* heaped in the hall that he had not got round to throwing away. She picked a crumpled tea towel, bearing the stains of the failed scrambled eggs, off the chair he offered her, and held it out to him. He apologised and put it on top of the pile of plates next to the sink.

He ran his hand over the work surface, as if he could sweep away its filth, but instead the grease from the eggs made the crumbs from the toast stick to his hand. He wiped his hands on the filthy tea towel, his back to her, feeling her rebuke as if she was his mother and he was a slovenly little boy.

'So,' he said, sitting opposite her.

'So,' she said. 'You look as if you'll be needing a maid, yourself.'

'I am.'

'I've heard your wife is unwell.'

'She is. How did you ...' But he knew how. He hadn't had a maid for three months, ever since Emily had threatened Caitlin, the last one, with a knife. Caitlin ran a better intelligence network than the British Army; no one would come near the place now.

'Nerves, is it?'

'I suppose you could say that.'

'Well sure living in a rubbish heap isn't going to make her better.'

He felt his face grow hot. Knowing that she could see him blush was almost as shameful as what made him blush.

'A man on his own,' he said. 'It's difficult, running a whole house.'

'After my Mam died, my Da ran an entire boarding house by himself with twelve bedrooms not counting our own. The day after the funeral he was back serving breakfast. Mind you, he had me to help.'

She was sitting up straight in the chair. He realised he was slouching, in a most unmilitary way, and scrambled to correct himself.

'How old were you when your mother died?'

'Fourteen.'

Fourteen. What was he doing when he was fourteen? Botching Latin prep and stealing Jenkins Minor's cocoa. He couldn't even get into the Second Eleven that year. This was quite a woman.

'It was three days after the war with Germany started,' she added.

'I had just got married myself when the war broke out,' he said, trying to re-establish himself. 'My honeymoon was cut short by it.' Cut short, too, he remembered, by a hysterical attack of crying by Emily when she heard the news. Other women courageously supported their men and their country; not Emily.

'A large number of my friends were killed in that war,' said the woman. 'Excepting the ones that refused to fight in it.'

Refused to fight in it. That was a luxury the Irish had. Sergeant Irving, he remembered, had been the son of a fisherman from Cromer who used to rise with the sun to load the thick tangle of nets onto his father's boat. Harry had seen his head blown off by a shell, and felt the flesh and the bone slap him in the face, and watched his brains drip down the front of his uniform onto his shoes. Private Parks used to work in the stables on Harry's father's farm, mucking out every morning with a whistled tune and an off colour joke. Harry had held him by the shoulders as he screamed for his mother, and then forced him forward at gunpoint. Ten yards later his stomach was ripped open by bullets and his insides emptied into the mud. Harry had listened to Captain

Thompson, son of the vicar who had married him and Emily, moan up and down all night as he died slowly ninety yards from him, tangled in barbed wire, both his legs blown off at the knees. Harry had seen the hands of drowned men he didn't know, or would no longer recognise if he did know them, reaching for him out of the churned ground. Harry had walked straight at a dozen machine guns firing at the tops of their voices, waiting for the bullets to rip through him, half wanting them to, but they did not. Harry had survived the war, but the men who hadn't loomed at him in his fitful sleeps, bursting unannounced into his dreams. Who was this woman to talk to him about the war?

'A large number of my friends were killed too,' he said. 'I watched most of them die in front of me.'

'Why did they go to the war, these friends of yours?' she said.

He felt his voice rise.

'Because they loved their country.'

'That's exactly why my friends didn't go.'

She was glaring at him, as if she was angry. It felt as if an argument was about to start. It had been a long time since he had had an argument with a woman; Emily no longer had the strength. Caitlin had never been like this. Caitlin had probably hated him for being English too, but she would never have said it to his face. And yet, Harry found, he liked this woman for standing up to him. He had what some of his brother officers thought was a weakness, and the shrewder ones knew was a strength; he liked the men under him to speak their minds, to have opinions of their own, even if they disagreed with him. He thought it made for better soldiering. He tried to calm matters down by getting back to the job in hand.

'You've not told me about your experience, Miss ....'

'O'Flaherty. Aisling O'Flaherty. I have, as a matter of fact. I've run a boarding house with my Da these last six years. Doing everything. Cooking, cleaning, washing, buying for it, accounts even. Spick and span,' she added, tossing a disapproving look at the sink. 'Men came from all over Connemara to stay with us,' she went on. 'All over Ireland. We had an American once. And we've had English, too. English officers. So I know what they're like. What you're like.'

She put her head to one side as if she was sizing him up, deciding if he was up to scratch.

'And you have a reference? From your employer?'

'From my Da?'

'Well, yes. If he's been your only employer.'

She clutched her shawl tighter to her. He saw tears well in her eyes; but she kept looking at him.

'My Da'll be writing no references.'

'Why not?'

'He's dead.'

'I'm sorry. How ...'

'There was a fire at our house. He died in it. I got out. But there was nothing left. So I thought, I'll come to Dublin. Start again.'

'And you have nothing, then? No proof of who you are or what you've been doing?'

'Nothing but what I've got in this suitcase,' she said. 'This is all that I could grab from the fire. But what I have,

Major Lovegrove, is what I can do. Do for you. Now, and in time to come.'

He felt a great sense of relief at being in his house with a woman who was not ill and who could speak up for herself. And the house felt different with her in it. It felt as if it might yet be restored to order; that it might still be possible for him to go on living in it. He didn't want to live in one room in a boarding house. He wanted to live with a woman who could make a home.

'I think you'd better meet my wife,' he said.

CHAPTER TWO

She shouldn't have talked like that, thought Aisling, as Major Lovegrove took her up the stairs, past the prints of Norfolk seascapes and the cathedral at Norwich. It was no way to talk to a man you wanted to give you a job, especially not when you were as desperate for a job as she was. And yet she hadn't been able to stop herself. It was like it was Da talking through her. He'd spoken like that to the recruiting sergeant who'd come to Clifden to take Irish boys to the war with Germany, and ended up nearly getting himself arrested. But sure he'd always taught her to stand up for herself. At least she'd managed not to cry too obviously when he'd asked her about Da; that was getting better. The whole thing altogether didn't seem to have put your man off. It looked like he wanted her, if he was introducing her to his wife. And, for all he was English, she had to admit she liked it that he'd let her speak straight to him, the same way Da always did. Anyways, she couldn't afford to be choosy any more. Two weeks she'd been in Dublin and not a sniff of work, with her having no reference to show. Her money had nearly run out. Much longer, and she'd be out on the streets. What if his wife did take a knife to her like Caitlin had said she would? Why would that matter after what had happened back in Clifden?

The Black and Tans - the scourings of English jails, murderers and rapists set free before their time to terrorise the Irish - had come to Clifden in the middle of the night, when no Christian soul was awake. It had been a glorious summer's day the day before, of the sort you didn't see so often, one when the very trees and hedgerows themselves seemed to sing with joy at being alive. After Aisling had served dinner to the guests at the boarding house and Da had done his accounts and gone out to O'Shea's, she had sat up late in Da's office typing reports for the Clifden branch of the Irish Republican Army, like she did most nights. She catalogued the guns received the week before from Dublin and now held in Flanagan's loft, and recorded the shooting of another policeman in Ballyconneely. As like as not it was Da that had done it; she'd heard him come back late that night. But she didn't know, didn't want to know. Though she attended the meetings in Flanagan's back room every Thursday night, and was known to have plenty to say for herself, the operational decisions were made in the field. That was as it should be. Da looked in on her when he came back like he always did, and gave her chapter and verse on the word from O'Shea's. O'Donoghue was after notching Flanagan up by a shilling, but Flanagan would none of it, and O'Donoghue would be singing to himself as Flanagan could get all he needed from your man Healy in Limerick now who was willing to make the journey, only Da hoped that O'Donoghue would swallow defeat as he was a good fellow who stayed at the boarding house four times a year and he'd be loath to lose him; Healy was travelling in pots and pans now – spades were no more for him since he'd fallen out with the Limerick lot, which was no surprise, given the temper on him – but he'd have an uphill walk with Corrigan, who was wedded to the old man and a slow fella for change; Sheehan, they said now, was on the point of being shown the door by his wife, on account of certain activities of his on the road which had to do with Mrs Coogan's daughter leaving town.

'It's as well you were never a priest, Da,' she told him. 'No secret of the confessional would be safe with you.'

'Sure and wouldn't I be without you if I had been?' he said, and he kissed her on the top of her head and squeezed her from behind like he did, his strong, hairy arms pressing into her light summer dress. A tentative breeze made its way into the office from the little window up high and cooled her face. She felt intensely happy. She wanted to go on like this, her and Da, running the boarding house and fighting the English together, knowing what everyone in Clifden did or said before they did it or said it, forever. Da went to bed, and she finished her report and tied it up with a treasury tag in a brown manila folder. She took it up to her room and put it under the mattress of her bed with the others like Flanagan had told her to. She undressed and knelt by her bed, took Mam's rosary in her hands and said a prayer for Mam's soul and a prayer for Da and a prayer for Ireland and a prayer for herself, and then she blessed herself and got into bed. It would be another warm day tomorrow; they'd want to open all the windows. There was a party of six come from Galway for the fair at Ballyconneely, so she would have her work cut out at breakfast, as those farmers were always after having extra bacon. Maybe later she'd have a walk with Sinead by the sea. Since Sinead had been walking out with Conor, she'd been awful stand-offish with Aisling. Aisling thought maybe Sinead was afraid she might be jealous. She needed to tell her that she didn't want a fella; Da was enough for her. But she didn't know how to tell Sinead that. Well, she'd find a way. She heard Da snoring next door as she drifted off to sleep. Hearing him snore always helped her sleep; it was a peaceful sound.

Four hours later, the Tans thrust themselves into her dreams. They were kicking in the front door. Kick, kick, kick, the door defiant, resisting, holding out against the odds. She sat up in bed. Suddenly, she felt sharp, concentrated, like a gun cocked and pointed, ready. She had known this time would come, Flanagan had told them it would, and now it was here at last. She felt a strange thrill run through her as she dressed automatically in the moonlight. With the last kick, the door gave in. She was on the landing now. English boots were clumping through the hall, English guns were sprayed out in all directions, half seen in the moonlight like an obscene growth, poking into the dining room, rattling round Da's office, emptying the drawers, throwing the papers on the floor, clattering through the kitchen, smashing a plate or three, thrusting up the stairs. Da was on the landing, too, also dressed, and the guests were coming out of their rooms in their pyjamas. Da walked up to Aisling swiftly and silently. He put his mouth close to her ear.

'The files. Burn them.'

Aisling slipped back into her room and closed the door behind her carefully, hoping the soldiers hadn't seen her. She threw back the sheets, and thrust her hand under the mattress. The covers of the files were rough against her hands as she dragged them out; they spilled and sprayed onto the floor, washing up against her knees. Everything they had done in the last four years, ever since the Easter Rising of 1916 had got them all going, was in these files; the dates, the names, the places. It was coming to a head. Things would be resolved tonight, one way or another. Maybe she would die for Ireland, and then she would be with Mam in Heaven. She heard two men taking turns to shout at Da on the landing.

'Where are the papers?'

'Would that be the *Clifden Post* you'd be talking about? I've not yet thrown out yesterday's if it's the racing results you're after.'

A slap, which Aisling winced at as she heard it.

'Fucking watch your lip, Paddy. Where are the papers? The Fenian papers?'

'I don't have any papers. Only my accounts for the boarding house, which you'll find are in good order. I pay my tax regular.'

'Fucking liar. We know they're here. Your mate McManus told us when we threatened his wife and kid. Three coppers dead. Three! What are you going to do about that?'

'I'm a boarding house owner. Nothing more. I've entertained officers of the British Army in my time. Fine guests, they are, too. But you'll see my current guests have been disturbed by you, and they need their sleep, as they've work in the morning.'

'Fucking Paddy liar. Where are the fucking papers?'

Aisling shepherded the files into a pile in the middle of the floor. There was enough moonlight through the window for her to find the matches by her bed. She wasn't feeling afraid. She was thinking only about the files and how to burn them without burning the house down. She felt strangely excited to be a soldier now it was happening at last. She couldn't wait to see how proud Da would be of her.

The door flew open. One of the soldiers had Da's arm behind his back. Another was holding a pistol to his head. With his other hand he shone a torch on the pile of files on the floor.

'What the fuck does that look like, Paddy?' he said.

'Burn them, Aisling,' said Da. 'Now.'

She wanted to go and drag Da away, take a bullet for him if she had to. But she also wanted to be a soldier, for Da and for Ireland. She picked up the matches, lit one, put it under one file, then carried the flame to another file, then another. The paper burnt fast. The soldier holding Da let go and jumped forward to snatch some files. Da pulled him back, took him by the shoulders, and kneed him between the legs. The soldier doubled up in pain. Good on you, Da, thought Aisling. That gave the flames long enough to reach the top of the pile. Soon, all the files were twisting in the fire, turning the words Aisling had typed black, crumbling, unreadable. They'd won.

'Right, Paddy,' said the other soldier.

He held his pistol to the back of Da's head and fired. The top half of Da's face flew out. Some of it splattered onto the face of the Madonna on the wall over Aisling's dressing table and the rest of it landed on the back of the doubled up soldier. Da fell forward, flat. Aisling felt a surge of hatred stronger than anything she'd ever felt before in her life, as if she herself was catching fire. She wanted to jump onto the soldier, grab his gun, kill him with it, then take the gun and kill all the other soldiers one by one, but the fire from the files had spread across the room, making a barrier between her and the soldiers.

'Finish her off and all!' said the soldier Da had kicked, now standing up, rubbing his crotch.

The soldier raised his pistol and pointed it at Aisling through the flames. She took a deep breath and blessed herself and said an act of contrition. She was ready. She would leap into Mam and Da's arms in Heaven. Then the soldier lowered his pistol.

'No,' he said. 'She wants to burn evidence, let's burn her. And while we're at it let's burn the whole fucking town. It's a nest of Fenians that needs smoking out. We'll teach them a lesson.'

'I want to get the bitch first,' said the man Da had kicked. 'Show her her Dad hasn't finished me. Show her my parts are still in working order.'

Aisling looked at the sergeant through a wall of fire. If he came for her, she'd push him into the fire and make him burn, like he'd burn in Hell soon.

'She's going nowhere,' said the soldier with the pistol. 'Leave her, Sergeant. Get the petrol cans from the lorry. That's an order.'

They went out, the sergeant kicking Da's body as he passed him.

Aisling felt the heat scorch her as the flames grew. They were reaching to the ceiling now. The smoke was making her choke and her eyes water. She could see Da's trousers burning. The flames had caught his hair, which was matted with blood and brains. His hair was thick and dark and when she was little she'd loved to sit on his lap and run her hands through it. He was a beautiful man, her Da, a beautiful man.

She reached under her bed and took out the suitcase Flanagan had told them all to keep packed and ready in case they needed to leave in a hurry. In it was a change of clothing, three slices of ham wrapped in greaseproof paper, half a loaf, and two pound notes. She took Mam's rosary off the bedpost where she kept it, kissed the cross, and put it in the pocket of her skirt. She opened the window to the street and threw out the suitcase. It clattered on the cobbles below, and spun a few yards across towards the church opposite. She stood on the window sill and blessed herself. It was now or never. She had to jump, or she would burn to death. She could feel the heat of the flames on her back. She jumped, landed on the street with a sharp jar to her knees, and rolled forward, banging her head on the ground. When she got up she found she could still walk, and had nothing more than a bruise on her forehead. She heard the soldiers inside the boarding house shouting orders about petrol and matches. She had to get away before they shot her, as they surely would. Maybe she could hide at the Flanagans' house till the soldiers had gone. She didn't feel afraid, she found; she just thought about the next thing to do. She ran down the street to the statue of Jesus and Mary, and turned towards the Flanagans' house. It was on fire too, the flames coming out of all three stories, licking at the night air. There were half a dozen soldiers in the street. Three of them were firing intermittently into the house. 'Come out, Paddy, you fucking coward,' one of them shouted. Sinead would be burning to death in there. She wished she'd been nicer to her, wished she'd been a better friend. She shouldn't have said that thing about Conor and his spots. It was too late now.

She looked back at her own house. The flames from her room were coming out of the open window now, and the dining room was roaring with flames, lighting up the street. The glass of the big window shattered, spraying and spitting onto the pavement. The guests were all out in the street in their pyjamas, herded together like sheep, three soldiers pointing guns at them. She saw Father Garvey come out of the presbytery in his night shirt and remonstrate with the soldier who looked like he was in charge. He was waving his arms in big circles in the way he did when he was angry in sermons. The soldier took out a pistol and shot Father Garvey in the head. Father Garvey fell back onto the pavement, his body sprawled in the gutter. Father Garvey, who'd baptised her and taught her her catechism. Father Garvey who'd said Mass in the church opposite her house every Sunday of her life. Father Garvey who'd buried Mam. He was a cantankerous old so and so, and they'd come dangerously close to falling out more than once with her being so outspoken, but he was the only priest she'd ever known. Another piece of her world gone, the world that was burning up before her eyes.

She fumbled in her pocket for Mam's rosary, took a handful of beads and clenched them in her fist. She wanted to be a little girl again, to be sitting in the kitchen eating Mam's fry and listening to Da's stories. For a moment she thought of walking up to the soldier and asking him to shoot her, so that she could be in Heaven with Mam and Da and Father Garvey, all together. But Da wouldn't want that. He'd want his girl to carry on his work, just as she'd carried on Mam's work when Mam had died.

In the warm, close night, she turned down the Galway road and ran, faster and faster, her suitcase banging against her legs, sweat breaking out on her forehead and dripping down into her eyes where it mingled with her tears. In snatched glances over her shoulder, she saw the destruction of Clifden. The Black and Tans were setting light to every third building and letting the fire do the rest. The flames rose up from house after house and shop after shop making the sky almost as bright as day. She could hear shots, and Englishmen's and Irishmen's voices shouting and women crying and some of them screaming. The windows were shattering in O'Shea's; Flanagan's roof was falling in; they were even smashing the windows of the church. She felt as if the inside was being ripped out of her. Every day and week and month of her twenty years on earth had been spent in that town, every man and woman and child she had ever known was from that town. She had nothing and no one now, except herself, the clothes she stood up in, some ham and some bread, two pounds and Mam's rosary. She felt as if she was naked, stripped before the night. But she kept running. She ran from the fire and the shouts and the bullets of the murderous English; she ran from the place where her mother lay buried and her father lay burning. But Mam and

Da were still with her, both of them. They would always be with her.

She spoke to Da in her head now, as she had often done in the last two weeks. Why should I be afraid of a sick woman? It gave her courage as Major Lovegrove ushered her into the bedroom. And by God the woman was sick. That was clear the minute Aisling clapped eyes on her, sprawled in the big brass bed in the corner. One of Da's speeches in Flanagan's back room, repeated almost monthly, consisted of his own grandmother's stories of the Famine, the English wilfully locking up whole barns full of corn for the sake of a few shillings of profit while men and women and children were lying down and dying in the fields, their skin all stretched thin as paper and their bones sticking out. Looking now at Emily's wasted body pinned to the bed, Aisling thought of Da's story. Once they starved us and now they're starving themselves. Is it that she feels guilty for what her race has done? And the room itself stank to high heaven, of sweat and stale urine and the unwashed clothes piled up in the corners as if they'd been thrown there in a rage. Not content with locking up and torturing the Irish, they now had to do it to their own women. Had neither of them thought of opening a window in here?

'Emily, dearest,' said Harry. 'This is Aisling. She's come to look after us.'

'Caitlin?' said Emily.

'No. Not Caitlin. Aisling. A new girl.'

'Caitlin was a wicked, conniving girl. She wanted to steal you away from me.'

'This is Aisling, dearest. Not Caitlin.'

Aisling pulled up a chair, sat down next to Emily, and looked straight into her startled face. Be bold, Da used to say; people respect boldness.

'Good morning, Mrs Lovegrove. I'm pleased to meet you now, and I'm looking forward to taking care of you and Major Lovegrove. I can see you're a handsome woman, and a gracious one, but you've not been looking after yourself like you might. Your husband has done his best, but there's only so much a man on his own can do, especially when his wife's not well. The first thing is these sheets will have to come off your bed and into the wash, and the same goes for your nightdress. You can't be sleeping in filth. It'll be a big wash as them clothes over there of yours and his are going in too. Dirty clothes can spread disease.'

She looked under the bed, and recoiled in disgust. 'Your bedpan will need a good scrubbing out. It's not enough just to empty it, pardon me for saying, Major Lovegrove. When all that's done you'll be needing a good bath, Mrs Lovegrove, and then it'll be time to start eating better. My Mam used to make me chicken broth when I was sick myself, so we'll begin with that.'

Emily's eyes, sunk back into her hollowed out face, seemed to burn into Aisling all through this. Da wouldn't have held back. The more difficult the person, the more he assaulted them with his charm until they gave in. And Mam wouldn't have tolerated this filth, for certain.

Suddenly, Emily sat up, grasped Aisling by the wrist, pulled her towards her, and planted a kiss on her cheek.

'Do what she says, Harry,' she said. 'She's going to look after me. She's going to make me better.'

Good. It had worked. Aisling felt a surge of energy. She had to be up and doing.

'We'll start by opening that window,' she said. 'It stinks like a grave in here.'

'Give her the key, Harry,' said Emily.

Major Lovegrove looked at Emily, and then he looked at Aisling, and a broad smile spread across his face. He thrust into his pocket and pulled out a bunch of keys. He held up a small one for the window lock, as if it was a trophy that he and she had won together. He pressed the keys into her hand. His hand lingered in hers longer than it needed to, she noticed, and he went on looking at her, still smiling. Now she saw that he had a gentle sort of a smile, one that made his face softer. Caitlin had been right about him being a handsome man.

'Welcome, Aisling,' he said. 'I hope you'll be staying a while.'

She'd made him blush with what she'd said about the house being a tip. Now she felt herself blush. She wished she wouldn't.

'Let's be getting that window open,' she said, pulling away from him. 'Is there a butcher's nearby for the chicken? Ah, don't worry, so, I'll find it myself.'

All that day Aisling cleaned and washed and scrubbed and shopped and cooked and threw things out and put things straight. She beat and pummelled Mrs Lovegrove's sweat soaked sheets and Major Lovegrove's filthy shirts with a scrubbing brush in the big sink in the scullery while Mrs Lovegrove took a bath, then pinned the sheets up to dry in the back yard against the sun. She carted out two buckets full of rotting abandoned food from the kitchen to the bins, and attacked the tops first and then the floor, driving back the grease like an enemy army. She fought with the ingrained tide marks, not giving in till they yielded and the bath and the sink shone at her command. She found her way to Grafton Street, the big street full of shops, and discovered that in Dublin there was more than one of everything. By a close scrutiny, she found the best butcher's and greengrocer's and baker's, took some things for herself and made arrangements for regular deliveries with the others. The baker's was the same that Major Lovegrove already used; the greengrocer's and the butcher's were new, and that meant swiftly expressing her regrets to the old ones. Major Lovegrove had given her two pounds for a week's wages in advance, and five pounds for housekeeping. She started keeping accounts in a notebook she bought from a stationer's in Grafton Street. She cooked a chicken in the newly shining oven that night. The three of them ate separately: Major Lovegrove sat up correctly in the dining room dismembering a leg; Mrs Lovegrove slurped greedily at her broth sitting up in her clean sheets and her clean nightdress, a napkin tucked into her by Aisling; and after they were both seen to, Aisling ate in the kitchen, looking round with pride at her work, tired but exhilarated.

So, she'd ended up living in the house of an Englishman, and an English soldier at that. Well, it would do her for now, until she found something else. She was glad to be working at least. He was well spoken, and polite; he was nothing like the Tans in Clifden. But then they could be the most dangerous of all, the polite ones. They were the ones who gave the orders to the likes of the Tans. Mrs Lovegrove was grateful though, giving Aisling a wintry smile when she served her her broth. When there was more flesh on her bones she'd be a fine looking woman.

The sky grew dark outside as she ate, thick clouds gathering. When she took her plate to the sink to wash it, there was a flash of lightning so bright it nearly blinded her, and, just after, a growl of thunder. Then rain came down in volleys. There was a knock at the door of the kitchen.

'Come in.'

Major Lovegrove was standing on the threshold, hands in pockets, shifting from foot to foot, looking like a little boy who'd been sent to see the Headmaster.

'I said come in.'

'I won't come in. This is your domain now. I just wanted to say thank you.'

'Sure I've only been doing the job you're paying me for.'

'Emily hasn't eaten so well in months. Nor have I. And the house ... I can live in it now. We're lucky to have you.'

'You could say I'm lucky to have you. I'd be out on the streets otherwise.'

'Do you have everything you need? In your room?'

'It's grand, thanks.'

The rain thundered on. He stood there, not saying anything. Aisling wanted to be washing up.

'Is there anything else, Major Lovegrove?'

'You. Your people. You have reason to hate us, don't you?'

'We do. We have reason enough. You're in our country and you shouldn't be. And your army's done terrible things. I've seen them with my own eyes, God knows.'

'I'm a part of that army. But you'll work for me?'

'I'd rather work than starve, Major Lovegrove.'

'Quite so. Well, I must go out now. I have to... meet someone.'

'Pint with your pals, is it?'

'That's it. There's a little group of us from the Castle. We meet up most nights.'

'My Da never missed a night. They had his stout waiting for him on the counter. Well, you have a nice time, now. You'll need your umbrella, so. Look at that rain. It's making up for today. I'll keep an eye on Mrs Lovegrove. She was asleep when I last looked in.'

'Thank you, Aisling. Good night.'

After he'd gone, she felt again the little ache of loneliness that had shot through her on the station platform when she'd arrived in Dublin. The house seemed somehow empty without him. She finished the washing up and went to bed in her little room at the top of the house, falling asleep to the sound of rain on the roof, wondering what time he would come home.

On the Monday she went out with her advanced wages and bought a summer dress, a couple of sets of underwear, and some monthly cloths in readiness. At the last minute, she bought herself a winter dress too. She hung up the dresses in the wardrobe in her snug tight little room in the attic, and then she stepped back and took a look at them to welcome them. Day by day, she began to feel at home.

Clifden wasn't completely gone, though. Every night up in the attic she knelt by the bed, took Mam's rosary in her hands and prayed for Mam's and Da's souls both now, feeling the touch of Mam's hands as she fingered the delicate beads, and sometimes the tears and the rage would come to her. She would smell the smoke and feel the flames on her face as the house burnt down again, Da with his face half blown off, powerless to rise. It would come on her at other times too, out of nowhere, when she was out choosing sausages or paying a bill, and then she would turn away from whoever she was with and rub back the tears with her wrist. She told them her Da was recent dead, and they would tell her they were sorry for her trouble, but she would never tell them how he died. She was in Dublin now, a new place, a new start. She didn't want the past catching up with her.

She remembered what Father Garvey had said to her at Mam's wake, that when someone you loved died you'd not to be afraid because they could look after you more powerfully from Heaven. Sure, that was true. Mam and Da were with her all the time. Mam was with her more now than in the years in Clifden after she'd died. She would peep over her shoulder as she made a stew, and tell her to add some salt, just as Da would remind her to look the Major in the eye and smile when he looked tired or down. When she inspected the kitchen all clean and straight, she felt Mam's pride; and when she felt lonely, she thought of one of Da's stories and she smiled to herself.

But for all Mam and Da were with her, as the summer went on the patches when Clifden faded grew wider and wider. She had her routines, keeping the house going on her own lines now the tide of filth and chaos had been driven back, and the Lovegroves had theirs, and they slid into one another remarkably well. She enjoyed the work, was glad to be busy. Mrs Lovegrove wasn't really getting better, was the truth. She was eating properly at last, and she had a little more strength, but still she lay in bed all day looking at the ceiling, tears in her eyes, never getting out, even to go to the bathroom. She used the chamberpot under her bed (now properly scrubbed), and Aisling had to wash her and change her nightdress in her bed. After a few days of being very grateful to Aisling, telling her how good it felt to be clean, how much better Aisling's food tasted than either Caitlin's or her husband's, and what a scheming minx Caitlin had been, out to poison her, she all of a sudden stopped speaking. One day Aisling saw her eyeing the knife she'd brought up for her to eat her lunch with, and after that she cut up Mrs Lovegrove's food for her.

Major Lovegrove tried to get his wife to talk; he did his best all right, but he could as well be talking to her pillow. She'd see him in their room sometimes, talking to Mrs Lovegrove slow and patient like, holding her hand and looking at her, telling her about his day at work: he'd seen Fitzgerald in Grafton Street and his wife had had a son at last; Winter and Wilson were squabbling as usual; Colonel Brind was back from his leave; it had been raining yesterday and now it had stopped. But he never got anything back. Da had had silent moments after Mam died, but they'd never lasted more than a quarter of an hour (and that was a long time for Da not to talk). Mrs Lovegrove had given up as sure as if her tongue had been cut out. So it was Aisling he talked to now; he had no one else.

Every morning after breakfast, as she cleared his plates away, he'd say, 'So, Aisling, what's on the agenda today?'

with a bright smile on his face. And she'd sit next to him in the dining room and go through all the business of the house with him, just as she used to do with Da. It was different the way he talked to Aisling from the way he talked to Mrs Lovegrove. With his wife it was like she was some visiting Duchess or something it was his duty to keep entertained. He'd sit up straight in the chair next to her bed. With Aisling, even though the dining room chairs were hard, he'd sit in his as if it was soft. When she was telling him about what would be the best fruits to go in the pie, he'd sit back and look at her all the time and then grin at her like he couldn't help himself, and she liked that somehow; it made her feel happy inside. There was never all that much to say, as he and Mrs Lovegrove never entertained, but somehow he'd spin it out, keep asking her questions. Often he'd tell her how sparkling clean the house was or how tasty the stew had been, and she'd blush like she'd done on the first day, even though she tried not to. It reminded her of Da's compliments the first time she'd looked after breakfast in the boarding house, words she'd never forgotten. She and the Major would soon run out of things to talk about, and he'd look down at his shoes as if he was going to tell her something, then he'd look up at the clock and say 'Is that the time? The Castle calls.' And he'd be gone. And always, just as on the first night, the house would feel empty without him, for all that Mrs Lovegrove was upstairs. They didn't go back to what they'd talked about on the first day, about the war and the Irish and the English; it was all about the house now. Sometimes she wished they could talk about something else. Some days she even felt like having a good argument with him. He was only her boss, but she liked talking to him was the truth, for all he was English. And when they ran out of things to say, she liked being quiet with him, too. It felt safe and warm at the same time.

He went out almost every night, like Da, but he came back much later, long after the pubs would be shut, long after she'd gone to bed. It was clear he wasn't seeing his pals. He must have a woman somewhere. Aisling felt sorry for Mrs Lovegrove, her being sick and all, but the funny thing was she couldn't find it in her heart to blame Major Lovegrove for what he was doing. Mrs Lovegrove was no kind of a wife for him, and a man must get lonely. Enough people in Clifden had asked Da when he would marry again, but he'd always said, 'Ah, sure, Aisling's enough for me.' But Major Lovegrove had no children, and no friends, or none that came to the house. His work seemed dull enough, too, from what she overheard him telling Mrs Lovegrove; filling in reports and pushing bits of paper around. It wasn't as if he was burning down buildings or shooting people or anything. He couldn't have much to do, as they didn't mind him getting up late and coming in halfway through the morning. If he could find some comfort elsewhere, well, why shouldn't he; wouldn't God forgive him, if he was making the other woman happy? And she would be happy, if she had any sense; he was a handsome, kind man, who understood women, she could tell that, and there weren't too many of them around. She wasn't even sure if it was a sin, him being a Protestant and all. That other woman was lucky, whoever she was. Aisling even felt a little envious of her.

She'd hear him sometimes when he came back, though he was awful quiet like, very considerate of her and Mrs Lovegrove. Once she heard the door opening and him coming in when outside St Teresa's was tolling three. Another time she got up for the lavatory in the night (a luxury, that; she had her own on the top floor) and on her way back to her room she noticed the door of his study was open and the gas light was on and she looked down the stairs and saw him sitting at his big roll top desk writing and writing and writing in a little black leather notebook. She stayed watching him a long time. She noticed how carefully and tidily he wrote and how he half closed his eyes and tapped the top of his pen on his mouth when he stopped to think. She noticed, as if for the first time, his hands, the left hand holding the book open, the right hand holding his pen. They seemed very strong and very gentle at the same time. Eventually, he looked up. He saw her watching him. The way he looked at her seemed to be asking her to come downstairs into the study, and apologising for something at the same time. Then he sighed, shook his head, put his notebook in the big roll-top desk, pulled down the cover, and locked the desk. She went back to bed. Neither of them spoke about it the next day.

For the first few weeks, Aisling would look at the Major's *Irish Times* each day after he'd gone out in the morning, reading the situations advertised, wondering when it would be time to apply for one. Then one day she put the paper back on the hall table unread. She realised she didn't want to leave. She couldn't be idle, never could abide it; she'd loved looking after the guests in the boarding house, making everything just so for them, and now here were two people who'd been in distress and needed her, and there was plenty she could do for them to set them right. She might even stay for a while; it might become her home, even. Maybe when Mrs Lovegrove was better there'd be babies on the way and she'd have more people to look after. She'd heard in Clifden of girls going to Dublin and staying with families all their lives, until the babies they'd looked after had babies of their own. Da was dead, Mam was dead, Father Garvey was dead, Sinead and her Da were most likely dead and Clifden was burnt to the ground, but God had spared her. There must be a reason. Maybe it was that He'd sent her here to start again, to make Mam and Da proud in the way she looked after this house. She could do a lot worse.

Outside the house, Dublin was a city at war with itself. Apart from that one night, Clifden was nothing but quietness and safety by comparison. On the streets there were soldiers everywhere, marching in groups, strolling in twos or threes, piling out of lorries, manning the entrances to banks and government offices, standing in front of barbed wire with guns. For the first few days she still jumped back from them instinctively, but they didn't notice her. Once, when she was in Grafton Street, she heard shots and shouting from a distance, and saw soldiers running, and she hurried the other way. But most of the time people looked through her in the street like she was invisible. That wasn't like Clifden either; there you could never pass anyone in the street without stopping to pass the time of day with them for a few minutes, even if your family and their family had hated each other for years. She knew that it was better to be anonymous, to keep herself safe from any Tans who might have telegraphed their people in Dublin. Even so, she wondered if she'd ever get to know anyone in the city. She'd swap a bit of chat with the people in the shops, but otherwise she had no one to talk to apart from Major Lovegrove. Not that she didn't like talking to him; she almost felt as right with him as she'd used to with Da. But she was alone during the day, and they had to eat separately, and he was still a boss when all was said and done. There were times she felt lonely, to be honest. She was like Da in that respect. She needed people to talk to. So it was a good day when, one sunny September Sunday, two months after she'd arrived in Dublin, she met Patrick.

CHAPTER THREE

She'd taken to going to Mass in the Cathedral of a Sunday. It was a good twenty minutes' walk from Lower Mount Street when St Teresa's was around the corner, but Mass was a time when she thought of Da, it being one of the things she did with him, and sometimes the crying came on, and it suited her to be in the biggest church in the city where no one would notice you or talk to you. The Sunday she met Patrick had been a bad one. She'd been shaking with tears all the way there, and as she'd sat down, she'd barely been able to swallow her breaths. People were looking at her, and she'd had to calm herself by force. She was glad when the bell rang and the priest came in and Mass started. The familiar ritual always took her out of herself. The priest was old and stooped, trailed by a couple of altar boys, one neat and upright, the other scruffy and fidgeting. The three of them took up their places and the distant mumble began. Ten Mass was popular; the pews were full, men in jackets and ties with their hats in their hands, women in shawls, twitching children. The saints around the walls, frozen forever in pain or ecstasy, stared unmoving at the people as they came and went Sunday by Sunday, while the high, curved roof loured over all of them, blocking out the light. Aisling liked the dark of the Cathedral; it went with its anonymity. There was nobody here she knew. It was peaceful. She felt calmer, her breath was slowing. One day she would be able to go to Mass without crying; one day she might even make Dublin her home.

Just after the gospel, she realised there was a man looking at her. She had a way like that, that she knew when someone was looking at her. Sinead said she was possessed. Da just said she was smart. When she turned round the man stopped, and looked at the altar. But then when she looked back at the altar he was looking at her again. He was wearing a trench coat, she noticed, a baggy one, tightly belted. He had a trilby hat sat next to him in the pew. And by God he was a good looking fella. Dark, full, curly hair and a slim face.A lithe, wiry figure with a kind of coiled energy.

The priest lumbered up the steps of the pulpit and slumped over the lectern. He spoke of the killings in the streets, and called on all good Christians to turn the other cheek. Aisling heard a snort. She looked across and the man was shaking his head, folding his arms in contempt. The priest paused a moment and looked at the man, sucked on his teeth, and went on talking about our need for forgiveness. The man gave the priest a thin smile, then saw that Aisling was looking at him, and turned to look at her, lifting an eyebrow. He had eyes that held you; eyes that seemed to worship whatever he was looking at. It was her he had been looking at, no doubt at all. Aisling blushed, and turned away.

When she went up for communion, the man followed her. She felt him, two behind her in the line, just after a woman helping her elderly Da with his stick. She kept her hands together and her looks down all the time like Father Garvey had taught them when he prepared them for their First Holy Communion, and afterwards she knelt in her pew with her eyes closed. Then everyone stood for the blessing at the end, and Mass was over. The Cathedral emptied, slowly, people staying on to pray. She sat for a few minutes. But he was still there, still looking at her.

She stood, genuflected hastily and made her way down the aisle. She had a little longer. She didn't need to be back at the house till twelve, to make the lunch. She'd go to St Stephen's Green and sit on a bench like she usually did after Mass, look at the ducks on the pond, clear her head.

'Miss.'

She was at the top of the steps outside the Cathedral, the gentle September sun on her face. She turned. The man who'd been watching her was leaning against the wall, slouching a little, hands in pockets. He smiled at her.

'Do I know you?'

He tipped his hat and walked towards her. He stretched out his hand.

'Forgive me. You must think me very impertinent. The name's Kelly. Patrick Kelly.'

Those eyes. When they looked at you, you could look nowhere else. The world narrowed to his face.

'Pleased to meet you, Mr Kelly.'

His hand clasped hers. Still his eyes held her. His hair seemed to have a life of its own, the curls bristling, almost fighting with each other. For a moment, she wanted to run the fingers of her other hand through the curls of his hair, to feel how thick and tough it would feel.

'But I don't know your name?'

'Aisling O'Flaherty.'

'Aisling. That means dream.'

'It does. My Da chose it.'

'Did he dream of you, so?'

At the thought of Da she felt the tears coming again. She had to stop him.

'Mr Kelly –'

'I have no excuse, Miss O'Flaherty. I have no reason to talk to you. I know nothing about you. Except that I know that lately you've been at ten Mass at the Cathedral and that I have too, and that the last few Sundays I've wanted to talk to you, and I thought this week, by God I will, before it's too late. Do you want to slap me so?'

He was still holding her hand. Aisling found that she was breathing deeply, and her face was colouring. The idea of slapping him was quite exciting.

'No. I don't want to slap you.'

'Would you do me the honour of taking a walk with me?'

He was a good looking fella all right. And what could be the harm in a walk? She rubbed her eyes with her spare hand as if she could make the redness of her crying go away. He must have noticed, but he didn't say anything.

'I've to be back at work at noon. But until then, yes. It's a sunny day. Let's walk.'

They turned down the little side street the Cathedral huddled in, Patrick striding out boldly, but taking care to keep at her pace, Aisling blinking a little in the full sun after the dark of the church.

'So it's always the Cathedral for you, is it, Miss O'Flaherty?'

'It is. I like it.'

'There's some say it's too big, too grand. They like somewhere quieter where they know the priest, know the people.'

'Ah, that's what I like about it. Not being known.'

'Sure, that's what I like about it too. So there's one thing we have in common already.'

He laughed, his laugh rich and strong, a laugh that was at home in the world. She laughed too, not knowing why, but enjoying it.

'It's different from home,' she said.

'Is that so?'

'Yes. Where I come from – Clifden, in Connemara – there, everyone knows everyone and everything. My Da knew what someone was saying even before they said it.'

Again the rich laugh. It seemed to fill out his body, make it bigger, make it fill the street.

'That's a good one. Is your Da still back at home?'

'No.'

'Has he been taken?'

'He has.'

'I noticed you were upset in Mass. Was it him you were thinking of?'

'It was.'

She looked down at her feet. Already, he had her talking about Da. Out of the corner of her eye, she saw his face crease in concern. Though he hadn't said anything she felt he wanted to know about Da, and she wanted to tell him.

'It was two months ago. There was a fire at our house. He died. I only just got out.'

She stopped there. She knew she had to, that it wouldn't be safe to say any more. And yet, she desperately wanted to tell him everything, about the meetings in the back room, about Da's night time expeditions, about the files she kept, about the Tans and the guns and the sack of Clifden.

'I'm sorry for your trouble,' he said. 'And your Mam?'

'She died six years ago. My little sister or brother – we never knew which – killed her before they were born.'

'You have no one older?'

'No. I have no one.'

Patrick looked across at her as they walked, and nodded. The pavements were filled with families jostling for space on the pavement on their way from Mass or to Mass, some of them talking softly, some of them arguing, some just being quiet together, and she felt her aloneness very sharply. From wanting to stroke his hair or slap him she went to wanting to be held by him, to be kept safe by him.

'This fire,' he said. 'It wasn't an accident, right?'

She gasped. How did he know?

'What do you mean?'

'There are a lot of house fires in Ireland these days. Nine out of ten of them are started by the English.'

They were on Sackville Street by now, the main street of Dublin, its enormous width stretching all the way down to the river. The widest street in Europe, they said. The bell of a tram clanged as it rattled past them. Opposite them was the

Post Office, left just as it had been after it was burnt down in the Easter Rising four years previously. People said the English meant it to stand like that forever, as a punishment and a warning. Only its front remained, nothing behind it, no roofs, no floors, just piles of rubble and twisted girders and scorched relics, open to the soaking rain. Aisling had been past it many times, and each time she thought of the Rising. It had been the beginning of her and Da's work for Ireland together, but even so, seeing the Post Office, symbol of the Rising's failure, always made her a little sad. It was like a gap-toothed drunk who had been full of promise when he was younger, but who at any minute might fall flat on his face.

Patrick nodded across the street.

'I was there, four years ago. Easter week, 1916. That week ended in the biggest house fire of the lot.'

Aisling felt the colour rise to her face.

'The Rising? You were in the Rising?'

Patrick was grinning to himself. She could see he wanted to tell her about what it was like being in the Rising. Well, she wanted to hear. So he told her.

'A hundred and fifty men marched down this very street,' he began, making a sweeping gesture as if he owned the street, his face lighting up as he spoke, 'through the sunshine on Easter Monday, with rifles, but no uniforms. Some of them arrived on a tram; and they made sure their fares were paid properly, so!' She laughed, feeling more relaxed in his company already. He pointed across the street. 'They pushed their way into the Post Office, there, through that door, past all the posh ladies buying stamps and the soldiers sending parcels home to England. Come on, let's cross.' He took her, to her excitement, by the hand, and led her across the wide street, running so they just missed a tram gathering speed, slipping behind a horse drawn cab. He made her stand outside the Post Office, and stepped back as if he was taking a photograph of her.

'It was on that very paving stone, that one you're standing on now,' he said, 'where Patrick Pearse himself, may he rest in peace, proclaimed the Irish Republic. Half the people paid no notice, but they'd be paying notice soon, right enough.' He pointed upwards, and she craned her neck back, feeling the sun hurt her eyes. 'Up there; that's where I lay with my rifle, picking off the English. I was there six days with barely a biscuit to eat. You see that shop there?' She shielded her eyes against the sun and looked back across the street at a cake shop. 'They came out of the slums and smashed its windows and helped themselves to cream cakes. I could have done with a few myself.' She laughed. He pointed to Lord Nelson, arrogantly surveying the city from the top of his pillar. 'There in the middle of the street, see, under Nelson's Pillar, there was a dead horse all week, covered in flies. I didn't feel sorry for him, though; he was an English horse.' She laughed again. Da used to make her laugh all the time, but she hadn't laughed once since she'd come to Dublin. She liked being with a man who made her laugh.

'Come on, let's walk,' he said. 'I don't like standing still.'

'Me neither,' she said. He walked fast. She liked that, too; she had never been one for dawdling herself.

'What was it like inside the GPO?' she asked him, really wanting to know.

'Sure, they were a holy bunch. I heard the rosary going day and night, and they say the fellas were lining up for confession with a priest they'd sneaked in. We weren't all like that, though; up on the roof, some of our jokes were not fit for a lady's ears.' He winked at her when he told her this, and Aisling blushed, but didn't mind blushing, and laughed some more, and said,

'No, but will you tell me the jokes some day all the same? I like jokes. My Da was a one for the jokes.'

'Ah, maybe one day, when I know you better. You know a strange thing?' he told her as they went past the Metropole Hotel, where a cab was stopping and a man in a peaked cap was holding the door open for a woman in a fur coat.

'What's that?' she said.

'My C.O. was my big brother, Sean. He was in there with me, giving me orders.'

He paused and looked away, suddenly silent. Aisling knew not to ask him about Sean, and felt in that moment as if she'd known him a long time. Then he thrust his hands in his pockets, and continued with his story.

'It was boring as hell, most of the time, if you want the truth. But that didn't mean it was safe. There was an English sniper up there, see, top of Trinity' – he pointed across the river to the round stately dome of Trinity College – 'he could reach us. He picked off Dermot O'Casey himself, a boy I was at the Christian Brothers with. He died two men down from me. I held him as he said his last act of contrition. He bled from the neck onto my sleeve, so.'

'You held a man as he died?' said Aisling.

'I did. His mother was glad to hear of it after.'

She thought of Da then, of his body stretched out on her bedroom floor. She wished she'd been able to hold him.

As they crossed the Liffey, its waters rushing impatiently to the sea, Patrick started to walk slower and his voice lowered. 'It didn't end well, though,' he said. He paused at the end of the bridge and made another sweeping gesture back to Sackville Street, cluttered now with trams and cabs and people. 'That whole street was in flames from the English shells. There were balls of fire, ten feet wide, flying into the air from the oil depot. You see Reiss's the jewellers there?' Aisling nodded. 'There were tongues of flame lighting up the night sky. I saw it from the roof. When the glass melted, there was something beautiful about it. It sounded like a waterfall crashing.'

His voice was shaking. He seemed to be on the verge of tears. She wanted to hold him in her arms, to comfort him.

'Come on, let's go,' he said, as if he didn't want her to see him upset.

They dodged round the back of another tram and ran across the street; again he took her hand. Then they turned past Trinity College and its playing fields as big as a farm, all scattered with the sons of the gentry baying at the oval ball.

'When the fire reached the Post Office it was too hot to touch anything, and all the water in the building turned to steam. The roof was falling in; we gathered downstairs and sang 'The Soldier's Song' Do you know it?'

'I do.'

They'd sung it at the end of every meeting in Flanagan's back room; it always lifted them, gave them courage for whatever lay ahead. He stopped, and looked out over the playing fields of Trinity. Then he began to sing, very softly, whispering the words, glaring at the posh Protestant boys on the rugby field as he sang:

'Soldiers are we
whose lives are pledged to Ireland,
Some have come
from a land beyond the wave.
Sworn to be free,
No more our ancient sireland
Shall shelter the despot or the slave.
Tonight we man the gap of danger
In Erin's cause, come woe or weal
Mid cannons' roar and rifles peal,
We'll chant a soldier's song.'

A platoon of English soldiers turned out of Grafton Street and wheeled right towards them. They were only a couple of hundred yards away. By singing that song, Patrick might as well have taken a gun out and pointed it at them. Aisling felt afraid and thrilled at the same time, just as she had on the night the Tans came. And as on that night, she felt ready to fight for Ireland. As Patrick began the second verse, she stood close to him, and sang it with him, as softly as she could. Their words and their breath mingled as they whispered the song to each other. They seemed to be exchanging secrets. People stared at them as they passed. One man winked at her; another gave her a discreet thumbs up. The two of them were together as one, defying the English.

'In valley green, on towering crag,
Our fathers fought before us,
And conquered 'neath the same old flag
That's proudly floating o'er us.
We're children of a fighting race,
That never yet has known disgrace,
And as we march, the foe to face,
We'll chant a soldier's song.'

They finished, together, on the same rising note, just as the English soldiers came into earshot. They stepped back and let the soldiers march past, their eyes to the front, their boots clumping, resentment on their boys' faces, as she and Patrick hugged their secret defiance to themselves. When the last soldier had passed, they turned to each other and laughed.

'Let's get moving before we get arrested,' he said.

Now they were in the smart part of the city, south of the river. The houses were high, with small windows at the top; families with servants.

'How did it end?' she asked.

'We broke out of the GPO, across Henry Street, the English firing all the time, into the houses on Moore Street. We had to smash our way through the walls with a sledge-hammer. How we managed it, God only knows; most of us could hardly stand after a week without sleep. It stopped at last when Pearse saw an old man dead in the street holding a white flag and knew it was time to surrender. That's the kind of man he was, Miss O'Flaherty.'

'Were you taken prisoner?'

'I was. The English kept us all night outside in Rutland Square at gunpoint. I won't go into the details, Miss O'Flaherty, but the plumbing's not so good there – we had to take our relief as we could.'

Again she blushed, and laughed, and felt a thrill at being admitted to the world of men.

'Then they marched us to the boats for England. I was a year in a prison camp in Wales. Boring as hell at first, when they kept us in solitary. But when they let us out of our cells, I made some friends for life amongst the fellas. There's one especially I'd go to the death for – name of Mick Collins. He is simply the greatest man I've ever met. No question. You'll be hearing more of him before long, Miss O'Flaherty, I can promise you that. No one knows who he is, but he has the whole of Dublin in his pocket.'

She wanted to meet this Mick Collins fella; wondered if he'd introduce her to him.

'Do you miss it now?' she asked.

'Sure, when they let us out, it was good to get home, and eat decent grub and be able to walk the streets, but I miss the fellas too. Still, I mustn't complain. I'm alive; which is more than can be said for the fifteen they shot, may they rest in peace.'

He blessed himself swiftly, and she copied him. 'I have a good job in a carpenter's. I like working with my hands. The only trouble is, it's a family business: Sean's still my boss!'

He laughed, and she laughed with him.

'Is that still as bad as it was?'

'Sure, he's been bossing me since the day I was born, and I'm used to it now. You know something, Miss O'Flaherty?'

'What's that?'

'Ireland will be free very soon. Her day is coming. We knocked the English off their perch that Easter week, and they'll never get back now.'

They'd walked as far as Merrion Square. Aisling, exhilarated by their talking and their singing and their laughing, looked resentfully up at the tall white houses. They seemed to gaze down at her and Patrick with haughty indifference, as if they knew nothing of the Rising or the struggle of the Irish people for freedom. She wanted to throw something through one of the front windows, to shake them out of their complacency.

'There were women too, weren't there? That's what my Da told me,' said Aisling.

'There were. Some of them – Connolly's lot - had guns.'

She had to tell him now. She couldn't hold back any longer. He might have been an English agent for all she knew, sent to smoke her out. But she couldn't stop herself.

'I did my bit too, you know.'

'In Clifden?'

'After the Rising. With my Da. He was in the local branch of the IRA. And I was the secretary. I kept all the notes. Until the Tans came for us. They killed my Da and burnt our house – burnt the whole town – but I burnt the notes before they could get them. And I got out.'

It felt like being able to breathe again. Being allowed to talk about it. Patrick looked at her, smiling, as if at some unexpected good news. She knew she'd impressed him, and she was glad of it.

'You got out, and now you're here. And you can fight on. Make your Da proud still.'

'What do you mean?'

'The war isn't over yet. And I think you'd make a grand soldier.'

'Them shootings ... what the priest was telling us about. Are they IRA?'

'They are. And he should know better than to bad mouth Irish boys who are fighting for their country.'

Nearby, the bells of St Teresa's began the steady ascent to noon. Aisling gathered her shawl about her. She didn't want to go.

'I'm sorry,' she said. 'I've got to go. I've to get back to work.'

'Have I made you late?'

'No, it's just there. Mount Street Lower. I'm a maid.'

'Will I see you again?'

Her heart gave a little leap. She'd wanted him to say that; she'd half thought of saying it herself.

'Yes. Please, yes.'

'Do you ever have cause to run messages in Grafton Street?'

'I do. Most days.'

'I have business there myself on Thursday morning. Do you know the Cafe Cairo?'

'I've been past it.'

'Can you be there at eleven this Thursday?'

'I can.'

'Well, until Thursday then, Miss O'Flaherty.'

'Aisling. Call me Aisling.'

'Call me Patrick.'

Just as when he'd introduced himself, he tipped his hat to her, and then he turned and walked away, his hands in his pockets, his face held up to the sun, smiling at it like an old friend. Aisling watched him go. On the corner of the Square, he stopped and looked back at her, as if there was something else he wanted to say. He stood like that for quite a while, then turned on his heel and walked briskly off. As she walked back to Mount Street, Aisling heard the gentle, insistent, courageous lilt of *The Soldier's Song* in her head, and felt as if a door had been opened onto a new life.

CHAPTER FOUR

Rory looked up from his dominoes.

'Where the fuck have you been?'

Four of them were round the old wooden table with the wobbly leg when Patrick walked in: Rory, Vinnie, Tom and Joe. They were always at dominoes, those four, every minute they got. They clutched and stroked the little black rectangles, holding them close like they were their children or something, only letting them go after much thought. They kept on with their game until they'd lost all their money, and then they lent each other money and started over again. When they were bored with playing, they argued. Apart from stalking and killing and arguing, they had nothing in their heads except dominoes. After an hour in Aisling's company, walking in on them was like walking in on a bad smell. Patrick remembered Aisling's voice lowering when she told him about her Da; remembered the way she tipped her head to one side when she listened to him, her thick auburn hair cascading down her shoulders, her face soft and open. Damn. It wasn't meant to be like this. She was meant to fall for him, not the other way around. Watch yourself, Kelly. But she'd been in the IRA, once. That could be good, or it could be bad. The natural thing would be to sign her up with the Cumann na mBan, the women's lot. But then he'd lose her. And he wanted to keep her to himself, for her to be his own private spy.

He looked around the room. This was where he lived, and it was a terrible way to live. What he did for Ireland. They had to share beds, and sleep top to toe. There were two bedrooms with three beds in each, and a wardrobe for their clothes in each room with a drawer at the bottom where they kept their guns under their shirts. There was one bathroom between the lot of them. The sink and the bath would get encased with grime and stubble because none of them would wash them out properly. About once a week Mairead, who looked after them a bit, would curse at them, shouting through the bathroom door as she scrubbed and sometimes they would be defiant and sometimes they would be shamefaced as if she was their mother. The dominoes table was also where they ate their meals. There were crumbs and a slopped tea stain still on it from breakfast. There was only room for six chairs around it, but still they all ate together. There was no kitchen, so Mairead brought their food in pails up the back steps, along with plates and cutlery. She had it cooked, and the plates and the cutlery washed up, in the restaurant next door where they didn't ask questions. The food was usually cold, and they grumbled and swore under their breath, and Mairead told them to mind their manners. The place stank. It stank of men. And for the last five weeks it had stunk, too, of Seamus' and Colm's unavenged deaths, which hung in the air like the stench of rotting meat. Patrick was going to do something about that, because no one else would.

He ignored Rory, unbelted his coat, took off his hat, and hung both on the hat stand in the corner. He sat in the one armchair, with a beaten, defeated cushion, picked up a newspaper that was lying crumpled on the floor, straightened it carefully, and turned to the racing page. Rory looked at him through a cloud of cigarette smoke that he had just exhaled.

'I said, where the fuck have you been?'

'I've been to Mass. And then I've been working.'

'Well so have we as a matter of fact. All fucking morning. Since eight, on a Sunday. Those of us who went to Mass went early.'

'Did you kill anyone?' said Patrick, not looking up from his paper.

'No. But we're going to on Wednesday. And so are you. And you won't have a fucking clue because you weren't tailing our friend Sergeant Casey today like you should.'

'Ah, give it a rest, would you?' said Tom, gleefully slapping down a double six. 'We're trying to play dominoes here. And it's Sunday. Give your man some peace for one day of the week.' Patrick liked Tom. He and Tom had traded stories of the fathers they'd wanted to murder over a few pints one night, and ever since it had felt like they had a secret bond.

'I'll give him some peace when he pulls his weight,' said Rory.

Patrick could feel the vein in his neck throbbing, as it did when he was on the brink of lashing out. *Save it,* Sean always said. *Save the anger, and let it come out through the barrel of your gun. Otherwise you'll miss.* He folded up the newspaper slowly and meticulously and leant forward.

'I've been pulling my weight,' he said. 'I've been doing something a damn sight more useful than sniffing after some poor benighted policeman and his girl. I've practically got in the front door of Major Harry Lovegrove, Esquire.'

'Who's he when he's at home?'

'Ask Seamus McCann.'

'I can't ask him. He's dead.'

'Ask his brother.'

'He's dead and all.'

'Exactly. My point exactly.'

He slumped back in the armchair and snapped open the paper. He didn't want to talk to Rory any more.

'Your point is what, Pat?' asked Tom. The dominoes were face down in front of them and they were all listening now. Patrick wanted to tell Tom, but he still didn't want to tell Rory. He went on reading, making them wait.

'Pat?'

He lowered the paper.

'My point is that it is Major Harry Lovegrove, Esquire, of His Majesty's Forces, whom we have to thank for young Seamus and young Colm being with their maker now.'

'How do you know that?' asked Joe.

Patrick put the paper on his lap and sat forward.

'The day after Seamus and Colm died, Sean sets me to tail Fitzgerald. I'm following him down Grafton Street, when our man Lovegrove sees him, shakes his hand half off, big grin all over his face. Tells him – I'm looking in a shop window while I'm listening – that he's had a good morning – "two problems have been solved in one go, thanks to some information I received yesterday from my new friend. They were indeed at Barry's Hotel." "So he was worth listening to after all, then," says Fitzgerald. "Good for you, Lovegrove, you won't be a major much longer." They have a bit more chat about Fitzgerald's wife's having a kid, then Lovegrove goes on his way and I carry on tailing my man. Barry's, I think – that's Seamus and Colm. When I get home I hear the Tans paid them a visit early that morning when they were sleeping and left them with a bullet in the head each.'

Patrick's voice lowered and shook a little. It had been Tom who had told him. Patrick hadn't even taken his coat off, the cold of the morning was still on his skin, but he'd seen the news in Tom's eyes as soon as he'd got in. 'Is it Seamus and Colm?' he'd said. 'How do you know?' Tom had asked. 'Oh, I know.' He'd felt as if it was his fault, as if he should have looked out for them. Jesus knew, they'd looked out for him often enough. They were like one person, always together, finishing each other's sentences, pushing and shoving each other as they walked down the street. And they'd as good as made him into a third twin. At the morning break at the Brothers, he'd lain on his front, Seamus on one side, Colm on the other, shoulder to shoulder, picking off Indians, defending the Alamo to the last man, while Sean sat on the wall, alone, just watching. When he'd got the strap from Brother Brendan, they'd taken a hand each and rubbed it till the pain retreated a little, Seamus doing Brother Brendan's stutter, Colm his twitch. In the Post Office, they'd lain at the window either side of him, just as they had in the playground; a sniper would have got one of them before he got Patrick. Now Lovegrove had got them. And by Christ he was going to get Lovegrove. That morning, he'd wanted to turn round, run down the street, find Lovegrove and put a bullet straight into his grinning face. Then he'd remembered Sean. *Save it. Let it come out through the barrel of your gun.* If he saved it, he might find out who the bastard on the inside was that did for Seamus and Colm.

'Did you tell Sean?' asked Tom.

'I did. Seamus and Colm could be eejits, I said, but they weren't that sort of eejit. Someone on the inside's passing on stuff to this man Lovegrove I saw in the street. We want to watch him and all.'

'What did he say?'

'He said nothing.'

'Nothing?'

He'd looked Patrick up and down like he was a cat that had brought a rotting mouse into the house, and had gone straight into reprimanding him, again, for having been five minutes late for a tailing the week before last. It had never been easy talking to Sean. All his life Patrick had been hanging around the edges of his dangerous games. Together, they'd lifted chocolates from the expensive confectioner in Sackville Street, him distracting the shopkeeper and Sean pocketing them, and then they'd taken them down to the canal where Patrick had stuffed himself till he was sick, his brown sweet vomit spurting into the dirty water. Sean had had two, pocketed the rest, and walked away leaving him doubled up in pain. Another time, on Sean's orders, he'd put a dead rat they'd found in the street in the drawer Brother Brendan kept his rosary in. When Brother Brendan had found it, and raged and screamed, Sean had said nothing; but somehow Brother Brendan knew, and Patrick had got six on each hand with the strap, the welts stinging him for a week. By the time he'd joined the Volunteers, Sean was already a commanding officer. When they drilled every Tuesday and Thursday night, it was always Patrick's uniform that wasn't straight, Patrick's gun that wasn't stripped right. But Sean was the only one who wouldn't go to the pub with the boys afterwards.

'Ah, you know Sean, Tom; when he doesn't want to talk about something. Anyways, on the Friday - the very day we buried those boys - I see Lovegrove in Grafton Street again. This time I follow him home. To Lower Mount Street – that's practically a barracks for English spies.'

'So Sean told you to follow him?' asked Tom.

Patrick pointed at his head with the index finger of his right hand.

'Not Sean, Tom. This. It's called a brain. We need to use it as well as our guns.'

Then Patrick pointed to his heart.

'And this, too. I loved those boys.'

Rory ground his cigarette into an ashtray as if he hated it.

'Love doesn't come into it,' he said. 'This is a war. You're a soldier. You obey orders.'

The others nodded, except Tom. He and Patrick exchanged looks.

'Rory's right,' said Joe, picking up his dominoes, 'give the heroics a rest, Pat. If for no other reason than that your man Lovegrove'll have a bullet put in your head and all.'

'She won't,' said Patrick.

'And who's she?' said Tom, grinning.

'The woman who has to cook his stews and wash his stinking underpants. Who better to find out what our man's up to?'

And help me kill him, he thought. Hadn't she reason enough when the English had killed her Da?

'You're humping his maid and all?' said Joe.

Patrick saw Aisling at Mass, her eyes red with tears, but her face still clear and pure and strong in the light from the high window. He liked humping women as much as the next man, but Aisling was not a woman you talked about humping. Joe, though, never talked about anything else.

'Let's just say I'm getting her sweet on me.'

'You crafty bugger,' said Vinnie, pushing some coins to the middle of the table. 'Mixing business and pleasure.'

Rory slapped down his dominoes.

'Mixing pleasure and being a fucking eejit,' he said. 'Did you not hear what I said? We're triggermen, Pat. The Intelligence boys, they sweet talk the maids, and the telegraph boys, and the clerks and all, and hand out the bribes and the threats and the slaps on the back and slip the lasses a length of cock if it'll get the job done. We're triggermen. We take orders from Sean, who takes orders from Mick.'

'When he and Mick are talking, that is,' said Tom.

'Shut it, Tom,' said Rory. 'The only time we follow a man is when Sean tells us, and then only to find the best time and place to put a bullet in his head. Jesus Christ, man, if we can't even run our own army, how are we ever going to run our own country?'

Patrick couldn't save it any longer. Anger crashed over him like a wave. He threw down the paper, stood, and stepped towards Rory.

'Are you blind or something? Did you not see the boys' mother at the funeral? Did you not see her faint and fall when they brought the coffins into the church side by side, practically bumping into each other? I had to catch her. Their Da's been dead these ten years. There was no one else. Do you want more women fainting and falling and so, until there's no one left to catch them? Leave Lovegrove alone,' he said, very low, breathing very hard, trying to hold down his anger, 'and more of us will wake up one morning with a bullet in our head. He's being left alone. I want to find out why.'

Rory took another cigarette from the packet, put it in his mouth and, without taking his eyes off Patrick, tried to light it. He couldn't. His hands were trembling too much.

'Ah, leave it boys, so, it's Sunday,' said Tom.

The door opened. Sean stood in the doorway and waited while they all stood up. He had his hands in the pockets of his coat and his eyes were on Patrick.

'So himself is back,' he said. He nodded at the others, and they sat down. He closed the door behind him and walked towards Patrick. 'Where do you think you've been?'

'I've been keeping us safe, Sean.'

'And how have you been doing that? By not coming on a reconnaissance mission? By putting yourself in danger tomorrow? By gadding about town, chatting to floozies and letting every man Jack know there's a dozen triggermen over a carpenter's in Abbey Street, just in case the English want to call by for a cup of tea and a chat when they're at a loose end so?'

'No. By getting intelligence on a man who's had two of us killed and'll have more of us killed if we leave him be.'

Patrick saw that the muscles by Sean's left eye were twitching. He'd first seen that happen when Mam had caught Sean stealing cake from the kitchen and he'd denied it, the crumbs still on his lips.

'Intelligence is my job, Pat. Execution is yours.'

'Fine, if you'll do your job.'

Vinnie whistled softly and Tom looked down at his dominoes. Rory grinned, and took a pull on his cigarette. Joe muttered something about needing a shite and left for the bathroom.

'What did you say?' asked Sean.

The two brothers looked at each other for a long moment. Sean was an inch taller than Patrick. Sometimes it felt more like a foot.

'Ah come on, Sean. Part of our job is to tail English spies, and then kill them when the time is right. We've been tailing McMahon and Newbury and Bennett and Ames and Baggally and Fitzgerald. We know where they live, where they go, who they talk to, where they sleep, who they fuck. But we've not laid a finger on one of the biggest of the lot. Major Harry Lovegrove, of 23 Lower Mount Street. He's one of them, Sean. He's one of the Cairo Gang. He had Seamus and Colm shot and God knows how many more. And I know for a fact he's got someone on the inside. I told you about him. Why aren't we tailing him?'

'You haven't answered my question, yet, Pat. What have you been doing?'

'I've been getting to know Lovegrove's maid. I watched her leave the house, I watched her go to Mass, I got talking to her after Mass.'

'And what did she tell you about Lovegrove?'

'Nothing. Yet. But intelligence operations take time, and patience. As I'm sure you know.'

Sean looked at him a little longer, then broke into a smile. He stepped towards him and slapped him on the shoulder.

'Good, Pat, good job. You go to it, boy. You're a natural. I'll tell Mick you're wasted here. He recognises talent when he sees it. He'll have you promoted to IO.'

Then he kicked Patrick on the knee, hooked up his leg with his foot, twisted his arm behind him and threw him on the floor, face down. He took a gun out of his coat pocket and pointed it at Patrick's head.

'Sean, no,' said Tom. 'The boy's done wrong, and all, and he's cheeked you, and all, but not that. He's no traitor.'

Sean put his foot on Patrick's neck.

'Patrick Kelly,' he said, 'you are a soldier in the Irish Republican Army and you will obey the orders of a senior officer. This morning you absented yourself from a reconnaissance operation without official leave. I'm suspending you from operations for two days. When you get up, you can get your stuff and take yourself to Annie's house and relieve Declan. He deserves a couple of days off. You don't. You can sit in the dirt and the grime there, sleeping on a chair and listening to the old witch go on about women this and women that. But you'll have nothing more to do with any woman apart from Annie until the day Ireland's free. On Thursday, you'll be in the Cafe Cairo at eleven as planned. You'll tail Fitzgerald till one, and after that you'll take part in the day's mission. When I've seen how you perform on that mission I'll make up my mind whether or not to report you to Mick. He decides... I decide who gets followed and who gets shot. I have good operational reasons for every decision. Question those decisions again and I'll put a bullet in your fucking neck even though you are my brother. Do you understand?'

Blood was trickling from Patrick's nose, down into his mouth. It tasted sharp and salty. It tasted like defeat. He wanted to throw Sean to the floor and stamp on him.

'I understand, Sean.'

'Now get up, get your kit and bugger off out of here.'

CHAPTER FIVE

Volunteers on guard duty in Annie's house got the armchair in concession to its need to double up as a bed, but it was not comfortable; it was lumpy, and had three separate holes, each with sharp springs protruding. Nothing was comfortable in Annie's house. Patrick had just used the toilet, which was even more encrusted with brown than the last time he had been there, and as usual the chain did not work; he had to stand on the seat and reach inside for the ballcock to make it flush. A few feet away from the lumpy armchair, Patrick's prisoner sighed and muttered what might have been prayers or might have been curses. Annie would not say anything about him, and Patrick would not ask. She confined herself instead to asking him if he wanted his eggs fried, scrambled or boiled, to querying why in God's name should it not be her with the gun in her hand and him in the kitchen scrambling the eggs, to reminding him three times that the key to the spare room was behind the clock on the mantelpiece (because otherwise she would forget herself where it was), and to asking after Molly. Annie always asked after Molly.

He hadn't thought of Molly in a while. It was in Annie's house that he and Molly had first met, back before the

Rising, when Patrick was young and eager to learn. The first evening they'd almost come to blows about the right moment to use physical force in the struggle; after that they'd barely stopped talking. They'd fired each other up with a rage for Ireland, arguing on long walks round Dublin about politics and the struggle and the Ireland to come. She'd given him books to read, and an education he'd never got from the Christian Brothers. She had him down for the first President of Ireland, with her his deputy; she'd given him all the worship no one ever had. But for all that she'd taught him, and for all the fire he felt in their talks, he could never worship her back. She knew that, and it just made her worship him harder. When she talked of the redundancy of marriage under socialism, he knew she was asking him to marry her. He'd thought of her when he was under fire in the GPO, wondering if she'd be throwing flowers at him when he and the boys marched triumphantly down Sackville Street. But they'd lost, and he'd been taken to Frongoch. After a bit, they were allowed to write letters, and other men wrote screeds and screeds to their sweethearts, but he couldn't find the words. Couldn't find the words because he didn't feel them, was the truth. Any words he wrote would either be unkind or a lie. She'd been his teacher, not his lover. When he'd got out, there'd been a letter waiting for him. She'd upped and gone back to Kilkenny and married the lad she'd been walking out with before she came to Dublin. Since Molly, he'd had a few quick, urgent fumbles round the back of pubs or in doorways, and the occasional visit to North King Street when he could afford it, but nothing serious.

He rubbed his nose. It still ached. You bastard, Sean. And you had to do it in front of everyone. Why? They'd been all right when Mam was alive. Sure, they'd fought and all, but Mam had always managed to keep the peace at the end. Since Mam had gone, nothing had been right. There had been nothing but war since then. His mind went back to the day Mam died, as it often did when he was angry or upset.

It had been a lively afternoon in early spring. Through the open window, he could hear the birds getting busy as he knelt on the hard wooden floor of Mam and Da's bedroom, her breath heaving out as if she was dragging it over broken glass. The priest was going hammer and tongs at the prayers as if he was running out of time, which he was. Sean was next to him, kneeling also. He wanted to climb into bed with Mam, but he knew Sean would laugh at him for being soft if he did. Mam stopped in mid-breath and the priest stopped in mid-prayer. The priest reached over and closed her eyes. Patrick felt as if he was frozen to the floor and would never move again. Sean stood up slowly and carefully, took the clock off the wall, placed it on the floor, lifted his foot and stamped on it, shattering the glass. Then he stamped on it twice more.

'Sean,' said the priest. 'Your mother's dead. Kneel, and pray.'

Sean didn't even look at the priest, or Patrick, or Mam. He walked out of the room, down the stairs, past Da snoring in his armchair next to an empty bottle of Power's, and out the door.

'Ah, let him go, son,' said the priest. 'He's taken it harder than you have, so he has.'

Then he started the rosary. Sean came back twelve hours later, and there was blood down the front of his shirt. He never explained why. With Mam no longer there to stop him, Da had drunk a bottle of Power's a day for the next six years until he fell under a lorry in Sackville Street on the way home from losing his job for being drunk. He and Sean did nothing but fight. With Da dead, Sean had moved on to the English, with occasional side swipes at Patrick.

School had got him away from Da and Sean fighting at least, though the Christian Brothers beat him in class for not knowing enough, and the other lads gave him a kicking in the playground for knowing too much. But then Seamus and Colm took him on; after that it was all right, in the playground at least. He couldn't think of Seamus and Colm separately, couldn't tell them apart in his head. They'd been born the same day and they'd died the same day. Colm had hidden a worm in Seamus's stirabout at school once. Seamus had picked it out and pretended to take a big bite, and said it was delicious, and Colm had laughed and laughed and laughed. There was always something innocent about them, for all the killing they did. If he'd done that thing with the worm to Sean, he'd have ended up with his face smashed in the stirabout. Seamus and Colm were the brothers he should have had. The truth was, he'd loved them more than he'd ever loved anyone, apart from Mam. And now they were dead.

He shifted in the armchair, and moved his gun from his right hand to his left hand. He felt a surge of anger at the thought of Seamus and Colm. God, he'd like to shoot Lovegrove now. Be patient, Kelly. You'll save more lives in the long run that way.

Since he'd overheard the conversation in Grafton Street, he'd been following Aisling for a month, on and off, whenever he could manage it. He'd known Lovegrove would have some sort of maid or another. It had been a simple enough matter to start with to trail Lovegrove from the Castle to home. Number 23 Lower Mount Street was a modest place, well kept but not loved, in the way of a property let out for short periods, three storeys high, squeezed up tight and narrow and clean and smart between the other houses on the street like a soldier on parade. Modest for an English officer, anyways, though it was luxury compared to the North Dublin two up two down, with the blocked chimney and the smoky fire, the leaking ceiling and the neighbours' arguments coming through the walls, that he and Sean had grown up in. Once he'd found it he'd had to turn tail, or Sean would have wondered where he was.

After that, he'd had to snatch his moments to get out from under Sean. The first time had been a rainy Tuesday morning just a week after Seamus and Colm had died, when he and Rory had been close to reaching for their guns over Patrick spilling Rory's tea, Rory said on purpose, Patrick said by accident. They'd all been on edge because it had been a good three weeks since any of them had killed anyone and they were going mad with boredom. Sean had told the two of them both to bugger off to different ends of the city and not come back till tea time; he didn't care what they did as long as they came back sober. Patrick had seized his chance and stood in the rain, collar up, hat down, for a good two hours outside Lovegrove's house till the girl had finally emerged. *She'll do*, he'd thought the first time he'd seen her. *I can do what I need to with her.* Somehow he had just known.

She'd been all wrapped up against the rain in her shawl and all, with a shopping basket and an umbrella up. And Jesus, hadn't she set off at a clip. He was out of breath just keeping up with her. It was like she was trying to outwalk the rain. McAvoy's for a loaf and a lump of butter. Gateley's for a dozen potatoes. Connolly's for half a dozen sausages. So, there could only be the three of them; Lovegrove, Lovegrove's wife, and her. Grand. She'd be lonely, being the only one, for all that servants could be at each other's throats half the time, especially the women. Plus there'd be no one else there to gab it about if he got her doing what he wanted. He thought of her cooking the sausages, turning them round delicately in the pan, serving them up on the Englishman's shining white plates, two each for the captain and his wife, and then two left over for herself to have in the kitchen. It must be nice to eat by yourself in peace like that once in a while, not elbow to elbow with the twelve of you round a table meant for six, all grunting and snuffling like a lot of piglets.

There was the question of a fella. If she had one his job would be a lot harder. She had a fine figure, her behind rolling invitingly under her skirt as he followed her, and he'd have thought she'd have been in demand. A Sunday afternoon would settle that. That was the time for girls and their fellas. But Sundays were also a day for tailings – targets had their defences down on the weekend, would give a lot away about themselves. The second Sunday after Seamus and Colm had died, though, Sean had decided there were too many of them tailing and they'd give themselves away, and had left half of them at the base. Patrick had told the lads with a wink and a nudge that he was after a girl and that they were to keep their gobs shut, and slipped out a quarter of an hour after Sean had left. It had been a sunny day and he'd been happy enough standing across the street from her house, feeling the warmth on his face and breathing air that didn't stink of sweat and farts and stale food. She'd come out of the house a little after two, but not with the air of looking for anyone. A girl like her would have a fella coming to the house, he'd thought. She'd gone to Stephen's Green, walked around a little, looked at the ducks, sat in the sun. It was a long time since he'd walked on Stephen's Green with a girl on a Sunday afternoon. Molly would have been the last one; the only one, if truth were told. Molly had always been nineteen to the dozen, but this girl was quiet, alone. He wouldn't have minded going up to her, sitting down next to her, enjoying the sun together, but no; he had to keep out of sight, bide his time. *Never strike until you've walked round and round your man from every angle*, Sean used to say, and the same applied to intelligence work. Sitting there, she'd looked like she was thoughtful or sad about something. Could be a fella had let her down; maybe she'd taken this same walk with him, sat on this same bench with him? That would leave the door wide open for himself; nothing easier to bag than a girl who's been disappointed in love.

Mass was next. Everyone went to Mass, and the Squad were no exception, though they'd not go every week. The Sunday after he'd followed her to the Green, he was on an afternoon tail, so he told Sean he'd get his duty over with in the morning, and Sean had nodded all right. He'd thought it would be ten Mass for the girl – that was a servant's time, between getting breakfast ready and making lunch – and he wasn't wrong. The street was dead quiet on a Sunday morning. It was full of English officers, and they were all sleeping off their beer or their spying or their whoring. She'd come out of the house at half past nine, a pious one's time, enough to give herself a good twenty-five minutes praying before Mass; she could get half a rosary in. But instead of going to St Teresa's, five minutes step away, she'd led him halfway across the city at her usual lick to ten Mass at the Cathedral. He sat at the back a little breathless, three rows behind her, and wondered why here. Was there someone at St Teresa's she'd wanted to avoid? Maybe the fella who'd walked with her on Stephen's Green? She was looking upset all right, fighting with the tears and losing, so it could be that. *Don't make up any stories*, Sean would say. *Stick to what you can see with your own eyes. Stories will lead you down a blind alley, and straight into the hands of the English.* Sean was right, but the fact of the matter was that he couldn't stop making up stories about this girl. More stories every time he saw her. He had to think hard about Seamus and Colm, so hard the tears came to his own eyes, to push the stories away. The woman next to him looked at him. She must have thought he was praying for a dead loved one; he proved her right by offering one up for the twins. When he'd done that, he made up his mind. He'd do it next week, after Mass. Do it for Seamus and Colm.

Sean put them on an early tailing, but he didn't want to change his plan. He couldn't wait any longer; he'd chance it, find a way to blag it with Sean later. He rolled out of bed before any of them were up and slipped out. He was opposite the house before eight, enjoying the crisp cold air, feeling the stories about the girl come into his head, not bothering to push them away this time. When she came out of the house, she was crying again, worse than last week. More stories rushed in. A letter? The Stephen's Green lad opening old wounds? Being upset didn't slow her down, though; it seemed to speed her up if anything. When she got to the Cathedral she sat and looked steadily up and ahead towards the crucifix over the high altar. A little shaft of sun from one of the high windows caught her face. It was then that Patrick realised that he had never properly looked at her face before; all this time he'd had to keep behind her.

He didn't have much to do with faces. Looking into someone's face meant getting to know them, and it didn't do to know that much about a man you had to kill; you didn't want to be looking into eyes you had to put a bullet between. With women of course – unless you were paying – you had to do that thing of taking an interest, and nodding and smiling and looking encouraging and all, but that was just a means to an end. Not that he'd ever done that with Molly; she had just talked all the time. But now he found himself looking at this girl's face like he'd never looked at a face before. In the sun from the high window it seemed smooth but hard at the same time, as if it had been carved out of marble and then polished to a shine. She was looking up at Jesus on His cross, but in a way that said that Jesus Himself would do what she told Him, or she'd know the reason why. There was a kind of power came out of her, that he'd never seen in a woman; hadn't seen in a man, either. For the first time that morning she was still, her hands on her lap and the sun on her face. He wanted to go on looking at her. He punched his hat and swore under his breath, making the woman in front turn round and glare at him. *Come on Kelly*, he said to himself. *You've a job to do. Remember Seamus and Colm. There's lasses enough to poke in Dublin without going and compromising a lead.* But it had got worse now he'd started talking to her, found out her name, found out she'd fought the English and all, had a Da who'd died for Ireland and not for Power's whisky. What did she think of him? She seemed to like him; he hoped she did. He realised he cared, and not just because of what he wanted to get her to do. Though he'd spent just an hour in her company without tailing her, it felt like he'd known her a long time; long enough to see what he'd been missing with Molly. Molly was all talk and ideas, a walking book, thin as a whippet, as if eating was a waste of time, and her body a nuisance. But when Aisling walked down the street, it was like she loved her body, and wanted you to love it back, only without showing off somehow. She'd be in Lovegrove's house now. What was it like inside? She would keep it a damn sight cleaner than this dump, for sure. He wondered what it was like working for Lovegrove; wondered if he was good to her; wondered how long it would take to turn her against him. What if she took Lovegrove's side? What if she turned him in to the English?

He shifted again in the chair. Christ, it was the lumpiest chair in all Ireland. They should put informers in it, and they'd be confessing all within the hour. He sighed.

He wished Aisling was here now. He knew how to charm women all right. He knew he was good at it. Normally, he told women about the Rising to impress them. But he'd told Aisling about it because he wanted her to know, and because he wanted to go on talking to her all day. Not in the way that he used to talk to Molly, which was just for the talking; no, he'd wanted to go on talking to Aisling to go on being with her. And then Sean went and ordered him to stay away from women.

Annie picked her way up the stairs between tottering piles of books with a tray of eggs, toast and tea.

'Would you have a couple of rashers of bacon for me, Annie?'

'Get away with you. I'll not kill another being in order to live.'

Patrick jerked his head towards the door of the spare room.

'What do you think's going to happen to himself?'

'Pigs are not imperialist oppressors, nor are they their agents.'

'That's what you think. Who's to say the English haven't bought them off?'

'But you're sure now you haven't had a word from Molly?'

'Not a word, Annie. She's her life in Kilkenny to live now.'

'Well. If you ever do. She had a fine mind, that girl.'

'Oh, there was nothing wrong with her mind.'

Annie shook her head, and went back downstairs, reciting 'The Lake Isle of Innisfree' in a singsong voice as she went. Patrick scraped off the burnt part of the toast, which was most of it. Sean had ordered him to be at the Cairo at eleven on Thursday. He'd obey that order. And if Aisling was there as she'd promised ... Well, hadn't Mick himself told him once in Frongoch that sometimes a soldier had to be smarter than his officers? That most battles were won by initiative? Mick would approve, he was sure. He'd do things Mick's way. And he'd say nothing to Sean.

CHAPTER SIX

So now Aisling had a fella. She couldn't deny she was glad of it, felt better for it. She and Patrick would meet at the Cafe Cairo whenever he could get away from his work at the carpenter's, squeezing into a corner table amidst the fug of cigarette smoke and the gossip of women and the competitive banter of soldiers. They couldn't meet in the evenings as she'd to be in to look after the Lovegroves, but the cafe she could slip into when she was out doing messages in the day. He never knew from one week to the next when they could meet, though; his boss was his big brother, and he was that strict that Patrick had to wait for him to be out of town seeing to an order before he could sneak away. They agreed that he would leave notes for her at Connolly's the butchers with the time of their next meeting. Connolly would hand them over tucked under her sausages in return for a squeeze of her arm and whispered details, which grew saltier every week, of his courtship of Mrs Connolly and a couple of other women before she came on the scene. It was exciting to think of Patrick leaving notes for her and skiving off work to be with her, as if they were having a secret liaison. It did mean that at the Cairo he was always looking round himself, twitching, eyeing the other men in the cafe as if one of them might denounce him to his boss, and once or twice he had to leave in a hurry. He was more relaxed on Sundays, when they'd sit next to each other at Mass in the Cathedral, and then take a walk on St Stephen's Green. Wandering the pathways and nooks and crannies of the Green, watching the trees shed their leaves, it seemed easier to open up than in the Cafe where he was never at ease. Even so, Sundays weren't reliable either as there were weeks he wasn't there, apologising with a note at Connolly's afterwards; he had an elderly aunt who was constantly on the point of dying and he and his brother would get summoned away to her at weekends.

He was nothing like the young men she'd known in Clifden. For one thing, apart from that first day when he told her about the Rising, he barely talked about himself; instead, he wanted to know about her. He encouraged her to talk about Mam, and was patient when she wept, offering her his handkerchief over the table in the Cairo. He got her talking about Da and the IRA in Clifden, though he made sure to wait till they were in the middle of the Green with no one around first. He asked would she be ready to fight for Ireland again, and she said yes, and he nodded to himself and looked as if he was going to say something, but then he spotted a soldier walking towards them with a girlfriend and he changed the subject to the foul weather that it always was in Dublin. He told her a lot of stories about the days before the Rising, when he was in the Irish Republican Brotherhood, as it was before it became the Irish Republican Army, but hardly anything about his life now, except that his work was dull and his brother a proper so and so. He seemed to miss his fighting days. He asked her a lot about her work, and ended up knowing all of Major and Mrs Lovegrove's routines as well as she did herself. It was clear he liked her from the way he looked at her, but he never so much as laid a finger on her, which was most unlike your average man. She sometimes wished he would. She even thought of making the first move herself. She felt there was a lot he was keeping back. She wished she could call in on him at his shop, but he told her not to as he didn't want his brother knowing about his midweek escapes. He lived, he said, in a boarding house with a pile of unmarried men, the biggest dive you'd ever seen, and he wouldn't shame a woman by letting her near it, so there was no calling on him there either.

But it was enough to be walking out with a young man, especially one as handsome as him, and to have someone to talk to, to be a little less lonely in the city. Major Lovegrove had asked her once, before she'd met Patrick, if she had a sweetheart and by the relief on his face when she'd said no, she'd figured out that he wasn't keen on her having a follower, so she didn't say a word of it to him. She often wished she could, though. She wanted to be able to share her excitement with him, felt sure he'd understand. For all they confined themselves to pies and sausages and Mrs Lovegrove's nerves, she felt she could say anything to him and he could say anything to her, if only they got the chance. A room felt different with Major Lovegrove in it. His smile when he thanked her for breakfast or let her know that Mrs Lovegrove was looking a lot better (though she wasn't) seemed to light her up somehow. She felt easy with him but also nervous at the same time, as if there was something about to happen between them but she didn't know what.

Patrick and she had not spoken about the future, though she often thought of it alone in her room at night after Major Lovegrove had gone out to his woman. She felt as if Patrick gave her something to hope for. One day he might set up his own carpentry business. One day she could be like other women, marry, have children, make a life together with him in an independent Ireland once the war was over. She felt guilty when she thought of that; she ought to be fighting in that war still, but she didn't know how. Maybe a chance would come her way. Well, as Mam used to say, what would be would be. She'd only known him two months after all. No sense in running before they could walk.

But what happened between her and the Major on the second Saturday night in November put all those thoughts out of her mind.

She'd been deep in a dream of Da on fire, the one she had a lot, when she heard the tap tap tap, quiet at first, then getting louder.

'Aisling.'

She could hear him through the door. He was almost whispering, and there was something in his voice she'd never heard before, as if he was ashamed or afraid even. Tap, tap, tap.

'Aisling.'

She felt scared all of a sudden. She climbed out of her bed, felt for her shawl in the dark, wrapped it round her and opened the door. The Major was standing on the landing, holding a candle. He was in his pyjamas and dressing gown, but he was as perfectly turned out as ever, the lapels of his pyjama jacket neatly spread over his gown.

'Aisling, I'm sorry to wake you. It's an ungodly hour. I... the truth is I don't know what to do.'

'What is it, Major Lovegrove? Are you not well?'

'No. Not me.'

'Is Mrs Lovegrove not well?'

'No. Not ... it's not that. Come with me, would you?'

He led her down the stairs to the landing where his and Mrs Lovegrove's bedroom was. He didn't say a word. He was walking fast, and the candle flame bent back so far it almost blew out. She walked fast too. She'd never been with him with the both of them in their night clothes. It felt like doing something they knew they shouldn't be doing, but wanted to do anyway. The door to the bedroom was open. The sheets had been pushed back and the bed was empty. Still holding the candle, he threw his hand out to the bed.

'Look.'

'Where is she?'

'She's gone, Aisling. I knew it would happen one day. Christ, I'm an idiot. I should have had her put somewhere safe. I was going to... until you came. What kind of a husband am I?'

'Have you looked...?'

'Yes. Thorough recce. I got back from... from seeing a friend... at two. I wasn't ready for sleep. I don't sleep much, you know, since the war. Happens to a lot of men who were out in France. So I worked for a bit in my study till three. Then I went to the bedroom. Expected to find her there like I always do. She's a good sleeper. I never wake her. But she was gone.'

'She's not in the bathroom?'

'Bathroom, living room, kitchen, dining room, my study, the spare room, the scullery. I've been in every room in the house. Bar yours, Aisling. You've not got her in there, have you?'

'No, sir.'

'There's nothing more I can do now till first light. By then it'll be too late. I've lost her. I should never have married her. What was I thinking? I should have seen the signs. Her father warned me. But I was transfixed. She was a beautiful woman. And she loved me, with a passion. It's hard for a man to resist that.'

He put the candle down on the table by the bed, sat on the bed, and buried his face in his hands. A sob, then a second, then a third, came out. He looked like a little boy who knew he was in trouble. Aisling walked towards the bed and sat down next to him.

'Sir?'

She put her arm round him. His dressing gown was smooth to the touch. She had ironed it that afternoon, taking care with the shoulders. They were always hard to get right, but she never let any creases get through. She began stroking his back with slow, circular motions. He looked up at her.

'What do you think of me, Aisling?'

His eyes were wet, and gleamed in the candlelight. She went on rubbing his back and reached out with her other hand and brushed the tears away from first one eye, and then another. His skin was smooth to the touch. She realised she was breathing faster, as though she had been running.

'Sir? I think... you're a good man to work for.'

'They all say that. At the Castle. Even... even some of the other people I work with say that.'

'I think you're a good man.'

'No one says that. Nor should they. Emily has never said it. Not that she says anything these days. Not that she ever will now.'

She took his hand between hers and held it.

'You were kind to me, sir. You gave me a job when I turned up on your doorstep with nothing, orphaned and desperate. I'd be out on the streets if it wasn't for you.'

'I'd be desperate without you, Aisling.'

He looked up at her now, his eyes clear of tears, firm and bright. She felt her face burning.

'Do you know what it's like? Do you know what it's like being who I am?'

'No, sir. I'm not sure we know that about anyone.'

He smiled at her. She smiled back.

'You're a wise woman, Aisling.'

'Thank you, sir.'

'A wise woman and an extraordinary one. I've seen you these last four months. I know what you've had to cope with. A household with no mistress. A man who's as good as widowed. You've kept us going, Aisling. More than that. You've given us our home back.'

'Thank you, sir. But I've only been doing my job. I enjoy it. I like keeping things straight.'

'It must be hard for you being so far from home. I miss England sometimes. I don't like the city. I grew up by the sea. Norfolk. A bleak, flat place on the eastern edge of England. Beautiful, though. Hardly anyone there. I liked that. Do you miss Clifden?'

He was close to her, talking very softly, almost whispering, as if he did not want to wake his absent wife. She could smell on his breath the sweet tobacco he smoked in his pipe. She looked down at his hand, the hand she had seen writing in the middle of the night. There were short black hairs on his wrist, that pricked a little into her hand.

'Yes. Every day.'

He waited a little. She waited a little. She noticed her heart beating faster; wondered if he could hear it.

'That fire. The one that burnt our house down. It was English soldiers that started it. My Da didn't die in the fire. He was shot in the head by an English soldier. The same soldier was going to shoot me as well until his officer ordered him not to. There've been days I've wished he'd gone ahead and done it.'

She felt as if she'd leapt across a great ditch and landed safely on the other side, telling him that.

Major Lovegrove breathed in sharply. She could feel his whole body tense. She squeezed his hand.

'Well thank God he didn't,' he said. 'Or I wouldn't have you.'

'Have you ever killed anyone, sir?'

'Yes. I'm a soldier. That's what soldiers do in a war. If you don't kill the enemy, they'll kill you. That's how it is. I'm talking about the war with Germany, of course. Nowadays all I do is shuffle bits of paper around in Dublin Castle. Dull, but peaceful. A welcome change.'

He made to pull his hand away from hers, but she held onto it tighter. Something had opened up between them and she didn't want to close it, for all she knew it was dangerous.

'What does it feel like? Killing a man?'

He made to turn away, but then he turned back and looked at her. He seemed to be weighing something in his mind. She desperately wanted to know what he was thinking.

'When you do it... it's exciting. It feels like... like going to bed with a woman... '

He looked at Aisling when he said that, and blood rushed into her face with painful, thrilling suddenness.

'But later, afterwards, when you think about what you've done, you feel ashamed. You feel haunted by the men's faces, as if they won't leave you alone, as if you've got them with you forever, even though they're dead. So perhaps it's like going to bed with someone you shouldn't go to bed with.'

She'd often noticed the draught that came in under the window when she'd been making Mrs Lovegrove's bed. Now it blew on the candle flame, making it gutter and flicker, throwing their shadows large against the wall behind the bed. The flame struggled, almost went out, then came back to life. She saw his face expectant, in a blaze of new light. She felt on the brink of something. Something that she had been expecting for a long time, but that had to happen now, that she could hold back no longer. That was when she reached for him.

She put her hands behind his head and pulled him towards her, pressing her lips against his. She kissed him deeply and greedily. She felt as if she wanted to be swallowed by him, to disappear inside him. Soon he was kissing her back, his arms round her, holding her tight, not letting her go. He pushed her down towards the bed. A warm shuddering feeling ran from her knees up to her head. She was on her back on the bed, and she could hear him moaning softly to himself. His thigh had thrust in between her thighs, rucking up her nightdress, and it rubbed against her as he kissed her. Through his dressing gown she could feel him hard against her thigh. She felt hot and wet between her legs.

She went over it in her mind many times afterwards, searching her memory like Father Garvey had taught them to in catechism classes, and she was quite sure. She couldn't blame him. He never touched her first. Maybe he'd spoken out of turn, maybe he'd said what shouldn't be said by a married man to a woman who was working for him, but she could have got up, left, thanked him and gone back to her bed, and in the morning it could have been forgotten like a disturbing dream. She liked being with Patrick, and he was a good looking fella, but this was nothing like being with Patrick. And, God forgive her, she didn't want it to stop. She wanted it to go on and on and on, and not stop until they were both naked and he was inside her.

But he stopped it. Suddenly, with no warning, he lifted his face from hers, and looked down at her with a kind of horror. He took his arms out from under her and pushed himself up from the bed. He stood up straight as if he was coming to attention, and loosened the cord of his dressing gown, and then tightened it so hard and so fast it must have hurt him. Still on her back on the bed, she felt as if she had been thrown out of a high window and was spinning towards the ground.

'Good God,' he said. 'What am I thinking of? What are you doing, Lovegrove? Your wife's missing, and you... '

He turned his back on her, and walked away to the window, thrusting his hands in the pockets of his dressing gown, seeming to look out of the window, though the curtains were drawn. Aisling sat up on the bed, pulled on her shawl, crossed her legs and hunched forward, wrapping herself tight. She felt terribly cold all of a sudden.

'I'm sorry, Aisling,' he said to the curtains. 'I shouldn't have woken you. You need your sleep. Go and get some.' She looked at his back. She wanted to go and put her hands round his waist and bury her face in his hair. 'It's at a time like this,' he went on, 'that I could do with a telephone. Brind wouldn't let me have one. Said it would draw attention...' She wanted to cry out at him, to shout and scream, to use all the cursing words she knew and then some. 'I can do nothing now,' he said, briskly, harshly, as if the curtains were a junior officer he was reprimanding for slack work. 'Nothing until daylight. Until the Castle opens for business. No point me wandering around Dublin in the middle of the night. One of us is enough. I'll just have to wait... try to...'

His voice tailed off. She walked towards him, slowly, furtively, one pace at a time, as if she was a burglar in his house. She held her hand out, three inches from his shoulder. She saw her hand was trembling. 'I should have had her put away. You bloody fool, Lovegrove.'

The moment she touched him, before she even had time to rest her whole hand on his shoulder, he spun round on his heel. She whipped her hand away, holding it up in front of her face, expecting a blow. His voice rose to a shout.

'Didn't you hear me? Get some sleep, woman.'

His face was red, and she saw his hands were shaking too. She turned, and walked out of the room as fast as she could without running. She took the steps two at a time up to her room, feeling as if she was being chased. She kicked the door shut behind her, threw herself on her bed and gave herself up to sobs. Sobs of shame, sobs of humiliation, sobs of rage, sobs that took her whole body and shook it up and down, from her head to her feet.

Oh, sweet Jesus, what had she been thinking of? What had she done? She'd kissed her boss. She'd kissed a married man. And then he'd gone for her. But she'd led him on. She'd tipped him the wink. Oh Mother of God. What would she do now?

But it had been sweet. Oh so sweet. She hadn't wanted it to stop. If he hadn't stopped, she would have gone on right to the end. Right to damnation itself. Oh God. And when he had pulled himself off and walked away, he'd as well have slapped her in the face. She wished he had. Because then she could have slapped him back. Because he deserved it. The bastard. To take advantage of her like that, and then walk off, talking about his wife and his care for her and all. When she knew he had a mistress somewhere else. They were all the same. The same as the ones who burnt down her house and murdered her Da. Murdering, raping English bastards.

Oh but dear God, but what if she'd fallen in love with him? Fallen in love with a man who was her boss and married and a murdering English bastard. And what if he was in love with her himself? Why in God's name else would he have got so angry?

Her sobs subsided. Her eyes hurt and her throat was dry. She could hear him downstairs in his study, clattering around, opening and closing his desk, talking to himself. She couldn't hear what he was saying, but it sounded as if he was giving himself orders. A little patch of moonlight through the window lit up Mam's rosary, hanging on the bedpost. *When you're in trouble*, Mam used to say, *any kind of trouble, go to the Lord. Tell Him what's on your mind.* She pulled herself up, knelt on the bed and took Mam's rosary in her hands.

Oh my God I am really sorry for my sin and I beg forgiveness, she prayed. *I firmly resolve with the help of your grace to sin no more. I firmly resolve. I firmly resolve. Firmly firmly firmly.* Ah, as if she could. As if it was any good. His face was in front of her, eyes gleaming, shimmering in the half-light between her and the little thin tortured body of the Lord on the crucifix at the end of the rosary. His tobacco breath was on her lips, mingled with her breath. She still felt the pressure of him hard against her thigh. How could she firmly resolve? He was in her, he was part of her now. She couldn't give him up like giving up sugar in her tea for Lent. But she had to. He'd probably sack her anyway. Get her out of the way. Oh dear God. She'd be out on the street.

She threw herself back on her bed and buried her face in her pillow. She cried some more, softly now, until she had no tears left. She felt as if she had been hollowed out from the inside and had nothing left except a dull ache. After a while, she fell into sleep.

It seemed like only a very short time before she was woken by a door slamming downstairs. He had gone out. She looked at the clock on the table by her bed. Twenty to nine. She lay back on her bed and thought. It didn't seem quite so bad now that she'd slept a little and it was light outside. She felt the need to do something. To turn out some cupboards. But she didn't want to turn out his cupboards. They would smell of him. *When you're heavy in your mind and prayer won't do the trick,* Mam used to say, *go to the confessional. You can trust a priest in the confessional. You're not talking to a man there, Aisling. You're talking to the Holy Spirit Himself.* It was Sunday. She would go to ten Mass in the Cathedral as usual, but she'd set out early so she could go to confession. Then she'd do whatever the priest told her to. Thank God Patrick wouldn't be there; he'd told her the last time they'd met that his aunt had summoned him and his brother again for that weekend. They were to meet next on Wednesday morning at the Cairo. She didn't want to think about what she'd have to say to him then.

She got off the bed and washed and dressed briskly, feeling her energy come back with action. She went down the stairs fast, almost running, not wanting to look into the bedroom. She didn't look in the living room either, where the Major sat in the evenings with his paper and his whiskey and his pipe, nor did she go into the kitchen, where she had cooked his meals. She'd have no breakfast today, because there wasn't time, because she wanted to go to communion after confession, and because she wasn't hungry. She pulled on her shawl and got out of the house as fast as she could. The sharp winter sun hurt her eyes which were still red with crying.

'Bless me Father, for I have sinned.'

The wood of the confessional in the Cathedral was hard under her knees. Through the tightly latticed metal grille she had a glimpse of a man pinned to the wall screaming in pain and another seated, hands in lap. The priest looked a little like Da; he had the same way of tipping his head to one side when he listened to her. *Ah, Da,* thought Aisling. *If you could see me now.*

'Go on.'

He had heard her pause. He knew this was not the usual disposal of daily failures, like sweeping burnt food into a bin. She felt relieved already, even before she'd spoken. He'd say the right thing, this one. He'd tell her what to do.

'I kissed a man.'

'Yes?'

'A married man.'

The head lifted from its side, nodding now, slowly.

'And did matters go any further, my girl? Was there nothing but what you said?'

She felt him pressing her down on the bed with his body, his lips against hers; felt him hard against her. His fingers were locked together in the small of her back, drawing her towards him, and she could smell the sweet tobacco on his breath, hear his heart beating in between the beats of her own. She was moistening between her legs, there in the confessional, in the middle of the church, in the presence of a priest. How could she stop herself?

'Nothing... no greater sin than that, Father. I mean, it didn't go to the next stage. He is very unhappy, I think. His wife is not well. She may be in some danger.'

'Well then the last thing he needs is temptation putting in his way at such a time.'

She squirmed a little, and felt herself blushing.

'I know, Father. I'm sorry.'

'That's good. Your sorrow for what you've done is a gift from God. How do you know this man?'

'I work for him. I'm his maid.'

More silent nodding.

'A dangerous situation indeed. And – from the sound of you – you're not from Dublin, are you?'

'No, Father. Connemara.'

'How long have you been in Dublin?'

'Four months, Father.'

'You're here on your own? No family?'

'Yes, Father.'

'What brought you here?'

'There was trouble at home. Trouble with the English.'

'Sure, we all have trouble with the English. How long have you been working for this man?'

'Since soon after I came to Dublin. I was surprised to be given the job – I had no references or anything.'

'There may be a warning in that. Could you not find another job?'

'I'm not sure I should leave him... with his wife the way she is.'

'You've not made things any easier for him.'

'He's far from home too. He's English. A Protestant.'

Deep breaths. A finger tapped on the nose.

'These are dangerous times. Just the other day, I saw a man shot in the street – gunned down in cold blood. I thanked God I was there to give him the last rites. But you're in the greatest danger of all – of mortal sin. Listen to me, my girl. I'm talking sense now.' She'd do what he told her. 'As soon as you can, find yourself another job. And find yourself a good, solid Irish boy, a Catholic, who loves his country and loves you. And when you do, be sure to -'

'I have one -'

He drew his breath in, annoyed at being interrupted.

'I'm sorry to interrupt you, Father. But I have a... well, a young man I'm walking out with. An Irish boy. A Catholic. A patriot.'

'That's grand. So you've no need to be fooling around with Englishmen, still less married ones, have you now? This fella of yours – I've a hunch the Lord's sent him to keep you safe in these times. And that's what a girl on her own in a city needs. Do you understand what I'm saying, my girl?'

'Yes, Father.'

'Will you stick with this lad? What's his name now?'

'Patrick.'

'Will you stick with Patrick? He's the one God wants for you. Will you do that now?'

She didn't want to stick with Patrick. She realised that now; it was clear to her. She wanted to stick with Major Lovegrove. She wanted to take up the space left empty in his bed by his wife. She wanted to show him she could be better than his secret mistress, wherever she was and whoever she was. She wanted to wake up with him and live with him and not be separated from him and she wanted him to be with her now, next to her, holding her. But this was the Holy Spirit talking to her, face to face, through this priest, like Mam had taught her, and if you sinned against the Holy Spirit you were damned whatever you did.

'I'll stick with Patrick, Father.'

'Good girl. And find yourself another job now. Make a good act of contrition, and for your penance say three Hail Marys and three Our Fathers.'

Aisling sank resignedly into the familiar words. *Oh my God I am sorry for having offended you.* She was sorry. She knew it was wrong. She wished it hadn't happened all right. But it had. *Because I dread the loss of heaven...* Though God knew Major Lovegrove's arms around her had felt more like heaven than anything else she'd ever known...*and the pains of hell.* Sure, she'd be punished if she went on with it. She'd deserve to be. *And I firmly resolve by the help of your grace to amend my life and to sin no more.* No more. That would need help all right. But no more. Stop now. Enough of it. Please God, let it be gone.

The priest wiped away her sin with a muttering of Latin and a brisk up and down and across of his hand, and she went and knelt in the third pew from the back and knuckled her forehead as she said her prayers. She would hear Mass and go to communion, and afterwards, she'd do what the priest had said. She would. He was right. She had to leave, get another job. Major Lovegrove would give her a good reference. He'd have to. She deserved it, apart from anything else. She'd worked hard. She'd looked after him, and his wife. On Wednesday at the cafe she'd tell Patrick that the Major had made advances at her and she wanted to leave and she would ask Patrick for his help in getting a new job. She had no one else in all Dublin to help her. She was alone. Everything depended on Patrick now.

CHAPTER SEVEN

Sister Coogan ignored Harry, and went on writing notes. Behind her, the ward was half lit, sepulchral, gas lights flickering and the curtains drawn although it was daytime now. Several of the women were tied to their beds. Two or three of them were moaning softly to themselves. One woman was shouting down curses alternately on Jesus and Mary. The others stared out as blankly as the bare walls they looked at. The ward smelt of disinfectant and boiled cabbage. In the far corner he could see Emily. He saw she was mumbling to herself, but he couldn't hear what she was saying. At least she was alive. And warm. And dry.

Finally Sister Coogan looked up from her desk.

'You've nothing to reproach yourself for, Major Lovegrove,' she said.

Except for kissing my maid in the middle of the night, thought Harry. While my wife was throwing herself in the river. Kissing my maid and wanting to go on, on to the end. Well, he'd managed to stop himself. That was something. But he wasn't sure he could stop himself again.

'Do you say that to all the husbands?' he said.

'Only when it's true.'

'Thank God she was found. Thank God there were men patrolling the curfew.'

'Amen to that,' said Sister Coogan. 'The policeman who jumped in after her deserves a medal.'

'I'll do my best to see he gets one,' said Harry.

'In November and all.'

'Can I see my wife now?'

Sister Coogan took Harry to Emily's bed. At least she isn't strapped down, he thought. Her words were running into each other now, and her eyes were drooping.

'See now, she's settling,' said Sister Coogan. 'That little injection Dr O'Dwyer gave her is calming her down. She'll be asleep like a baby before we know it.'

There would be some who would say that all this was God's punishment, thought Harry. But it had happened before he'd kissed Aisling. Though not before he'd wanted to kiss her. He'd wanted to kiss her for weeks, kiss her and more, almost since the morning she'd come, walking into his house like an angel. He'd lied to himself that there was nothing to it, that she was just a pretty girl he enjoyed talking to, but the truth was that he couldn't get her out of his head. He had to stop himself following her round the house. He found himself thinking of her when he should have been concentrating on prising information out of an informant or giving a report to Brind; it was starting to affect his work. It wasn't like Mrs Collett, the war widow who'd buzzed round him at home when Emily had got ill. It was like Emily at the beginning, only more so, much more so. Night after night he would lie in bed, Emily asleep next to him, longing to hold Aisling in his arms. What had happened was going to happen sooner or later. And, he realised with a leap of joy, she had been the one who had started it.

'When you go to church this morning, you need to thank the Lord that your wife's safe, Major Lovegrove. The cold of those waters could have killed a man ten times her strength,' said Sister Coogan.

Kissing Aisling – or rather, her kissing him– had felt more like God's reward than God's punishment. God's reward for having put up for so long, so faithfully, with the misery of his wretched, pointless, lying marriage. At last, a woman who wanted him. Who didn't freeze up in terror at his touch. Who wasn't mad. Who would talk to him. Who reached for him, who pressed her lips to his.

Emily was mumbling now, her mouth twitching a little.

'She's going to need longer than we can keep her here,' said Sister Coogan. 'I'll be fetching Dr O'Dwyer, and he can advise you of what to do next.'

Emily's head tipped to one side on the pillow, and her eyes closed. She was snoring slightly, as she did. She won't tell me why she did it, he thought. Aisling, though, could talk; Aisling could talk beautifully. They said that about the Irish, that they knew how to talk, and she did, but in fact it was more that he could talk to her. He felt as if he could go on talking to her all day, that they'd never run out of things to say. And yet there were a hundred things he still wanted to say to her that he hadn't dared say yet; about the waste of the last six years with Emily, about the dead men who haunted his dreams, about what it was like being a secret soldier, lying and bribing and blackmailing in a dirty filthy war against her people. About what it was like to live in an empty marriage. He'd been ready to start telling her those things when she'd reached for him. But she was the wrong nationality and the wrong station in life and the wrong religion and he wasn't married to her.

Dr O'Dwyer strode in. He looked like a man who was used to people listening to him and doing what he told them. It must come from being surrounded by women.

'Major Lovegrove?'

'Dr O'Dwyer. Thank you for seeing me.'

Dr O'Dwyer looked over his half moon spectacles at a clipboard.

'Your wife has made a good recovery from the physical shock of her fall – or rather, her jump – into the waters of the Liffey. However, it has either triggered, or was triggered by, a mental disturbance which is more serious. She is likely to need intensive care for some time. Some considerable time. Potentially – let me be frank with you, man to man – the rest of her life. You may have to be without a wife, Major Lovegrove. You may have to make other arrangements. Do you understand my meaning?'

'I believe I do, doctor.'

'Well. The English are famously resourceful in these matters. Now, we need to talk about practicalities. I know of a fine place in Kingstown, lovely spot by the sea, easy to visit from Dublin, but far from the bustle and care of the city.'

'St Mary's?'

'That's the one. You've already considered it, perhaps? I think your wife could find peace there; and you yourself could find peace of mind. She'd be well looked after. What do you say, Major?'

You may have to make other arrangements.

'Thank you, doctor. That sounds an excellent proposal. I'll put it into action straight away.'

Which would mean he and Aisling would be alone in the house together. He felt a sharp thrill at the thought; he felt himself growing hard.

When Harry got back to the house, he picked the *Irish Times* off the doorstep, as he did every morning. Nothing in Dublin yesterday, but more killings in Cork. It could only be a matter of time before there was a full-out war. Perhaps then they'd put him in a uniform again. At least that would be more straightforward and honest and manly than lurking the streets at night like a whore, picking up tittle-tattle here and there. He hated all that.

He went inside. The hall with the umbrella stand and the table for post and his pictures of Norfolk was the same. But the house felt different. There was no Emily to look in on upstairs. He gave a little sigh and shook his head. He hadn't been such a bad husband. He had loved her once, truly, when they were first married. He'd tolerated her wild swings of energy and emotion. When she'd got ill, he'd talked to her every day, he'd been kind to her. He'd provided for her. Though he'd been to visit prostitutes, it had been to gather intelligence, not to use them, not like half the men at the Castle, including the married ones. He'd been faithful to her. Until last night.

'Aisling?' he called out, tentatively, more a question than a command. No answer. He walked down the hall to the door to the kitchen. The kitchen was her domain. He never set foot in it. Going into the kitchen would feel almost as thrilling and dangerous as pushing her down on the bed. He tapped gently at the door.

'Aisling?' Almost a whisper now, a confidence in a lover's ear. Still nothing. He took a deep breath, grasped the handle and opened the door in one brisk motion. The scrubbed table was empty, with the chairs tucked under it. The cloths for drying the dishes were all hung straight, to the same length. A row of pans on a shelf gleamed back at him. Stone jars labelled for tea and coffee and butter and sugar sat on another shelf. The cooker shone in the sunlight, free of blemish. Aisling was impeccably neat and tidy, always.

Except for last night. She hadn't been very neat and tidy then, when she had surged at him like a wild animal. He remembered her nightdress falling away and her thighs parting under him and again he felt himself growing hard at the thought. And then he'd shouted at her and made her cry and run from the room. Oh God, he wanted her here now. He wanted her in his arms. His conscience had told him to push her away but his conscience was a fool. Why wasn't she here? Had she run away? Should he go up to her room and see if her things were still there? What if she had thrown herself in the river as well? He didn't know what he'd do if she had left.

CHAPTER EIGHT

Aisling was outside on the doorstep. She took her key out of her purse and looked at it. She remembered the priest's words. *I've a hunch the Lord's sent him to keep you safe.* She thought about Patrick. Patrick was interested in her. He liked her. He'd never shouted at her to go and get some sleep. He'd fought bravely against the people who'd killed her father. He wasn't English. He wasn't a Protestant. He wasn't married.

But the *Irish Times* she had stepped over on her way out had been picked up. That meant Major Lovegrove was back. He was only a few feet away. She wondered if she should turn round and leave now, find a cheap boarding house for the night, come back later for her things on Monday when the Major was out. The truth was she didn't want to. Instead, she wanted to swing open the door and jump into the Major's arms. *When you're tempted*, Father Garvey used to say, *think of the pain that giving into the temptation would cause. Sin always ends in pain, one way or another.* She pushed the key into her hand, the sharp edges cutting into her, making it hurt. Right. She would do it now, properly, honestly, face to face. She would give her notice, apologise for the inconvenience, gather up her things. She could forfeit her wages; she'd put by enough to keep herself for a week or two while she found another situation. She took a deep breath, put the key in the lock and turned it.

The Major was standing at the other end of the hall, in front of the kitchen door, staring ahead, looking guilty, like a little boy caught raiding the sweet jar. What was he doing there? He never normally went near the kitchen. There were dark stains under his eyes, as if the flesh had been dragged down. He walked towards her briskly, his whole face sagging into a smile.

'Aisling. Where have you been?'

'I've been to Mass, sir. I always go to ten Mass on Sunday.'

'Of course. Of course you do. I'd completely forgotten about church. Forgot to go myself. Went clean out of my head. The vicar will have noticed. Might call in at evensong – tell him something came up at work. I thought you'd left too, you know. You as well as Emily. Thank God you're back. I need you, Aisling. They found Emily. In the docks. They had to fish her out. Don't leave me now, Aisling. I need you. Don't leave me.'

She embraced him, there in the hall. He put his head on her shoulder and held her and wept. She stroked his fine dark hair and told him she was sorry for his trouble. She couldn't leave now. There could be no harm in it, in staying a little longer. The man's wife had just died. He'd be going home, packing up the house, back to England; they'd not make him stay here. And she'd have the perfect reason to move on to another place, start again. Even so, she didn't want to stop holding him. Holding him made her feel strong, and weak at the same time. Holding him was bringing back the previous night. Holding him made her go moist between the legs. Holding him was an occasion of sin.

'They heard the splash,' he said, lifting his head from her shoulder, looking down at her, his face wet with tears. She stepped back from the embrace, brushed her hands on her skirt, as if getting something off them.

'Who did?'

'Thank God they heard the splash. Two policemen, patrolling the curfew, at half past two. They told me in the Castle, when I went in. It'd have been... just the time I was waking you. At Sir John Rogerson's Quay. It's only ten minutes walk away. She must have been walking around the city for hours before she did it.'

'Did they get to her in time?'

'One of them jumped in after her. Jumped in! In November! Held her up, carried her up the steps. They wrapped her in their coats. One of them ran for a car. They took her to the Mater. She's there now. I've been to see her. She's in a terrible state. I mean, they've got her warm and dry and everything, but she's muttering to herself and talking all kinds of nonsense. She didn't recognise me. The doctor said she couldn't be left. She's to be watched all the time. He says he knows of a place in Kingstown. Specially for ladies. Very good care. Very reasonable rates.'

Then he stopped talking, and looked at Aisling, as if he was wondering what to do next.

'Oh, sir. I'm so sorry. She was a good woman.'

'She's still alive, Aisling.'

'Yes. I'm sorry. She is a good woman.'

'She's still alive, but the truth is I don't love her any more. I did once, but I don't any more. Does that make me a monster, Aisling?'

'I... you're not a monster, sir.'

'The truth is...'

He's going to tell me he loves me, she thought. What do I do then?

'The truth is what, sir?'

'The truth is I don't know what to do.'

Something collapsed inside Aisling. She felt like crying. Instead, she reached for activity.

'Have you had any breakfast, sir?'

'No.'

'Sit yourself down in the dining room and I'll make you a nice plate of fry.'

She was glad to get into the kitchen. He never came into the kitchen. She filled a kettle and put it on one of the hobs of the stove. She couldn't leave the man now, she told herself. Who would look after him? She took down a pan, put it on the other hob, sliced off a lump of butter, and dropped it in the pan. Poor man. On his own. Still, he'd been on his own before, as good as. She reached for the eggs, and cracked two in a bowl. She realised she was as hungry as he must be, and cracked two more in. She began chopping some mushrooms. He'd have to stay in Dublin if his wife was in a home here. God only knew when she'd get better, or if she'd get better. She took down the packet of bacon, peeled a couple of rashers off, remembered herself and peeled two more off. The butter was sizzling nicely now. She dropped the bacon in the pan, swept in the mushrooms off the chopping board, and added the eggs. No, someone else could look after him. She wasn't the only maid in Dublin. And she could look after someone else; this wasn't the only house in Dublin. The white of the eggs hardened slowly. She pushed the food round the pan a little. She saw Patrick's face. Saw his eyes. He had beautiful eyes, no doubt about that. *I've a hunch the Lord's sent him to keep you safe.* She wasn't sure she wanted to be safe. The kettle was boiling. She took down the teapot, poured a little water in, swished it around, poured it in the sink. Then she reached for the tea. As she reached for it, she saw the Major through the door into the dining room. He was looking ahead as if he was thinking very hard. He seemed to sense her looking at him, and he turned to her, and when he turned, he smiled. It was the smile of a man who'd been away a long time and had come home at last. She smiled back. For a moment, she felt completely at peace. This was her home. She had no other. Clifden was gone, burnt to ashes. And it seemed to have become more truly her home now Mrs Lovegrove's silent misery no longer weighed down on the house. Now there were just the two of them. She remembered the fry. It was just exactly ready. She took the pan off the stove, made the tea, divided the fry into two plates, poured the tea, and went into the dining room. She placed one plate, one cup of tea, one knife and one fork in front of the Major. He looked up at her for a long time, that same smile on his face. He didn't look like a nearly widowed man. She didn't want to go back to the kitchen.

'Thank you, Aisling. Thank you for everything.'

'Eat that up, sir. You need it.'

She made herself go back to the kitchen. She closed the door behind her so she wouldn't see him any more. She poured herself a cup of tea, took down her plate of fry and began to eat it. She could hear the sound of his knife and fork on the plate through the door. Something hurt inside her, like a pain in her stomach, though she still had her appetite. She tried to think of Patrick's face. She found she couldn't.

When he'd finished eating he knocked on the door from the dining room to the kitchen. She opened it. He stood there shyly, like a little boy, not like a man in his own house. His face looked very soft.

'Thank you, Aisling,' he said. 'That was delicious. In fact, I think it was one of the best meals I've ever had in my life. I'm going out now. I have to take a train out to Kingstown, to pay a visit to the home Mrs Lovegrove will be staying in. She will have to be there a very long time. Maybe the rest of her life. After that... I have people I have to see tonight. I'll be dining out, coming back late, no need to wait up for me at all. So you have plenty of time to get the house straight. Not that it needs getting straight. You keep us... you keep the house very straight. I'm sorry I shouted at you last night, Aisling. I was overwrought.'

'Don't you worry, sir. I don't blame you in the slightest. I'm sorry that... '

That she'd kissed him? That she wanted to kiss him again, now, here on the threshold between her kitchen and his dining room?

'No, Aisling. You have nothing to be sorry for. Nothing at all.'

He stood there a little longer, as if he was waiting for her to say something. Though a thousand words were dancing in her head, she didn't say anything. He turned, and went into the hall, and put his coat and his hat on and went out. She stood still where she was. After a while, she went into the dining room and picked up his plate and his cutlery, and took it back into the kitchen to wash along with hers. When she'd tidied up in the kitchen, she set about ironing some of his shirts. She wanted, desperately, to talk to Da, to tell him what was on her mind. But then again, even if Da was still alive, she couldn't have. Because what was going through her mind was not something any girl could talk to her Da about.

CHAPTER NINE

Patrick was early for Aisling in the Cafe Cairo on Wednesday. He ordered a tea. The bottom half of the big windows was steaming up with the rain. Outside, on Grafton Street, people walked briskly, heads bowed, hands in pockets, eyes down. Every few minutes the door clanged open and the sound of the rain came in and a whiff of stewed tea and baking and cigarette smoke escaped, and a man with a turned up coat and a dripping hat or a couple of soldiers made an inch or two taller by their uniforms or a cluster of tightly wrapped women would step inside, collapsing their umbrellas and shaking the rain off themselves like animals reaching dry land. They would sniff around the room till they found a table they could settle at, remove their soaking outer clothes, hang them on the stands by the door, and settle to scouring menus and lighting cigarettes. Each time the door clanged, Patrick looked up, hoping it would be Aisling, feeling, to his annoyance, a little slump in his shoulders when it wasn't.

He'd taken things slowly with Aisling on purpose, getting to know her, getting her to talk, listening to her, keeping his hands to himself so she thought he respected her. It was hard snatching time away to be with her without Sean tumbling to him, but she didn't seem to mind; it added to the romance for her. It was important to build up her trust before he made a move. The last thing he wanted was to be in the situation where she went blabbing to Lovegrove. There'd been one time on the Green when she'd been telling him about her Da and the IRA back home and her eyes had lit up and he'd thought of doing it, but then an Auxie and his girl had walked past looking at him suspiciously and the moment was gone. Well, as Mick had said to him once, revenge was a dish best served cold. Seamus and Colm were at peace now, and there'd be time enough to give Lovegrove what he deserved. Only, the thing was, it wasn't just about Lovegrove; it was about the man Lovegrove had on the inside, who had to be stopped. And time was running out on that one, because there was the big one coming, next Sunday. Sean was adamant that they'd not be told anything till the last minute, but they all knew. They knew that the Squad would be paying a visit to each and every English spy in Dublin, Lovegrove included, as they lay in their beds on Sunday morning, and would be sending them to their Maker before they even had a chance to put their pants on. A knockout blow. In one fell swoop, the English spies silenced forever. A turning point for sure. The war as good as won. It was pure Mick Collins, bold and brilliant. The man was a genius. But if Lovegrove had a man on the inside, the whole thing could be blown, and there would be Tans waiting for them and the entire Squad would end up in an English jail, or at the end of a rope, or lying in the gutter with their brains blown out. Patrick had to move now, today, and move fast. His little solo operation could make the difference between life and death for every man in the Squad.

Except there was a complication. The complication was that, just as he'd feared, he'd only gone and bloody well fallen for Aisling. That wasn't how it was supposed to be. But that was how it was all right. He'd never felt like this about any woman he'd known. She wasn't like any woman he'd known. She was bold and brave and strong and she loved Ireland as much as he did. Molly had loved Ireland too, but she was more like a walking book than a woman. Aisling was a woman, a beautiful woman, but with a man's strength of mind, and it sent his head into a spin just thinking about her. For all he held back saying anything or doing anything, that being what the operation demanded, he just wanted to reach for her and tell her what he was feeling and what he was doing and why. Maybe he could, maybe he would, once it was all over and Lovegrove had been dealt with. She'd be out of a job then, after all, with Lovegrove dead, and his missus presumably off in an asylum somewhere. He could sign her up for Cumann na mBan, and they could fight together, side by side. He'd known fellas in the Rising who'd had sweethearts in Cumann na mBan, and who'd married them once they'd got out of jail. Only Sean wouldn't let any of the Squad have sweethearts. He was for them living like priests, giving all that up for the fight, so there'd be no wife and children to grieve for them when they were taken. Well, if he brought in the traitor who could blow Sunday, surely to God Sean would let him have what he wanted, or if he didn't, Mick would. But he had to get the traitor first. He had to concentrate and not let his feelings get in the way of what had to be done. And he had to do it today. With luck it would all be over in a week, one way or another. But Jesus,

Aisling was a hell of a woman. He didn't think he could bring himself to do anything to hurt her.

He was not the only one watching the door. Fitzgerald, who was, after all, the one he was supposed to be watching, always sat at a corner table with Baggally and McMahon. It was so they could watch the door too. That was smart enough, but what wasn't so smart was that they were regular in their habits, the last thing an agent should be. Hence Sean switching him and the boys around on watching duty. The three Englishmen, Fitzgerald, Baggally and McMahon, would stop in almost every day on their way to the Castle, where they were not expected till noon, still rubbing the sleep from their eyes at eleven in the morning. They might have been out on the town last night for all anyone would know, but Patrick knew they'd been sitting in pubs with a slow glass and an open ear, following curfew-breakers home, standing outside houses counting which lights were on, passing discreet coins to street women in return for names and descriptions, stalking the streets of Dublin sniffing out Patrick and his kind. Now their pockets were bulging with scribbled notes and their stomachs were rumbling for food. The kitchen at the Cairo knew to keep back breakfasts for them and they fell on plates of bacon and eggs and fried bread, washed down with strong tea. Then they would push their plates away and settle back with cigarettes and slide a sliver or two of their separate nights out of the side of their mouths in between their chat about women and cricket and the last war and who was up and who was down at the Castle. Patrick was there to follow Fitzgerald once their breakfast was done. Nine times out of ten he'd head straight for the Castle with the others. But there would be the tenth time. The time that would lead him to one of Fitzgerald's sources. More than one man had died on the streets thanks to Patrick's following. It was worth doing.

Baggally and McMahon were bachelors. Fitzgerald's wife was back in England, in a place called Sussex, which, according to his overheard chat, was blessed with no rain, no Irish, and deferential servants. It was useful them being womanless; men with wives had breakfast at home, went out less, were generally harder to follow. They talked a lot about the war with Germany. According to them, it was a much fairer contest, because the enemy wore a uniform and you could see who they were. They had all been out in France; one of them, Baggally, had had his leg blown off by a German shell, and dragged a wooden stump round Dublin. Some days he seemed to think that he'd lost his leg to an Irishman disguised as a German, and he was here for his revenge.

Patrick sat three tables away them. *Stay as far away as you can without losing your man*, Sean told them; *you're not there to listen to his chat, just to follow him.* Still Patrick listened; he always listened. If he hadn't listened, he wouldn't have found out about Lovegrove and Seamus and Colm. He spread the *Irish Press* out on the table in front of him. *Take a newspaper*, Sean said. *Always have a newspaper. A man with a newspaper has his mind busy; he's not looking at or listening to what's going on around him. Better, take a pencil and circle the winners on the racing page. Then you're doubly busy. Never let them see you looking at them. You've been on early shift, you've got a break, this is what you do with it; afterwards, you'll be down the betting shop, spending your wages. Your job is to stay close, but not too close,* Sean told the fellas. *To see where your man goes. To see where he lives, who he lives with. See, above all, if there's a moment when he's on his own, or, best of all, a moment when he's on his own but in a crowd. Kill a man when you're both on your own, and it's obvious who did it. Kill a man in a busy street, and in seconds you're just part of the street, and you live to kill another day. You're no use to us in a prison cell or at the end of a length of rope. The longer you live, the more of them we can kill. And that's what we're here for; to kill the bastards before they kill us.*

Racing Demon for the 1.20 at Cork, thought Patrick, trying to concentrate on horses to stop himself thinking about Aisling. 2/1 wasn't great – the bookies were getting tighter, he was sure – but she'd run away with everything at Limerick last week. There shouldn't be any stopping her. He'd put down a shilling. Then another bob on Morning Glory for the 2.30.Worth a shot at 12/1.If Sean gave him ten minutes off to lay the bet. He looked up. Fitzgerald was wiping the egg off his moustache. Baggally said something about the rain and Fitzgerald nodded. Patrick sucked his pencil and looked over the results from yesterday. Nothing doing at Limerick – the track was flooded. When he looked up again he saw Aisling coming through the door, and felt a smile leap to his face in spite of his best efforts.

She was clutching a canvas bag close to herself. He saw a couple of chops wrapped in brown paper sticking out of it. She didn't have an umbrella. She'd wrapped her head in a scarf. A strand of her hair had slipped out of the scarf and lay sprawled across her face, dripping from the rain, letting a drop run down her smooth cheek. Patrick wanted to reach across and push her hair back. She looked around the cafe. When she saw Patrick he stood up. He came round the table and pulled out a chair for her.

'Have a seat. You must be glad to get out of that rain.'

'I am.'

'And I'm glad to see you.'

Grand. It was good cover meeting a girl, and on top of that he felt ten times better to be with her. He'd missed seeing her at the cathedral on Sunday, really missed her. Once a chore, going to Mass was the highlight of his week now he got to sit next to her. And the chat afterwards was good, better than he had with anyone else; would be better still if he could say what he really felt, tell her who he really was. Still, they'd had two policemen to kill on their way out of Mass at St Dominic's on the other side of the city, and there was no way Sean would have let him off. One of the policemen had been with his wife and his little daughter, no more than three she must have been, and she'd started screaming and wouldn't stop. He could still hear her half a mile away. Sean told them, as he always did, to think of all the boys and girls the English had orphaned. Even so, Patrick found it was getting harder each time. Maybe the thing with Aisling was turning him soft. Jesus.

Out of the corner of his eye he checked on Fitzgerald. Fitzgerald had finished his breakfast now, but he was lighting a cigarette, and spreading his own newspaper on the table. He had a fresh cup of tea. He should be good for ten minutes at least, maybe fifteen. Patrick hoped he'd settle to some chat with his pals, get a bit busy. He looked over at Aisling. She seemed nervous, ill at ease, and very tired. She'd told him Lovegrove didn't want her having a fella. Had he found out about them?

'What is it you'll be having?' he said.

He caught the eye of a waitress across the room. Plump, elderly. She bustled importantly over and pulled out her notebook.

'Just a tea for me,' said Aisling.

'That's all I'm having, too,' said Patrick.

There was a silence between them. For a moment it seemed as if the little square table between them was an island where they had been washed up together, and that they were all alone on it. Aisling looked as if she wanted to say something and didn't know where to begin. Patrick, too, had something he needed to say, to begin the process of recruiting her, but for a moment he forgot about the IRA and the war and Fitzgerald and McMahon and Baggally and Sean and saw nothing but Aisling and her tired eyes and her face flushed with the warmth of the cafe and heard nothing but the rain. He didn't want to recruit her. He wanted to hold her in his arms. He wanted to look after her. In the end it was Aisling who broke the silence.

'Patrick. I need your help.'

'With what?'

'I need to leave the Lovegroves.'

Jesus wept. Disaster. She can't leave, mustn't leave. Not until Sunday, at least.

'Why would you be doing that? Didn't you say your man was good to you and all? Every time I see you you can't stop talking about what a top fella he is.'

He saw tears come into her eyes. He reached over the table and took her hand, which he'd never done before. He squeezed it, and she squeezed back.

'He is... he was... he is... but...'

'But what?'

'Mrs Lovegrove... you know about her nerves?'

'As if they were my own.'

'On Saturday, she went out in the middle of the night and threw herself in the Liffey.'

'Mother of God. She'd not live through that in this weather.'

'Some policemen found her and fished her out and took her to the Mater. But it was the last straw. The Major's putting her in a home.'

'So he's laying you off now you've no longer to look after her? He'll give you some notice, surely?'

The waitress brought their teas. Aisling took two sugar lumps, Patrick noticed, and stirred them in greedily. Normally she only had one. Fitzgerald had begun an argument about cricket. He maintained that if the Irish were forced to play it, we'd have no more trouble from them. Aisling looked down at her tea for a long time, and then she swallowed hard and looked up at Patrick.

'That's not the thing,' she said.

'Then what's the thing?'

'The thing is... when Mrs Lovegrove went missing... he woke me up... and...'

'And what?'

'And we... and he kissed me.'

Patrick snatched his hand away, made it into a fist and banged it on the table, making Aisling's tea spill into the saucer.

'The bastard!'

Baggally looked over, and Patrick lowered his voice.

'Was that it? Did he try anything else?'

'No. Nothing else. That was it. But I can't stay there. Not on my own.'

Patrick sighed angrily and sat back. Just as when he'd overheard Lovegrove bragging in Grafton Street, he wanted to march down to his house right now and put a bullet between his eyes. The fucking bastard. Not content with killing our men, he has to molest our women. Truth was, though, he'd seemed mild enough when Patrick had seen him in Grafton Street. But that was the English all over. All smiles and charm as they kicked your head in. Calm down, Kelly. Save the anger. Let it come out of your gun, but at the right time. There's too much at stake here. On Fitzgerald's table, the argument about cricket was getting louder. Baggally was almost shouting about something called leg before. McMahon was calling for another pot of tea. They were distracted. Now was the moment. Now or never.

'Don't leave, Aisling,' he said.

'Why not?'

'There's something I've got to tell you.'

'What?'

'Do you know exactly what it is that Major Lovegrove does?'

'He's in the army. Though I never saw him put on a uniform. He spends all day in Dublin Castle, doing paperwork, nothing more. He hates it, but it's safe. He goes out till very late every night. He says he's seeing his pals. I reckon he has a woman.'

Patrick leaned forward, putting his face close to Aisling's. He realised he was close enough to kiss her. *Concentrate, Kelly. You've a job to do.* He lowered his voice.

'It's not a woman he's after at night, Aisling. I'm going to tell you what it is he really does.'

He let his eyes stray to the misted up windows, let the sound of the rain be heard for a moment. He seemed to see Seamus and Colm walking down Grafton Street, pushing playfully at each other. He held up his right hand and twisted the three middle fingers together. He counted them off as he spoke.

'Me. Seamus McCann. Colm McCann. Those two were brothers, twins, but I was as good as a third twin. We were like that. At the Christian Brothers. Sean, my own brother... he's never walked an inch for me. Those two as good as saved my life, in the playground and in the classroom, more than once. They died on August 13th this year.'

'The two of them? Together?'

'Yes. They were buried together and all. The Mass was at the Holy Innocents, the church they grew up in. The church I grew up in. Their mother's a widow. Three elder daughters, two in America, one in Liverpool, all married. They were all she had left. When she saw the coffins come in, side by side, shoulder to shoulder, she fainted. I had to catch her.'

'What happened?'

Patrick could see tears brimming in Aisling's eyes again. Good, it was working. He wanted to reach over and brush her tears away, kiss them away. But he had a job to do.

'They were shot by the Tans as they slept. One bullet in each of them. In their heads. Same as your Da, Aisling. No warning. No chance to defend themselves. No charges, no trial, no process of law. Just a bullet. That's the language the English speak.'

'Why?'

'Because, like your Da – like you - they fought for Ireland.'

Aisling sat back and examined him for a while. She picked up a napkin and wiped her tears away with it.

'You fight for Ireland, don't you, Patrick?'

'I fought for Ireland in the GPO, yes, and I'm proud of it...'

'No, I mean now. I mean you still do. You're not just a carpenter's clerk, are you?'

Patrick let his eyes move warily to Fitzgerald's table. Fitzgerald had poured himself a second cup of tea, and was lighting a cigarette. They'd moved on from cricket to French women. Baggally was making them laugh now, and slapping his wooden leg, as he did when he was excited. He'd got to the bit about the local baker and the baguette. Once he'd reached the priest and the holy water he'd be at the end, and they might laugh and leave. Patrick would have to hurry, even if it meant taking a risk.

'You're a smart girl, Aisling. So I won't try to fool you any more. Yes, I fight for Ireland, but not in a way I can tell you or anyone else about. And that's what I want to talk to you about. You said you wanted to fight for Ireland. That you fought for Ireland back in Clifden. That if you'd been here in Easter Week you'd have picked up a gun like Countess Markievicz herself.'

'I would have.'

'Well now you can.'

'How?'

'When Lovegrove comes home... from being out at night... does he ever write things down? Take notes or anything?'

'Yes. In a little black leather notebook. He writes in it in the night. He says he can't sleep. He has bad dreams about the war with Germany.'

'Where does he keep this notebook?'

'Some mornings he puts it in his pocket and takes it to work with him. Other days he leaves it in his desk.'

'Does he lock the desk?'

'He does. It's one of them roll top ones.'

She mimed the opening and closing of the desk. Patrick looked anxiously across at Fitzgerald.

'Do you know where the key is?'

'He hangs it on a hook inside his wardrobe. I've seen it when I've been putting his shirts back.'

'Are you ever in the house on your own?'

'Mrs Lovegrove was always in the room. She never got out of bed. But now she's in the home, and staying there. So I'll have the place to myself during the day.'

'Can you copy in a good hand?'

'Back home I used to do Da's accounts.'

'Those notes he writes up.... they're not just notes. They killed Seamus and Colm.'

'What are you saying, Patrick?'

Laughter exploded at the English table. Fitzgerald, impatient to go, was grinding his cigarette in the ashtray and reaching for his wallet. Patrick lowered his voice.

'Harry Lovegrove is an English spy. He doesn't spend his nights with a mistress. He goes out after dark to spy on men who are fighting for Ireland. He writes up what he knows, takes it into the Castle, and the men in the Castle give orders for those men to be captured and tortured and shot in cold blood. I know this for a fact. The morning my friends Seamus and Colm were shot I heard him, out there in Grafton Street, boasting to a pal of his about having told the Tans where to find them. He's not such a nice fella as you think. He's a murdering English bastard the same as the murdering English bastards that did for your Da and burnt your home and your town. That's what I'm saying.'

Aisling looked down at her tea. She swilled the sugary dregs in the cup, but did not drink.

'But you can stop him,' Patrick went on. 'You can save lives, just by doing a little copying. That's why you've got to stay, just a little longer, for all that he's done what he's done to you.'

She went on looking at her tea. Patrick almost felt as if he had stopped breathing for a moment. Fitzgerald was calling for the bill now. He would have to hurry her.

'You have to choose, Aisling. Whose side are you on? Theirs or ours? It's a war. There's no middle ground.'

Aisling looked full at Patrick. She tightened her fist round her teaspoon as if she was about to attack him with it. He knew he had one last chance.

'What would your Da want you to do, Aisling?'

She put down her spoon, swallowed what was left of her tea and banged her cup down on the saucer.

'He'd want me to do it.'

'Grand. Good girl.' Fitzgerald was paying the bill. 'Now. Do you have a notebook? Something you use for accounts and shopping lists and so on?'

'I do.'

'Will you be on your own in the house this afternoon?'

'He comes back at six every night, never earlier.'

'Open his desk. Copy all you can into your notebook. Put everything back exactly where you found it, good and neat like. He mustn't know what you've been doing. Meet me tomorrow outside Reiss's in Sackville Street, at eleven, with your notebook. We'll both be looking at jewellery.'

'Which we can't afford.'

'Not yet. But when Ireland's free, who knows? Look, I've got to go now. But Aisling –'

'What?'

He wanted to tell her he loved her. It was the moment. She knew who he was now. He'd never felt closer to her. But he had to wait. Wait till Lovegrove was dealt with.

'Nothing. I'll see you tomorrow, all right?'

He left two sixpences for the teas. She pushed one away. He picked it up.

'Until tomorrow,' he said.

The Englishmen were fiddling with their coats and umbrellas. Baggally lumbered out first, his injury giving him priority. Fitzgerald and McMahon went after him, muttering confidentially about racing. Patrick folded his paper until they were out of the door, then followed, snatching his coat, thrusting it on, briskly turning the collar up against the rain.

CHAPTER TEN

As Aisling let herself into the house the gutters in Lower Mount Street were overflowing, and the rain was still coming down in sheets, muffling everything. For the last three days she and Major Lovegrove had tiptoed round each other, avoiding each other's eyes, passing each other a yard apart for fear of touching, using as few words as they could get away with. She had stayed in the kitchen longer than she needed to, cleaning and polishing till the taps and the sink wore out. He had stayed in his study when he was in the house, and gone out earlier than usual, coming back later than usual. At night she'd prayed to Mam and Da and St Jude for help and then lain in bed wide awake, her mind racing, her body twitching and turning, sleeping only in snatches. She'd delivered her meals to him silently. Each time she'd stood next to him in the dining room she'd felt a torrent of words bubbling up inside her and had had to force it down with an almost physical effort. Altogether it had felt like living with an unexploded bomb in the house that could go off at any moment. She'd counted on Patrick giving her a way out. Well, now he had. It just meant staying here a little longer, that was all. She'd do it for Da. She hadn't been able to save any Irish lives in Clifden, so she'd do it here instead. Then the minute she'd finished her copying, she'd give in her notice, and would insist Patrick found her a job. She could tell he was sweet on her; she could get him to do it.

She went through to the kitchen and put her shopping – two chops, some vegetables, a couple of packets of tea – away in the cupboard. If she finished her copying today, she could even give in her notice tonight. No point in letting the chops go to waste, though. She'd cook them when he came back from the Castle tonight. For him and for her. To eat in different rooms, as they did. She went into the dining room, and sat down in the chair that Mrs Lovegrove should have sat in but never did. Mrs Lovegrove. Mrs Aisling Lovegrove. What nonsense. It didn't go, an Irish name with an English name. And in any case, there was already a Mrs Lovegrove. She got up and returned to the kitchen. She closed the door to the dining room. She wished she could lock it.

She took her notebook and pencil out of the pocket of her pinny, where she'd left it hanging up by the stove. Then she remembered she'd just washed and ironed the Major's shirts. There was no point in leaving them in the scullery if she was going up to his room. She picked them up. She found herself pressing the top one to her face. It was a fine white linen shirt from a tailor's in London. He must have had it delivered to Norfolk. It felt crisp and soft. Even after it had been washed and ironed it seemed to smell of him, of his breath when he'd held his face close to hers. She worried she would crease it. She wouldn't have time to iron it again. She had too much else to do before he came back. She carried his shirts up to his room at arm's length.

On the threshold of the bedroom she hesitated. She looked around the room. There was a print of Norwich Cathedral on the wall, and on his side of the bed there was a glass of water, a book by Rudyard Kipling and a photograph of his mother. On Mrs Lovegrove's side there was a picture of her father and mother, and a novel that she never read. Her father was wearing his Colonel's uniform. Her mother looked like a soldier too, though she was not in uniform. For all that she'd scrubbed and cleaned and changed all the linen after Sunday, Mrs Lovegrove's stale, sick breath still haunted the room. She hadn't quite left yet. The sheets on his side of the bed had been thrust back and it didn't look like he'd slept in them much last night.

She put the shirts down on the chest of drawers and opened his wardrobe. The key to his desk was there, hanging on the inside of the door. She went over to his bed, plumped up the pillows and shook out the sheets. There was still the whiff of the sweet tobacco he smoked on them. She went round the bed tucking them in tight. A made bed always looked a little bit forbidding, she thought, as if you wouldn't want to get into it for fear of making a mess. She looked at the picture of his mother. She had a nice kind smile. She looked like the sort of woman who'd never get angry. He'd taken after her, she thought. She'd never seen him angry, with her or Mrs Lovegrove. Except for the one time.

She picked up his shirts from off the chest of drawers and put them in the drawer at the bottom of the wardrobe. Mrs Lovegrove's dresses and coats were still hanging up in there, untouched. They'd been untouched since she'd come; Mrs Lovegrove had never got out of bed. Now her side of the bed was empty for the first time in four months. The bed seemed a little lonely without her. Aisling took the key off its hook and put it in the pocket of her pinny, next to the notebook and pencil.

In his study, Major Lovegrove had a leather chair with a low back and a seat that had kind of dimples in it. The chair was on wheels, and you could spin it round if you wanted. Aisling pushed it away from the desk and spun it this way and that a little. Then she pulled herself back to the desk. The desk was made of varnished wood. He'd asked her to polish it once a week; he'd told her it was his father's. He always kept it locked. She ran her fingers over the slats on the cover. She sat for a bit longer looking at the desk. Then she took the key out of the pocket of her pinny and put it in the keyhole. It turned very easily. She rolled up the cover. On the desk there was some blotting paper in a cover, an ink well and a pen. There were lots of little drawers. Aisling opened one of them. It was full of paper clips. She opened another. It was full of pencils. He kept his desk tidy, like a military man should, though he'd been incapable of keeping his home tidy till she came along. She remembered the first day, what a stinking tip the place had been, how good it had felt to clean it out. How he'd followed her everywhere, though he'd pretended not to. How he'd talked to her in the kitchen that night, not wanting to leave. She opened a third drawer. In it was the little black leather notebook. She sighed with relief. She looked at it for a while. She remembered watching him writing in it in the night; the way he'd looked up at her. She'd known then, though she'd not admitted it to herself. She took the notebook out and put it on the desk and looked at it some more. She picked it up and flicked through it. His writing was small and precise and careful and easy to read, as neat and tidy as the way he dressed. She saw some dates. She would start with the most recent entry. She took the notebook and pencil out of her pinny. She held the notebook open with one hand while she wrote with the other.

Visit to Mrs O'Connor's establishment, North King Street, Saturday 13th November, 1920. I arrived c. 11 pm, masquerading as a client, and asked specifically for Bernadette, as Newbury had told me she was a good source. Once in her room, I offered her five shillings in return for information about any of her clients who had been engaged in any kind of illegal activity, with the promise of another five if it turned out to be accurate. She told me one of her regulars was a man called Joe (he had not given a second name, nor did I expect him to). She described him as a short, rather weedy man with curly red hair and a high pitched voice. He had a nervous habit of rubbing his nose with the back of his hand. She further described him as 'a show-off, with nothing much to show off about'. On his last visit, which had been on the previous Monday, i.e. November 8th, he had asked her to perform an act which she was not prepared to perform, at least not for the fee he was offering. He had told her that if she knew who he was and what he was capable of she would not be so high and mighty with him. When she asked him what he meant he told her that he had put a bullet in the head of an English soldier in broad daylight in Grafton Street that morning. This would appear to refer to the murder of Lieutenant Ford in that location on Monday 8th November. It is of course possible that he had simply heard tell of the murder and had appropriated it to himself in order to impress the woman in question, but his description does accord with that given by witnesses to the murder. I pressed her for more details of Joe. Did she know what he did for a living, or where he lived? He had told her he was a full time soldier for the Irish Republican Army. One day, soon, they would free Ireland from the English and he and his like would be recognised as heroes. Until then he had to operate in secret. He told her that very soon they would all be hearing from the I.R.A.; that something big was going to happen, something that would echo round the world. This mention of 'something big' does accord with the intelligence of my earlier source, from whom I have not heard in a while (see above, August 12th) and lends a greater weight of credibility to the same, credibility which had already been vouchsafed by the successful raid on Barry's Hotel. He (Joe) told her that if she cared for her life she should entertain no more English gentlemen.

In spite of his boasts, she continued to decline to perform the act he had requested, and he left in a huff. I gave her five shillings for the information, with the promise of another five on its independent verification. I told her to say nothing to Mrs O'Connor or to any of the other women in the house of our transaction. I also asked her that, should the man Joe visit her again, she should be as accommodating to his needs as she could find it in herself to be, and should use his good favour to extract as much information from him as possible, in particular where he was living, and anything he could tell her about the imminent 'something big' of which he had spoken. I promised her a very significant financial reward, sufficient for her to abandon her current profession and to begin again in a more respectable line of work, should her information lead to the capture of more than one member of the IRA and the thwarting of the proposed operation.

I stayed a little longer with her speaking of inconsequential things in order to make my visit of a plausible duration. At c.

11.30 pm, I came downstairs and paid Mrs O'Connor the sum of ten shillings. I expressed my satisfaction with Bernadette's services and asked her to treat Bernadette well, because I had every intention of returning to enjoy those services again on a future occasion. I left Mrs O'Connor's establishment and walked home, returning at about midnight.

My expenses are detailed below:

Fee to Bernadette (source) 5s
Fee to Mrs O'Connor (employer of source) 10s
Total: 15s.

Aisling put down her pencil and rubbed her wrist. She wasn't used to writing for such a long time. So Patrick was right about what the Major did at nights. He spoke to whores. And, if Patrick was right, he got men shot in their beds. Men like Joe. Though Joe treated those poor women at Mrs O'Connor's like dirt, while the Major had been quite the gentleman, it seemed. But he had Irishmen killed for all that. What was this 'something big'? Would it finish the war? Would it finish the job Patrick and his friends had started that Easter? She rubbed her head. It was hard to think straight. She'd barely slept in four days. Perhaps everything would be clearer when she'd copied some more. *See above - August 12th.* That seemed important. She flicked back a few pages till she found it, and took up her pencil again.

Thursday 12th August. It is not my custom to meet contacts during the day as a rule, for fear of exposing my work to public view, but in this case, given the intelligence gathered below, I believe the risk taken to have been more than repaid. This contact first made himself known to me by means of a note pushed through the front door of my house during the morning of Wednesday 11th August and discovered by myself on leaving the house. The note was enclosed in an envelope marked 'Personal and private: for the attention of Major Harry Lovegrove'. It read simply 'If you want to know more about Mick Collins be at the east pond on Stephen's Green at one tomorrow.' I discussed the contents of this note with Colonel Brind. After some persuading on my part, he reluctantly agreed it was worth pursuing, but that I must be careful not to be gulled by a fantasist. He mentioned, once again, though with ample justification, the unfortunate episode of the barman at McGarry's.

I was by the pond on St Stephen's Green at one o'clock. At ten minutes past one, a tall, slim, handsome, man with dark curly hair in his mid to late twenties dressed in a baggy trench coat and a trilby hat approached me and asked for a light. As I lit his cigarette, he said, 'Is it Mick you're after?' I nodded, and he said, 'Then let's go for a walk.' We walked around the Green as we talked. I asked him for his name and he said simply, 'Call me Patrick.'

He spoke at length of the Intelligence Director of the I.R.A., Michael Collins. Mr Collins's role in the organisation is of course no secret to us; the difficulty for us is in locating and apprehending him. He is generally known as 'The Big Fella'. To some this is a term of approbation, indicating approval of his physical size and strength, and his commanding personality. To Patrick, however, it was a term of contempt. He described Mr Collins as 'a big-mouthed gobshite', a man who is 'up his own arse', who, in Patrick's most pungent phrase, 'would tell God Himself how to make the world.' Patrick acknowledged his effectiveness as a leader, but questioned his motivation. Collins, he said, had no love for Ireland, only for himself. He wanted to free Ireland from British rule only to set himself up as 'King Michael', which would be 'a sight worse than King George.' He gave me a number of examples of times when he had been treated unfairly and publicly humiliated by Mr Collins. He feels that he has given much to the organisation, but that his dedication and talents have not been recognised, and never will be. I encouraged him to give vent to his feelings about Collins, which are clearly extremely bitter, in the interests of winning his trust.

I asked him how he knew the location of my house. He said 'We know where all yous are', and implied that it would be a simple matter to launch an attack on me and my colleagues, though when pressed he would give no details of any other British agents known to him. He declared that he had been watching me for a while, and that he had formed the impression that I was a man he could trust, not like the others. I flattered his judgement with a view to reinforcing this sense of trust. I asked him why he had contacted me. It became apparent that he was motivated to co-operate with us not by hope of financial gain, but out of a sense of resentment towards Mr Collins, and a desire to avenge perceived slights. I tried to steer him towards giving me more concrete information regarding Mr Collins's whereabouts. At this he became cagey, and would only say that he was 'here, there and everywhere', and that 'the cunning bugger never sleeps in the same place twice.' I suspect that he does not in fact know as much about Collins as he would like to make out. I asked him if he wanted Collins to succeed in his campaign. He said no, he could think of nothing worse. I asked him how Collins could best be stopped. He said that at the moment the men of the I.R.A. think that Collins 'walks on water', but that if he could only be seen to fail in some way, he would soon be overturned. I asked him what would be the most significant failure imaginable. He spoke of 'something big' coming soon; an operation which would eliminate all the British agents in Dublin (including, doubtless, myself) in one fell swoop. If it succeeded, Collins would be unassailable, and would probably win the war; but if it was betrayed, he would be finished. I pressed him for more details. He frankly admitted he had none as yet. However, he assured me that, despite the ill feeling between him and Collins, he would, by virtue of his position in the organisation, be briefed fully when the time came.

I asked him when this operation was likely to take place. He told me towards the end of November. I urged him to pass on to me anything he knew as soon as he knew it. I told him of the lives that would be saved if he did, and reminded him of how humiliated Collins would be. This last thought gave him much pleasure, and he spent some time in gleefully imagining the consequences for his superior. Mindful of Colonel Brind's strictures, and anxious to ensure that the reliability of such momentous intelligence should be vouchsafed, I asked him if he could present me with some smaller, interim intelligence as proof of his veracity. He considered for a moment, and then chuckled to himself. 'The twins,' he said. What twins? I asked. He told me of two twins, Seamus and Colm McCann, who he said were 'Mick's little puppies, ready to run around and do his bidding and thump the floor with their tails when he came in the room.' He said their removal from the organisation would deal a blow to Collins. These two men are of course already on our wanted list. They are in one sense easily identifiable, given that they are identical twins and that they invariably operate together. They are most ruthless killers, and have on their hands the blood of at least six soldiers and policemen. Such is their fame that policemen have been known to move to defend themselves on sighting any pair of twins in the street. However, despite their distinctive appearance, they have as yet evaded capture, principally by their stratagem of continually changing their overnight location. I asked Patrick if he could tell me their whereabouts. He told me that if I wanted to pay Mick's little lapdogs a visit they would be sleeping at Barry's Hotel tonight.

We had by now spent something like one hour and a half in conversation; fortunately, there being a persistent drizzle, there were very few people on the Green and those who were passing through did not linger. I thanked him for the information and asked where we might meet when he had information on the larger operation of which he had spoken. At this point he became very nervous and agitated. He looked at his watch, and expressed concern that he had been away too long, and that he would be a dead man if he was seen talking to the likes of me. I suggested an alternative strategy. He knew where I lived; he had been able to leave me a note there. He could record what he knew in writing and post it through my door when he was passing. He seemed satisfied with this, promised to let me have more when he had it, to 'stitch that bastard Collins once and for all', and took his leave in some haste.

My recommendation is that we should act forthwith on the information regarding the McCann brothers. Should it prove reliable, we can be reassured that Patrick is a well connected source, and further communications from him should be taken seriously.

I incurred no expenses on this occasion.

Aisling put down her pencil and closed the black leather notebook. So Patrick was right. No doubt about it. The Major gave the order for Seamus and Colm to be shot in their beds. The same man who talked so patiently to his corpse of a wife and wept that he didn't love her enough. The same man who'd held her down on the bed (though hadn't she pulled him down there herself?).The same man who danced before her eyes in the night, with his gentle smile and his quiet manner and the strong arms that she wanted to be held in. He'd made those boys' mother faint with grief. She saw her own mother's coffin alone and proud and sad before the altar in the church in Clifden, and remembered holding Da by the arm to stop him from collapsing. Then she remembered Da six years later lying on the floor of her own bedroom with his face blown off by an English soldier.

Who was this 'Patrick'? Was he her Patrick? The description matched all right. But why would he have asked her to spy on himself? And this 'something big' – did it mean they would be pushing past her on the way to shoot the Major in his bed? Could she stop them? Should she stop them? Would she stop them?

CHAPTER ELEVEN

As Aisling was copying out from his notebook, Harry was in his cramped little box of an office in Dublin Castle, trying to work and failing, the rain beating against the one small high window he was allowed. Normally, he completed his reports with legendary efficiency and dispatch. He'd get them done in the night when his nightmares from France wouldn't let him sleep. His insomnia put him streets ahead of other men; he never missed a deadline. But now his report on enemy morale was a day overdue, and Brind would notice. Aisling had been in his head since she'd come, but he'd managed to work through it, mostly. Since Sunday, it had been impossible. She'd been avoiding him, and he'd been avoiding her. But sooner or later, something would have to be done or said. He couldn't go on like this, sitting impotent at his desk, unable to put one word next to another.

He remembered the feel of her in his arms as she had held him in the hallway on Sunday morning, her soft hands running through his hair, her breath on his neck. He felt her thick auburn hair brushing against his face. He'd desperately wanted to run his own hands through her hair, to smell it, to feel it, to take her face in his hands and to kiss her long and deep.

The King stared down at him gruffly from his portrait on the wall. In his last talk to the men before they left for France, General Spragge had told them, *Whatever situation you're in, in or out of uniform, the first question to ask yourself is: where does my duty lie?* Harry knew where his duty lay. He was an officer and a gentleman, married to a Colonel's daughter, serving in a war against the Irish. Carrying on with one of the enemy whose family had been killed and burnt out by his side and who would have every reason to hate the English was definitely not where his duty lay.

'I said, are you in the middle of something? If you are, it's not work. You're bloody miles away, man.'

Newbury was standing in the doorway, leaning against the jamb. There was barely room in the office for a desk, a chair and a filing cabinet. Newbury's presence shrunk it still further.

'Sorry, old boy. Family troubles.'

'Leave them at the gate. That's what it's there for.' Though Newbury was only a captain, he sometimes acted like Harry's commanding officer. Harry had never quite known how to stop him doing this. 'Anyway,' said Newbury, 'I brought you something.' He reached into the pocket of his jacket, pulled out an envelope and tossed it onto Harry's desk. It was addressed in a neat hand to a Miss Sinead Rafferty, and had a County Cork address. The flap at the back had been steamed open. 'Thought it would be in your line.'

'What is it?' said Harry.

'From a man called Ryan. Fancies himself as a respectable solicitor, for all he's a Mick. Not a Fenian himself. But his nephew, Thomas Byrne, is. Disappeared two years ago. Almost certainly in Collins's Squad now. That letter could find him.'

'What does the letter say?'

'Things he wouldn't want Mrs Ryan seeing. Been a naughty boy with the maid. Got her up the duff. She's gone home to County Cork, had the kid, but he still sends her money and sweet nothings once a month. There was five pounds in the envelope. I put it in the kitty for the Christmas party.'

'GPO?'

'Those boys earn their money. We should invite them to the Christmas party. Serves the Fenians right for blowing up the old one.'

'So what do we do?'

'You know what to do, Harry, old boy. You've done it often enough. Bring Byrne in. We'll do the rest.'

'And Ryan?'

'If screwing your servants was a capital offence, half of Dublin would swing. Us and them. Leave him alone once we've got what we need.'

Newbury rubbed his eyes.

'Got to go. Reports to write. I was up till two this morning chatting to ladies of easy virtue, and not allowed to lay one finger on them. Some of them weren't bad, either. Still, you've got a wife. You don't have to worry about these things.'

He kicked the door shut behind him as he left. Harry felt like calling him back. Calling him back and punching him in the face.

So I'm doing what half Dublin does, according to Newbury. Doing what Newbury does, no doubt. Or wanting to, rather. Except I'm not. It's not like that at all. If it was, it would be a damn sight easier to give it up. Oh Christ.

He sighed, pulled the letter out of the envelope, spread the pages on the table, and began to read its words of guilt and desperate longing. *My darling girl, you have lit up my life... for all what we did was a sin, it was the sweetest time of my life... I miss you every day and yearn for you by my side... do you still have your hair in those pigtails?... I hope the enclosed will help you to get by, on your own as you are... if you can send me a photograph of wee Seamus, you will gladden my heart...* There was plenty here he could use. It should be a simple matter to locate Tom Byrne, though he didn't want to think of what they'd do to him once they had him. He was glad they didn't let him work in the cellars any more. He wasn't up to it.

He turned back to the report on enemy morale, but still he couldn't concentrate. How could he threaten Ryan when he was guilty of the same thing himself? He remembered the story from his childhood about not casting the first stone. This morning, when Aisling had picked up his breakfast plate, her arm had brushed against his wrist, and he'd wanted to snatch the plate out of her hands and take her in his arms there and then. A fine way for an officer and a gentleman to carry on.

The door opened, and Newbury came in again.

'Just passed Brind's office. He wants to see you. Now. Bollocking on the cards, old boy,' he said with satisfaction.

Brind's office was not a relaxing place to be. It was as stripped of ornament and clutter as his speech. A desk with sharp angular edges; an in-tray and an out-tray, never more than one piece of paper in each; a fountain pen, always laid exactly parallel to the desk's edge; one medium sized portrait of the King behind his back; one chair behind his desk, two chairs in front of it. He was reading a report as if he was angry with it.

'Enemy morale?' he'd said. 'Where? Due yesterday AM.'

'I know sir. I'm sorry.'

The Colonel scrutinised him with a fixed gaze.

'Look unwell,' he said.

'I feel unwell, sir.'

'Report to the MO?' added the Colonel.

'It's not that, sir, it's...'

'What? Spit it out, man.'

'My wife. She's been unwell. With a nervous complaint.'

'Know that. All bloody Dublin knows that. Change in her condition?'

'On Saturday night she threw herself in the Liffey. She was trying to kill herself.'

'Succeed?'

'Mercifully, two policemen on patrol found her. They took her to the Mater Hospital. But she won't be coming home for a long time.'

Brind nodded, once. This was unusually expressive for him.

'Wife trouble. Bugger of a thing. Plays hell with a man's work. Compassionate leave?'

Compassionate leave would mean staying at home all day with Aisling. That was what he wanted more than anything else. It was also the last thing he needed at the moment.

'Thank you, sir, but no. I don't want to be at home all day in an empty house. I find that work takes my mind off things, for all I've not been pulling my weight this week. I'll try to buckle down more.'

'That's the spirit. Return to the charge. But if you haven't done enemy morale yet, stick it at the bottom of the pile. Something new's come in, more urgent. Full write up of that man of theirs Patrick you managed to turn. Heard any more from him?'

'Not yet, sir. He said he'd be back in touch when he'd been briefed about the big operation. Said it was due towards the end of November. Should be any day now.'

'Exactly. That's why the Viceroy's interested.'

'The Viceroy?'

'He's just back from leave, and he's got the scent. Takes him a while to pick things up, but when he does, he worries away at them like a dog with a bone. Wants the lot. Nothing left out. All the facts and figures. On his desk by the end of the week. If you can get more out of the man, he's talking promotion, gongs, all sorts. McGarry's a distant memory. Good enough? Up to it?'

Harry nodded. This was the longest speech the Colonel had ever made to him.

'Of course, sir. Thank you, sir. There's just one problem...'

'Being?'

'Unfortunately, sir, I don't have my notes to hand.'

The Colonel's face clouded with anger.

'What? Where are they?'

'They're at home.'

'Bloody hell are they doing there? You leave top secret material lying around in your house?'

'Not exactly, sir. I lock my notebook in my desk, and conceal the key in another part of the house. I took the judgement that it would be better to minimise the number of times I carried the notebook to and from the Castle, in the event of my capture by the enemy. As I believed I would be working only on the morale report today, I decided this morning to leave my notebook at home.'

This was not true. He hadn't been fit to decide anything that morning. He'd had to get up and walk out without touching the breakfast Aisling had made him in order to stop himself kicking open the door to the kitchen and seizing her and telling her he loved her. He hadn't thought about the notebook at all. He'd just forgotten it.

'Intelligence should stay within these walls,' said the Colonel. 'Got a maid, haven't you?'

'Yes, sir.'

'Can she read? I know half of them can't.'

'She can read, sir.'

'Well what if she's got a boyfriend who wants to kill us all? Most of them have.'

Harry winced at the thought of Aisling having a boyfriend as if he'd been hit.

'See my bloody point, Lovegrove?'

'I do, sir.'

'How far do you live?'

'I can be back here in forty-five minutes, sir.'

'Right. Leave of forty-five minutes granted. Go home, get it, bring it back, keep it here. And don't leave tonight till you've done the Viceroy's report. He wants it on his desk first thing tomorrow.'

Harry stood and saluted.

'Thank you, sir.'

He turned and left the Colonel's office. Forty-five minutes, there and back. That was assuming he could avoid talking to Aisling when he got home. If he got talking to her – talking to her properly – it could be more like forty-five hours. He might never come back.

Aisling was still copying when she heard Major Lovegrove come in downstairs. She stopped in mid sentence, put the notebook back in its drawer, closed it, locked the desk, went back to the bedroom and hung up the key. She quickly took the shirts out of the wardrobe so that she could be putting them back in when he came into the bedroom. She heard him coming up the stairs.

'Good afternoon, Aisling,' he said.

'Good afternoon, sir.'

'I'm sorry to interrupt your labours. I had to come home to get something from my desk. For the office.'

'But your desk is in your study.'

'Quite so. However, I keep the key to it hanging in my wardrobe. On the inside of the door, there, just there. Would you be good enough to pass it to me?'

'Of course, sir.'

As she placed the key in his hand he closed his hand over hers and looked at her, just as he had on the first day when he had given her the key for the window. He pressed her hand hard this time, so hard that the cold metal of the key buried itself in her flesh. For a moment she forgot Ireland and Patrick and Da and everything and felt only the press of his hand and his eyes on her face and she wanted to pull him towards her and kiss him. Then he took his hand, and the key, away. She felt a little ache inside her when he did that. He went on looking at her for a long time. He held up the key and nodded towards his study.

'I have to go, Aisling. I have to go back to work. Colonel Brind is expecting me. He has given me exactly forty-five minutes leave of absence to fetch what I need. Colonel Brind is not a man one should cross lightly. I cannot stay talking to you. I have spent too long talking to you already.'

He left the room. Aisling started putting his shirts away for the second time that afternoon. She wanted to throw them open and bury her face in them. After a minute he returned, the little black leather notebook in one hand and the key in the other. Again, he stood in silence for a while, looking at her. Aisling studied him. She knew that if he would only kiss her, she would do whatever he wanted, even though it meant betraying her country and her Da and God and everyone. At last, he spoke. She thought afterwards that if he had just waited another five seconds before speaking she would most certainly have kissed him.

'Well,' he said, 'as I said, Colonel Brind is waiting for me. I will have to walk very fast back to the Castle. Almost run, in fact.'

He put the key in his trouser pocket, and patted the pocket.

'I will keep this with me from now on, I think,' he said. 'Can't be too careful. These are dangerous times, Aisling. For all of us. Dangerous times.'

She carried on putting his shirts away until she heard him close the door downstairs behind him. Then she sat down on his bed and wept.

CHAPTER TWELVE

Sean was outside Wynne's Hotel in Lower Abbey Street at one o'clock like they'd agreed. Vinnie and Rory and Joe were with him. They always took five on a job. Patrick and Vinnie would do the job. Vinnie would fire first, to get the man down. Patrick would finish him off with a shot to the head. Rory and Joe would be there in case they needed covering fire, or if their guns jammed. Sean would hang back and watch from a distance. They switched it around between jobs so that everyone knew how to do everything, except that Sean was always at a distance. Sometimes Patrick wondered if Sean was keeping an eye on them as much as he was keeping an eye on the police and the soldiers. They all had to lose themselves in the crowd afterwards. The more of them there were, the harder it would be to lose themselves, the harder to pretend they didn't know each other. Five was the right number.

Vinnie wasn't grinning, for once. Joe was shifting from foot to foot as if he was cold although he had his coat on. Rory threw down his cigarette and ground it under his heel.

'Where did he go?' asked Sean.

There was still bad blood between him and Patrick, but it had to be forgotten. They often quarrelled, all of them, living so close in that place, but the way it was, when you were on a job, quarrels had to be forgotten. You couldn't afford quarrels when lives were at stake.

'Breakfast in the Cairo till half past eleven. Then a stop in the Bank to get some money out. Then into the Castle. I waited outside in the rain, till it stopped, but he wasn't coming out again.'

'Who was with him?'

'Baggally and McMahon.'

'The bugger with the wooden leg?'

'Himself.'

'The whole time?'

'All the way into the Castle.'

'Ah, they're thick as thieves, those three. We can't do a thing as long as they stick together. Unless...'

'Unless what, Sean?'

'Unless nothing. You'll know when you need to know. Right, let's go. Time to take care of Sergeant Casey. You've remembered your gun at least?'

Patrick patted the pocket of his coat.

'I have.'

Sergeant Eammon Casey of the Royal Irish Constabulary had been warned. They were always warned, at least if they were Irish they were. Either give it up, or work for us, tell us what they're up to. Casey had had a visit. It had been noted, had been pointed out to him, that he was after getting married next year, that he should be thinking of his fiancée, thinking of the family they might have. Nothing doing. Casey was firm. 'I've taken my oath to the King. When I take an oath before God, I keep it. And I uphold the law. I'll not give in to a gang of murderers.' It was Joe who'd warned him. He'd reported the conversation word for word. A gang of murderers. 'The bastard deserves everything he gets,' Rory had said. 'Kill one and ten more give it up,' Sean had said. 'And soon there are none left, and Ireland's ours again.'

It was Rory who had tailed him, with a patience and a care that had surprised them all, that didn't seem like Rory. But Rory was a good soldier when all was said and done, he could control his feelings well enough when a job demanded it, provided the rage wasn't in him. Casey had Wednesdays off in return for working Sundays, and he had lunch with his fiancée, Siobhan, and her parents, in their house in Upper Gardiner Street. He'd done well, had Casey. Siobhan's father was a doctor. His name plate was by the door of their house, his surgery in the front room. Her parents had put up a fight at first, but they'd given in in the end. The way he'd fought for her and not given up was one of the things that Siobhan loved most about Casey. They knew this because Rory had sometimes been close enough to Siobhan and Casey on their walks to hear their conversations. He'd told the others with a laugh and a sneer about Casey fighting for Siobhan when he should have been fighting for Ireland. Patrick had said nothing, but had found that he hated Rory for bringing the woman into it.

They'd talked about whether it was right to shoot him in front of Siobhan. Sean had said it set a good example to the others; it let them know that they weren't safe anywhere. Rory had enthusiastically agreed. Patrick hadn't said anything; he was starting to have doubts about it all, but he didn't dare show them to the fellas. After lunch on Mondays, Casey and Siobhan always took a walk together by the Liffey, along Bachelors' Walk, up to the Ha'penny Bridge and back. They'd do it on Bachelors' Walk. That was a good place, because there were always a lot of people walking there, and because it was on Bachelors' Walk that four civilians had been massacred by the English six years before. These things matter, Sean had said. It lets our people know and their people know that what they do to us we'll do back to them. Rory had said he'll be a bachelor for all eternity after we've finished with him. If it had been raining, Casey and Siobhan would have stayed at home, and the whole thing would have had to have been put off a week. Luckily the rain had stopped in good time.

Patrick and Vinnie were standing fifty yards apart, on the pavement opposite Siobhan's house. It was a big grand house, three stories high. It wasn't as grand as Merrion Square, but it was about as good as an Irish Catholic family could hope for. Doctors did well for themselves. Rory and Joe were another fifty yards up Gardiner Street, outside the Jesuit church, the smart one, Joe leaning disrespectfully on one of its proud imposing pillars. Sean was on the pavement opposite the church, looking at his watch. Once the target was in view, or about to be in view, it was important none of them had anything to do with each other, until the moment before they did the job. Patrick and Vinnie were both smoking, to calm their nerves and to give themselves something to do.

The front door opened and Casey and Siobhan came out. He was a slight, dapper little man with a neat moustache and tidy hair, good looking in a clean sort of way, who looked like someone who took pride in everything he did. He was wearing a suit and a tie under his coat; Patrick thought he must have to try hard to impress Siobhan's parents still. Siobhan was holding his hand tight and leaning on his shoulder. She was quite a small girl, a little bit plump, but with a lovely open face. She was smiling up at him and he was whispering something in her ear. Whatever it was made her laugh. Patrick could tell she was laughing not because what Casey had said was funny but because she was happy. Aisling laughed like that sometimes when she was talking about her Da, telling one of his stories. His stories made Patrick laugh too. He'd like to have met her Da.

He made a slight signal to Vinnie with his cigarette and the two of them set off, following Casey and Siobhan on the other side of the street. Rory and Joe and Sean followed them behind.

Keep your man in view, always, Sean said, *but don't go breathing down his neck. If you do, he'll know what you're up to, or if he doesn't, others will.* It was a good time Sean had picked because a lot of people were on their way back to work after lunch and Abbey Street was good and full, so the five of them weren't noticed. They walked past the Abbey Theatre. Something by Mr Shaw was playing. Shopkeepers stood smugly in front of their shops, aprons on, their names on awnings above them. Tom had told Patrick once that when they'd kicked out the English, there would be no more private property. He couldn't see it happening. These buggers wouldn't be giving anything away. Vinnie was about six or seven paces ahead of Patrick, Rory and Joe were on the other side of the street, Sean was well back. Patrick could see Casey and Siobhan well enough, arm in arm, talking and laughing. Then she went a bit serious like. He'd be telling her some story about when he was in mortal danger, trying to impress her. But she wanted to be impressed; was already impressed. He remembered his first walk with Aisling, telling her about the Rising. She'd seemed impressed enough. Joe always bragged about how his war stories never failed to get a lass into bed. Joe didn't care what the lass thought of him once that was accomplished. That was Joe for you. But the funny thing was that the thought of bed barely crossed his mind when he was with Aisling, for all she was a gorgeous woman.

Grey clouds loured above them, threatening to rain. It was always threatening to rain in this bloody city. You could smell rain in the air. He wondered what Siobhan would think if she knew what mortal danger Casey was in now. He wondered if she'd love Casey more if he somehow managed to shoot his way out of this one. He wondered what she would think of Casey when Casey was dead and gone. He shouldn't be thinking these things; a soldier shouldn't think of the enemy like this. But he found he couldn't help it. Next he found himself wondering what Aisling thought of him now. What she would think if she knew what he was about to do? Would she admire him for it? She was willing to spy for Ireland, but what would she think of killing men in the street? He realised he cared a lot what Aisling thought of him. More, if he was honest with himself, than he cared about getting her to spy on Lovegrove. That was a worrying thought. Dozens of men's lives depended on her spying on

Lovegrove. Maybe he should keep it short at Reiss's tomorrow. Just hand over the copying, thank you, and goodbye. Try and forget about her. Get her out of his head.

Siobhan and Casey passed Wynne's Hotel and turned left into Sackville Street. Vinnie turned after them, and Patrick followed. At the end of Sackville Street they crossed the road and set off to the right of the bridge along Bachelors' Walk, down by the Liffey. The sun peeped out between some clouds and the puddles of rain on Bachelors' Walk glistened a little. There was a tugboat on the Liffey, heading out to sea, belching black smoke. Vinnie picked up his pace and began to close on Siobhan and Casey. Patrick closed on them too.

Casey had his arm around Siobhan's shoulder and she had hers around his waist, leaning into him as they walked. He was smiling and she was laughing. Vinnie strode towards them, making no attempt to hide now, keeping between them and the street so that their only escape was into the river. Casey and Siobhan didn't notice him. They were too interested in each other. Vinnie overtook them. He wasn't smiling or laughing now like he usually was. He turned, and stood directly in front of them. He pulled the gun out of his pocket and pointed it at them.

'Get back, Miss,' he said.

Siobhan screamed and buried her face in Casey's chest. He held her to him and stroked her hair.

'Put it down,' said Casey.

'It's no use,' said Vinnie. 'I've a man behind me, and two more on the street. Let her go.'

Casey held Siobhan tighter. She was sobbing.

'You'd shoot a woman?' he said.

'No, I wouldn't,' said Vinnie. 'And I wouldn't use one to shield me either. Let her go.'

Casey cradled Siobhan's face in his hands.

'I love you,' he said. 'I'll always love you. You'd have made me the happiest man that ever lived. Pray for me every day. As I'll pray for you. Now run like hell home.'

'No,' she said. 'I'm going nowhere. I'd as soon throw myself in that river. If you're dying, I'm dying with you. I'll not live without you.'

'Go,' said Casey.

'No,' said Siobhan.

Patrick was standing behind them, but they hadn't noticed him. Vinnie was holding his gun at arm's length, and his wrists were trembling a little. He twitched his head, nodding at Patrick. Patrick did nothing. Vinnie twitched his head again.

Patrick took out his gun, stepped up to Casey and pointed it at his head. Casey lifted Siobhan up and kissed her, long and deep. When they had finished kissing, she buried her face in his chest again.

'We're safe,' said Casey, looking Vinnie full in the face. 'Even those Fenian bastards wouldn't shoot a woman. You're the bravest woman alive, Siobhan.'

Patrick fired. The bullet came out between Casey's eyes and made a huge rip in the top part of his face. Some flesh and some blood and some bone and some soft grey bits of brain flew out to the front and to the side. None of them got onto Patrick. A large lump of flesh landed on Siobhan's head, and blood began to pour down from the top of Casey's head, soaking into her hair. Casey buckled at the knees. For a moment Siobhan held him up, his shattered head now the same height as hers. Then she buckled with him. She laid him out on the ground and looked at his ruined face. She let out a howl like a wounded animal, and beat on his chest with her fists, hard, again and again like a drum. The blood that had come from Casey's head was running down into her eyes and mixing with her tears.

Patrick and Vinnie lowered their guns and looked down at what they had done. Patrick had done this before. This was his seventeenth time. He'd done it all right. But it had taken two twitches from Vinnie. It was harder to concentrate. Harder because Aisling was in his head, and when he looked at Siobhan he saw Aisling. It had never been like this before. Molly had never got into his head like this and nor had any other woman. He wasn't sure if that was a good thing or not.

A little short fat man carrying a parcel was walking with his wife, who was much taller than him, on the street above them. She stopped, and would not move. Her face seemed to freeze into a mask. He kept tugging at her arm, whispering to her to come away. More people passed. They blessed themselves and walked a little faster, as if they had seen this before, which many of them surely had. One woman, heavy with make up and cheap jewellery, said 'You cowardly bastards!', spat on the ground and walked on. Two little boys in filthy clothes with holes in ran from the other side of the street to look.

Rory shouted at them from fifty yards away.

'Run, you fuckers! Run like hell!'

CHAPTER THIRTEEN

Waiting for Patrick outside Reiss's the jeweller's in the cloudy chill of the next morning, Aisling felt almost warmed by the luxury of the shop. Her eyes moved greedily over the window, from one thing to another, like a starving woman in front of a cake shop. There were necklaces of pearls that shone against the lowering grey sky above; there were brooches and clasps sitting self-confidently on their stands, inviting you to be their guest; there were gentlemen's watches that would not only tell you the time, but tell you what to do with it; there were single rings, sitting plush and ladylike on plump cushions, that seemed to wink at you.

Dublin had not stopped both entrancing and frightening Aisling with its wealth and variety. When a couple got married in Clifden, they'd have rings if they were lucky, if the farm or the business was doing all right, though there'd still be voices that would say that was a wicked waste of money. But that was it. You'd never see anything else on anyone. Father Garvey's vestments were the only bright things anyone ever wore.

Patrick came and stood next to her. He said nothing for a while. He was looking at her rather than at the jewellery.

'Do you like what they have here?'

'I've never seen the like. I have never, ever seen the like.'

Patrick looked from her to the window, and back at her again.

'Maybe one day you might have something from there.'

'And when would that be?'

'When Ireland's free.'

'Will that solve all my problems?'

She'd been awake till just before dawn, wearing out Mam's rosary with prayers. She'd fallen asleep to the birds singing, still with nothing resolved. She'd woken late, and had to scramble through making Major Lovegrove's breakfast, though she never liked rushing a job. He hadn't even looked at her when she'd put it before him, and that had hurt.

'Ireland being free? Or you having a ring?'

'Which is more likely?'

He pointed to a ring, in the middle of the window. It sat up clear and proud with a glistening red stone on top of it.

'That one. There.'

He took her left hand by the wrist and held it up to the window.

'Suits you grand. Goes with your eyes.'

And he turned his eyes on her. She felt a little afraid. Yes, he was a good looking fella. But he wasn't the one she wanted to marry. And what if he was the traitor she'd read about? Could he have called her here to put a bullet in her head? She tried to change the subject.

'How long till Ireland's free?' she said.

'Not long now. As long as we all do our bit.'

He let her hand fall.

'Come on,' he said. 'Let's walk.'

They walked side by side down Sackville Street. If Reiss's dazzled her with its colour and light, Sackville Street overwhelmed her, still, with its size. It seemed to roll down towards the river like a great river itself, carrying people in an endless stream, with Nelson on his column in the middle of it like a tree clinging on in the stream. Everyone was in a hurry; the stream was flowing fast today. She saw the priest who'd preached at the Mass when she'd first met Patrick shuffling along with a stick, a packet tucked under his arm, and she thought of what the other priest had said to her in the confessional, about the Lord sending Patrick. A lorry with half a dozen Black and Tans in the back swivelling a gun on a tripod lumbered past on the other side, and both she and Patrick looked away with a shared instinct of disgust.

When they got to the bridge they turned right on to Bachelors' Walk, by the river. That morning, when she'd been buying sausages, Connolly the butcher had told her that a man had been murdered there the day before. 'His head blown off as he held his fiancée in his arms,' he'd told Aisling. 'What it is that'll happen next now, only God Himself in heaven could say.' She wondered how many men Patrick had killed. She felt a little thrill of danger to be walking next to him. Of an evening, Bachelor's Walk was full of courting couples, but now, halfway through a cold November morning, it was as empty as Sackville Street was full.

'So,' said Patrick, as soon as they were away from anyone who could hear, 'did you do it?'

'I did.'

She had her notebook in the wicker shopping basket she was carrying, tucked under the sausages from Connolly's. She could just give it to him. But still something made her want to hold it back.

'What did you find out?'

'I found out he went to prostitutes.'

'What I'd expect from a man who jumps on his maid.'

'That's not how he is.'

'What do you mean?'

She'd spoken without thinking, angry at Patrick. She didn't want to tell him that it was she who'd made the first move with the Major.

'I mean he didn't go there for what most men go to prostitutes for. He went to get information from one of the girls.'

'And did he get any?'

'The girl he spoke to had had a visit from a lad called Joe.'

Patrick gave a short little laugh.

'Joe?'

'Yes. He'd been there. He was boasting about killing a soldier in the street.'

'He was bragging about it, was he?'

'He was. To get the girl to do what he wanted. Not that she would.'

'Bloody idiot.'

'What?'

'Nothing. Good girl. You've done a grand job. Anything else?'

Aisling walked in silence for a while. She could leave it there. She could say nothing more. She could apologise that that was all she could find, make her farewells, go home to the Major, put her notebook in the fire. Have nothing more to do with Patrick. She wanted to protect the Major, to look after him. But then she smelt the choking smoke filling her bedroom in Clifden, and saw Da's shattered face staring up at her. She felt a surge of rage like a sudden pain. Did they bury Da? Did he even ever have a decent funeral? Who would take it with Father Garvey dead? Sure, if Patrick was shooting men like the one who killed Da he was doing God's work.

'You were right,' she said.

'About what?'

'Major Lovegrove told them Seamus and Colm were sleeping at Barry's. Told them to "act on it".'

Patrick thrust his hands deep in his pockets.

'Bastard,' he said.

'Only it wasn't him that found out. He was passing on something someone else said to him.'

'Who?'

'Someone inside the IRA. A man who met him on Stephen's Green.'

'Who?'

He looked like a little boy, pleading for something he'd been promised.

'He said his name was Patrick.'

'Well it wasn't me.'

'He sounded like you. Tall, dark curly hair, slim, mid to late twenties. Handsome, the major said.'

'That's me, is it?'

'Ah, I didn't say that.'

'What else did this Patrick fella tell him? Apart from where to go and put a bullet in Seamus and Colm's heads?'

'He talked about Collins.'

'Mick? Mick Collins?'

'Himself. You've told me about him enough times.'

'I have. With good reason. So what about Mick?'

'He hated him, this Patrick fella. He wanted to do him down.'

'There's some do. Even in the IRA.'

'That's why he was blabbing.'

'He's a traitor, so. A traitor because he can't stand Mick being bigger than him. When we find him...'

'What? When you find him, what?'

'What do you think happens to traitors, Aisling?'

'Would you do it? Would you put a bullet in his head?'

'I'd do it, so. I'd be glad to do it. Anything else? Anything else he said?'

'He said something big was going to happen. The end of November. It'll be soon now.'

'What sort of big was that?'

'All the English agents. Killed.'

Aisling winced when she said this. She didn't want to say any more to Patrick now. She felt exhausted, as if the information had been dragged out of her. She stopped walking, abruptly. The round towers of the Four Courts loomed directly above them; grey, stony, immoveable, the givers of law. On the other side the Liffey rushed past, preoccupied with its own business. Patrick stopped next to her, and said nothing for a while. She started walking again, to break the silence as much as anything else, and he walked with her.

'Could your man know you've been reading his notes?'

'I don't think so. But he came home when I was in the middle of copying.'

And if he'd stayed home another five seconds she would have kissed him again and then God alone knew what would have happened.

'He saw you copying?'

'No. I locked up the desk and got out of the room in time. But he took the key. The key to his desk. He took it from the wardrobe. He put it in the pocket of his trousers.'

She remembered the feel of his hand on hers as he took the key.

'So you can't get back into that desk again. Not unless you get into his trousers.'

She only just stopped herself from hitting Patrick then and there.

'Ah, shut up, will you.'

'About what?'

'About getting into your man's trousers. What do you think I am, some kind of whore?'

Aisling looked away from him, at the river. The water looked grey and cold. She felt cold, all of a sudden. Then Patrick touched her on the shoulder. It felt repellent, and she pushed him away.

'I don't think you're a whore, Aisling,' he said. 'I'm sorry I said that and all. All I meant was, you're in his house, and you wash his clothes and do everything for him, and as long as you can find a way to get at his papers without him knowing you could as good as win the war for us. You're better than ten men with guns, Aisling. Will you keep at it?'

A flock of birds took off from behind the Four Courts. They lifted and wheeled left, flying down the length of the river, heading out towards the sea. Aisling watched them go. *When Ireland's free.* She owed it to Da to keep at it. And then she owed it to God to get out of that house as fast as she could before she was tempted any more. She reached into her basket under the sausages, and pulled out her notebook. She turned back the pages she had written on, and tore them out, briskly, neatly.

'Here. Word for word. I have a nice hand, don't I?'

Patrick looked round nervously, glanced at the papers, folded them twice, and thrust them into the pocket of his trenchcoat.

'Good lass.'

'Patrick.'

'What?'

'I don't want to stay in that house, all right? I need to leave.'

'I know. I know you do. But this.., this operation. The end of November thing. I can't talk about it. But it's big, very big. You need to look at every letter that comes through the door. Steam open any that are suspicious. If your man blows it, dozens of men will die and we've lost the war. The English are here forever, and you can be sure they'll kick us even harder once we're down. Do you want that so?'

'No. No I don't.'

'Think of your Da.'

'You don't have to tell me to think of him.'

'That's grand. So stay in there, just a few days more, till we've got the traitor. Then I'll get you out of there, find you another job. I'll make sure you're safe. Are you worried he might jump on you?'

She was more worried she might jump on him.

'No. I'll be all right. I can look after myself. But I don't know for how much longer.'

'Days. No more. After Sunday you'll have nothing more to worry about.'

'What's happening on Sunday?'

'That I can't tell you. Can I see you tomorrow?'

'Where?'

'Stephen's Green. By the pond. Same time.'

'Where the Major and the traitor met?'

'It's a good place to meet. Open, full of people but not too full.'

'All right. Tomorrow.'

'Watch everything. Remember everything. Tell me everything. I have to go now.'

'You're always in a hurry these days, Patrick.'

'After Sunday it'll be different. After Sunday we'll have time to talk.'

'What about?'

'I'll tell you after Sunday.'

He looked at her for a long time. She thought he was going to say something, but then he turned and walked away, along by the river, the way the birds had flown, towards the sea. She stood watching him as he went. The Lord had sent him, the priest said. He was a good man. He was on the right side, fighting for Irish freedom, risking his life. Da would have loved him. If only she could feel for him what she felt for the Major. But she didn't. The truth before God was that she didn't.

CHAPTER FOURTEEN

Sitting in Brind's office in the Castle that morning, Harry realised that Brind was looking pleased. Brind never looked pleased. It was quite frightening.

'The Viceroy lapped up your report. Positively lapped it up. And he insisted. Anything else comes in, he wants to be briefed by you, in person. Don't often say it, but bloody well done, Lovegrove.'

'Thank you, sir.'

Brind leant back in his chair and studied Harry.

'You're a man with a future. One day, your own regiment. One day, even, a province in India. Sky's the limit. Job's not over, of course. Disposed of the McCann twins, but that's just the beginning. Have to head off this attack that's coming any day now. Above all, have to get Collins.'

Brind picked up a pencil and held it with one hand at either end.

'Get that Irish bastard by the throat...' He snapped the pencil between his hands, making little bits fly onto his desk, '... and they're broken. Lot of them.' He put the ends of the pencil in the bin next to him, and started carefully sweeping up the bits with his hand. 'I'm giving you full charge of the operation, even though there are plenty here who outrank you and who'd bite my hand off if I offered it to them.'

'Thank you, sir.'

He felt warmed by Brind's praise, felt as if he was back to being a proper soldier again.

'But no more notebooks in the house. This is too high calibre for that.'

'Absolutely not, sir. All my notes are locked up in my office from now on.'

'You said you have a maid?'

'Yes sir.'

Aisling. Aisling was still in his thoughts, all the time. He'd barely been able to stop himself from kissing her when he'd gone back for his notes yesterday. He'd had to look away from her when she'd put his breakfast in front of him that morning for fear he'd blurt out what was in his mind. He'd noticed she'd been crying, and had wanted to hold her, to console her. Aisling was stopping him being a proper soldier.

'Have to go,' said Brind.

'Sir?'

'Maid. May be innocent, but can't take the chance. Too much at stake. Just in case.'

'Dismiss her?'

'That's what I said. Use the wife trouble. Say you've got the compassionate leave and you're taking Mrs L back to England.'

Dismiss her. Tell her to go. Remove her from the house. It would solve the problem. And then he could concentrate on his work. Get his promotion. Get out of this country. Go home. Start again somewhere new where Emily could be properly looked after. Forget Aisling. Forget her once and for all. Do his duty. He didn't want to get rid of Aisling. He didn't want to, remotely. But Brind was offering him a way out of the firing line of his obsession, handing him a ticket home. He would be a fool not to take it. He stood to attention and saluted.

'Sir!'

CHAPTER FIFTEEN

Mick would see him right, thought Patrick, lying on his bed back at the Squad's HQ that evening, Sean's words of rebuke for his absence that morning still echoing in his ears. Mick would take his side of it. He was coming some time tonight, they all said. They didn't know when. They never knew when. Truth was, they didn't really know if he would come. No one, not even the men who stood at his right hand day and night, knew what Mick would do next. That was how he kept out of the hands of the English, how he kept one step, no, one leap ahead of them all the time. Two Black and Tans had kicked open the door of the room where he'd been sleeping with a woman, and found her sitting up holding the sheets round herself, and the window open and him gone, no sign of him up the street or down the street, even though they'd heard him and her at it as they came up the stairs. He'd sat in a bar jawing with a couple of Auxies about racing for an hour and a half, and left them with two or three good tips and the bill for the drinks and them thinking he was the best of fellas, until someone had told them who he was. He'd stopped the Chief Constable himself in Sackville Street, right outside the GPO, and asked after his daughter's

First Holy Communion and remarked on how lovely her red sash had looked and hadn't Uncle Paddy been in fine voice at the do at Vaughan's afterwards before he got back on his bicycle and flew off, pedalling as if he hadn't a care in the world before the man could stop him, or find out how he knew all that. He could talk all night and never be tired, or he could be silent for an hour while others talked and then remember every last word they'd said. No one saw him write anything down, but he knew where you were and what you'd been doing and who you'd been doing it with on a Thursday afternoon five months previous better than you knew it yourself. He could be laughing and slapping you on the back as if you were his best pal one minute and screaming and swearing at you like a banshee the next. Everybody knew who he was, but nobody knew where he was; everybody knew what they thought of him, but nobody knew what he was thinking. And when you were on a job, you'd sooner get a bullet in your head than come back and tell him you hadn't done it like he wanted it done. That was the Big Fella for you. That was Mick Collins.

Mick had been Patrick's inspiration in the camp in Frongoch; Mick had brought him into the Squad in the first place; and now Mick might be Patrick's last chance. Mick might be what stood between him and getting drummed out of the IRA. Only nobody left the IRA. The only way you left the IRA was when you left this world, sometimes with a bit of help from the IRA itself. Patrick wondered if Sean might be ready to provide that help.

It wasn't even as if they'd been out on a reconnaissance that morning. They'd been sitting around playing dominoes and smoking and arguing and scratching their balls. He'd told Joe he was going out to buy some smokes, and he'd slipped out at five to eleven, and he'd been back by half past, and Joe hadn't even finished his hand of dominoes but there was Sean, standing in the corner, hands in pockets, like he'd been hoping this would happen. Rory had said, 'First time you made a fuck last half an hour,' and Joe had had to stand between them. Then Sean had spoken. 'Did you have to take the boat to England for your smokes, so?' he'd said. Then worse. Talk of disobeying orders a second time, of letting Ireland down, of not being fit to be a soldier. Of how deliberately disobeying orders was next door to treachery, and they all knew what happened to traitors. His face, red and twisted, right next to Patrick's, half whispering, half shouting. The others had sat and said nothing and looked at their shoes, because they knew better than to interrupt Sean when he had a gas on. He'd sent Patrick to his room, like their Da used to do to the both of them. Told him to stay there while he decided what to do with him. So here Patrick was, lying on the bed he shared with Vinnie in the dark of the early winter evening, with (on Sean's orders) no smokes, no food, no light, listening to Joe and Rory bicker at each other outside about shoe polish as they clacked their way through their thousandth game of dominoes. He hadn't even tried to tell Sean what Aisling had told him. He'd save that for Mick. Mick would be here soon, and Mick would see it his way.

He'd read Aisling's extracts from Lovegrove's notes again and again until it had got dark. Her precise, careful hand was easy to read. If someone put a match to the papers now he could write them out word for word. What a job she'd done. And in a house with a man who'd jumped on her. Come Sunday, that bastard Lovegrove would be dead, and he'd get her out, and tell her what he felt for her. He'd hinted with the ring. Gone too far, probably. She'd been mighty cold with him after. Maybe she was nervous about the whole spying thing. There was plenty to be nervous about, God knew. It'd be different after Sunday, he was sure. When they'd got through Sunday he and she could get on with some bloody living.

'Is this how you're going to throw the English out? By beating them at dominoes? Use your double six like that and they'll be here another hundred years.'

A Cork voice. Soft, a little held in, a little held back, but with a sharp edge behind it, because that was how Corkmen were. That was how the greatest Corkman of them all was. Mick was here. Patrick grinned to himself in the dark. He swung his legs off the bed and pushed open the door. He blinked in the flickering gaslight a little. Mick was sitting with his chair tipped back at a dangerous angle, his feet on the table and his hat covering half his face. Rory and Vinnie were clutching their dominoes protectively as if he might take them away at any moment. Sean was leaning against the wall, his arms folded, as far away from Mick as he could get.

'Mick,' said Patrick.

'I gave you an order,' said Sean. 'Get back in your room.'

'You sent Pat to his room with no supper, so?' said Mick. 'Jesus, Sean, you love to throw your weight around with your little brother, don't you? Is it so you get to eat his leftovers? Come over here, Pat! Let's have a look at you.'

He swung his long legs off the table, sat forward on his chair and tipped his hat back. He pulled a chair round, and gestured for Patrick to sit on it.

'What did Sean send you to your room for?'

'He disobeyed orders by absenting himself without official leave,' said Sean.

'I wasn't asking you,' said Mick, without looking at Sean.

'I had a reason,' said Patrick.

'I thought you'd come to talk about Sunday,' said Sean.

'I'll decide what I talk about. Pat here is a good boy. I've known him since Frongoch. He wouldn't do something without a reason. Come on, Pat. Let's hear your side of it.'

Patrick sat down opposite Mick. He felt bigger, stronger already to have Mick's undivided attention.

'I met a woman.'

Mick whistled, and slapped Patrick on the knee.

'You sly dog, Pat.'

'No women!' said Sean. 'I gave an order.'

'Shut it, Sean,' said Mick. 'I think Pat had a reason. And not the one you're thinking of.'

'Mick,' said Sean, 'you should be disciplining him, not listening to him. What does it say to these boys if you –'

'I had a reason all right,' said Patrick. 'I think I've found a traitor.'

Out of the corner of his eye, Patrick saw Sean shake his head and look away. Mick jerked his head sideways at Rory and Joe.

'You two, bugger off. Take yourselves down to the pub for the night. And take the rest with you. Me and Sean and Pat here need to talk. Go on. Do it. Some time before Christmas. Maybe a few pints will improve your dominoes.'

Rory and Joe looked at each other. Then they pushed their dominoes into the centre of the table, mixing them up, and carefully pocketed the coins they had won. They stood up, took their coats from the rack, and pushed open the doors of the bedrooms one by one.

'Come on, lads. We're off to Nelligan's. Orders of Mick.'

In a clatter of trench coats and trilbies and soft, happy curses the room emptied itself of men. Mick picked up Rory's chair and placed it on the other side of the table, next to Patrick. He beckoned to Sean. Sean moved reluctantly, heavily across the room, looking around him as if for an escape. At last he sat. Patrick felt Sean's discomfort, even as he felt proud to be favoured himself by Mick. Mick took out a packet of cigarettes and offered them to Sean. Sean shook his head. He offered them to Patrick, and Patrick took one. He took one for himself, lit it, then lit Patrick's with the same match.

'So, Pat,' said Mick. 'Who is she?'

For a moment, for all his wish for Mick's approval, Patrick didn't want to tell him. He wanted to keep Aisling to himself. Keep her from this world of smokes and farts and fists on tables and filthy jokes. Mick took a drag on his cigarette. He punched Patrick's knee.

'Who is she, Pat? Who's the young lady? Tell Mick.'

He was smiling at Patrick. That didn't happen too often. When Mick smiled at you, you'd do anything, tell anything.

'Her name's Aisling O'Flaherty. She's a maid in Major Harry Lovegrove's house, in Lower Mount Street.'

'A maid or the maid?'

'The. She's the only one.'

'They're not rich, some of these spies. How did you meet her?'

'I followed her a few times. Then I got talking to her after Mass.'

'You crafty devil. What started you on her?'

Patrick looked over at Sean. Sean was looking away from both of them. Patrick took a deep breath. He felt almost as keyed up as he did on the way to a shooting.

'Back in August, when I was tailing Fitzgerald, he bumped into Lovegrove in Grafton Street. Lovegrove told Fitzgerald he'd tipped the wink to the Tans about Seamus and Colm. Told him he'd got someone on the inside.'

'Someone on the inside?'

'Yes, Mick.'

'Did you tell Sean?'

'I did, but –'

'Once triggermen turn IOs they lose their nerve,' interrupted Sean. 'You can't have triggermen taking notes on what people say, or they won't be fit to kill any more. They get too close.'

Mick turned his head slowly towards Sean and held his gaze on him silently for a moment. Then he turned back to Patrick.

'You did, but what?'

'But he ignored me.'

'So.' Again Mick looked at Sean.

'You got talking to this girl after Mass?'

'I did.'

'What did you find out about our friend Lovegrove?'

'Nothing the first time. But we arranged to meet again. We've been walking out together since August as a matter of fact.'

'What?' said Sean. 'Walking out? You disobedient bastard!'

'I know you're surprised to hear a woman might want to walk out with me, Sean,' said Patrick, feeling the anger rise in spite of himself. 'I know you've never had so much as a touch of a woman in your life.'

Sean stood up, knocking back the chair he was sitting on.

'Sean!' said Mick. 'Sit down. I said I wanted to hear his story, and I will. In full. Go on, Pat.'

Sean picked up the chair and sat, slowly, reluctantly.

'On Wednesday, I thought it was time to spill a few beans. I didn't tell her I was in the Squad or anything, but I told her about Seamus and Colm, told her what Lovegrove really does, got her to agree to spy on him. She has cause. Back in Connemara, the Tans burnt her house and murdered her Da. So she told me about a desk in Lovegrove's house. Where he keeps his notes.'

'Has she got into this desk?'

'She has, so. And she copied this.'

Patrick reached into his pocket and pulled out Aisling's notes. Already, they were looking worn from all the times he'd read them, from how tightly he'd folded them in his pocket to keep them safe.

'You didn't tell me about this,' said Sean.

'You didn't ask,' said Patrick.

Mick flicked his eyes from one brother to another. He took the notes from Patrick and unfolded them. Patrick watched him as he read them. Part of him didn't want Mick touching what Aisling had touched; part of him was proud. Mick read fast, with total attention. Patrick and Sean sat, not touching, saying nothing. Once, Mick looked up from the notes and looked first at Sean, then at Patrick, then back at Sean again. Then he went on reading. When he'd finished, he stubbed out his cigarette in the ashtray on the dominoes table and sat back in his chair. He spread Aisling's notes out on his knees and looked down at them thoughtfully.

'Brilliant,' he said. 'Fucking brilliant, Pat. Nothing less than a fucking gold mine.'

He looked up at Sean.

'Why didn't you know about this, Sean?'

'He's a soldier, Mick. He disobeyed orders.'

'Well maybe the orders weren't so good. Here's one order you'll give the boys, and it will be obeyed. No more visiting knocking shops. Tell Joe from me that I know what he's been up to at Mrs O'Connor's and who he's been blabbing to, and that I will personally cut off his prick if he does it again. They can talk to their right hands if they're feeling lonely. Understood?'

'Yes, Mick.'

'More important. There's a traitor in the ranks, and he could blow Sunday. He could blow all of us. He's doing it because he hates me. I don't hate him. I just hate traitors. I need to know for sure who he is. Pat, are you seeing this girl again?'

'I am.'

'Again? Despite my order?' said Sean.

'We're past that, Sean,' said Mick. 'When?'

'Tomorrow, eleven, by the pond on Stephen's Green.'

'Grand. You be there. You be early. You keep close to her. You do everything you have to do to find out who the bastard is who shopped Seamus and Colm, and who is going to shop the rest of us. Understood?'

'Yes, Mick.'

'And you bring everything you've got direct to me. Liam is at Vaughan's at the moment. The minute you have something, you go there, you ask for him, and then you ask him for me. He'll have orders to take you to me. You don't say anything to anyone until you've seen me.'

'Not even Sean?'

'Not even Liam. You don't even read anything she copies until I have. Understood?'

'Yes, Mick.'

'One last thing, Pat. Are you sweet on this girl?'

Mick was looking straight at him. He couldn't lie when Mick was looking straight at him.

'I am, Mick.'

'Is she sweet on you?'

Patrick paused. He had to tell the truth to Mick, to himself.

'I don't know, Mick.'

'She will be, soon. When the war's over and Ireland's free, I'll be best man at your wedding. Until then, you put duty before love. Do what you like with her, but do nothing that'll hurt Ireland. Nothing. Understood?'

'Yes, Mick.'

He folded up Aisling's notes up and put them in his pocket.

'Good man. Now you get down to Nelligan's with the rest of them. You deserve a pint. I've things to discuss with Sean. And not one bloody word to anyone, you understand?'

'Mick.'

'What?'

'Thank you.'

'Ah, bugger off, will you.'

CHAPTER SIXTEEN

Aisling stood at the stove, flaking the haddock into the pan, feeling the flesh of the fish soft and crumbling in her hands, waiting for Major Lovegrove to come home. She would find a way, she thought. That key would have to be somewhere in the house. He wouldn't keep it in work. What would be the point? His desk was here. Even if he kept it in his trouser pocket all the time eventually he would have to go to sleep. She could feel her way into the bedroom in the night when he was asleep and get it then. Feel her way into his bedroom. The thought sent a little shiver through her that ran up from her thighs to her breasts. But what if it turned out there was nothing in the desk any more? *Can't be too careful*, he'd said. *These are dangerous times.* She peeled off the shells of the boiled eggs and sliced them into little slivers, dropping them into the pan with the haddock and the rice. If he stopped keeping secrets at home, what good could she be as a spy? She might as well leave now. But Patrick had said dozens of men would die if she didn't stop him. Should she follow him at night time? That could be dangerous. That could get her shot. But who would miss her when she was gone? And wouldn't she be first in the queue for heaven as a martyr for Ireland? Wouldn't it wipe away all her sins, so?

She stirred the egg in with the haddock and the rice. She listened to the gentle bubbling and let the smell of the fish rise to her. Kedgeree was his favourite. He'd had it for breakfast at weekends when he was a boy, he'd told her once. Now he liked it any time. It would put him in a good mood, maybe. She needed to keep him in a good mood so he would trust her. And also because the thought of him being angry with her made the tears start to her eyes. She wiped her eyes with the back of her hand. He was a bastard, she told herself. He was one of the ones that had killed Da and burnt her house down, and he'd taken advantage of her. Only he wasn't. And he hadn't. Oh, Jesus. What was she to do? What would Patrick say if he knew what was going through her mind now?

She scooped up the last of the butter from its dish and flicked it in, threw a sprig of parsley on top and folded a cloth over the top of the pan. When she'd kissed him it had been long and deep and had seemed to reach down inside her. He'd pushed her onto the bed. And yet he was so quiet and careful like. So thoughtful. Not like any other man she'd ever met. The way he talked to her, as if he was afraid she might break or something. As if he was afraid he might break. He was a gentleman. People said that, but it was true about him. He was gentle. Except when he was sending young Irish lads to their deaths. But then wasn't he being a soldier, the same as Patrick was? Just for his country instead of ours? He was gentle to his wife. His wife. Aisling wondered if she was lying in her bed in the madhouse now, thinking of her husband, wondering what he was doing. If she missed the smell of her husband. There was a rich, almost leathery smell seemed to come off his skin. It was a strange thing. As she'd been changing the sheets earlier, she'd thought that everything in this house smelt of him. She'd picked up a corner of one of his sheets and held it close to her face, and felt as if she was holding him.

She lifted the cloth off the pan. The kedgeree was ready. She heard his key in the door. She took the pan off the heat and put it on the side and went out into the hall.

'Let me take your coat, sir.'

'No thank you, Aisling. I'm going straight out again. I've got to work.'

He wasn't looking at her. He was looking at his Norfolk seascape on the wall. King's Lynn in a storm.

'I made kedgeree. I made your favourite.'

'Well I'm very sorry, Aisling. I'm afraid you've laboured in vain. I'll be dining out tonight. Not coming back till late.'

He still wasn't looking at her. She was starting to feel a little afraid.

'It'll keep till tomorrow. You can have it for your breakfast. Like you did when you were a lad.'

He turned to look at her.

'Aisling.'

'Sir?'

'There's something I have to tell you.'

She couldn't tell if he was angry or sad. He seemed to be both.

'What's that, sir?'

'I've been talking with Colonel Brind. We've both agreed that I cannot do my work satisfactorily while Emily is so unwell. It is hard for me to concentrate. He's agreed to grant me leave. To take Emily back to England, where she can be treated by the very best nerve doctor. In London.'

She felt a lump rise to her throat.

'How long are you going to be away?'

'I'm not... we're not coming back. The Colonel has got me a desk job in London.'

He was leaving her. He was leaving her in the lurch. Now he'd had his fun, he was leaving her for his wife. Bastard.

'Wouldn't you rather be here? Where you can kill some Irish?'

'That's not what I do, Aisling.'

'Oh no. You get other people to do that for you.'

It was a foolish thing to say. Foolish to give away what she knew. But she couldn't stop herself.

'What are you talking about, Aisling?'

'Nothing. I'm talking about nothing. So you're giving me notice? Is that what you're saying?'

'I'll see you're fully paid up.'

'I don't doubt you will. You'll give me enough to keep me quiet.'

'Keep you quiet?'

Would she stop doing this? She couldn't.

'Wouldn't do now to get out that an English officer had jumped on his maid, would it? Wouldn't do much for his promotion prospects.'

'I think you'll find, Aisling, that you jumped on me.'

He said this very quietly, breathing hard and slow. She could see a vein on his temple throb. It scared her to see that. Still she kept on with her boldness, just as she had on the first day they'd met.

'Ah, you're right, so. What a bloody fool I was to do it. When do you want me gone?'

'We're leaving on Monday. You need to be gone by then. I'll see if there is someone at the Castle who can find you a position. I'm sure I can twist a few arms.'

'Just tell them you'll have them shot if they don't give me a job. That should do the trick.'

She turned and ran up the stairs, taking them two at a time. She remembered the kedgeree. She'd taken it off the heat, it wouldn't be ruined. Thinking of the kedgeree made the tears spring to her eyes. She kept running, holding the tears in until she'd got to her room, and then she slammed the door behind her, threw herself onto her bed, and gave herself up to angry sobs; as angry with herself as she was with him.

She heard the door close behind him. He might be shot while he was out. Shot by Patrick, maybe. She might never see him again, and the last words they spoke would have been words of anger. It had been terrible when Mam had died and when Da had died, but at least she would always know that they loved her. If he died tonight it would leave a great gaping wound in her that would never heal. She suddenly felt terribly, terribly tired, as if a great weight was crushing her. She held the pillow close as if for comfort. Sleep, which had evaded her for the last three nights, now ambushed her from all sides.

CHAPTER SEVENTEEN

Harry had sent a note to Ryan to meet him at O'Hea's at ten. O'Hea's was in the darkest, deepest north of the city, where men drank more than they ate, women had more children than they could count, and the children had never seen shoes. It was down a back street in the Monto where the sun never shone and the damp dripped from the houses. Whores would let their customers take them up against the wall outside, because they had nowhere to go and neither did their customers. It was no place for an officer and a gentleman, and no place either for a respectable solicitor specialising in the wills of wealthy widows living in Merrion Square. That was why Harry had chosen it. No one would recognise either of them. When he sat down with his glass of porter, ten minutes early as ever, he saw a couple of men at the next table, gap toothed, clothes torn, half-bearded, staring at him. Must be after a rough, cheap whore, they would be thinking. They were half right.

He hadn't thought of eating at O'Hea's. O'Hea's didn't serve food. The clientele either couldn't afford it or weren't interested in it. He'd gone first to a chophouse in Dame Street not far from the Castle, a smoky, intimate place that served substantial plates of meat cooked rare to men on their own. It was run by a Protestant who welcomed Castle men. He could perfectly easily have dined at home, but he'd decided before he got home to say what he had to say to Aisling, and then go straight out. Job done. Problem solved. It hadn't been like that, though. As he'd picked at his chop, chewing it reluctantly, leaving most of it, he'd thought things over. He'd imagined that dismissing Aisling would sort everything out. She would pack her bags and be gone from the house and then she would be gone from his mind. But then she'd turned on him, and it had hurt. Hurt more than a rocket from Colonel Brind; hurt more than Emily's mad rantings; hurt more than he could have expected or imagined. She wasn't stupid. She'd worked out what he did at nights. And she was right. He wasn't a proper soldier. He no longer pulled the trigger himself. He got other men to do it, and when they did the bullet went into the back of the man's head while he was sleeping. What sort of a war was that? He felt more confused and unsure than ever; not a good state for a soldier to be in. Well, he told himself, they had to fight it that way because that was how the Irish fought. One day, as like as not, he'd get a bullet in his head when he was sleeping. It would be nothing less than he deserved.

He sighed, and sipped at his porter. It was not a drink he enjoyed, but it was less likely to poison him than the cheap gin that was the only alternative here. He looked around the room, adjusting his eyes to the dark, taking in the low, despairing mutters of the men, the thickening pipe smoke and the stench of sweat and drink. The men at the next table had stopped staring at him, and were hunched back over their gin. It was true what he'd said in his anger, that Aisling had started what had happened. But he'd followed, and willingly. More to the point, he'd wanted to carry on. It was only by a mighty effort of will that he'd stopped. And when he thought of Aisling going for good, he didn't feel relief. He felt nothing but a kind of emptiness and despair, as if he was about to topple into a deep hole with no bottom, chained all the while to poor Emily. *You may have to make other arrangements*, the doctor had said, as if he was writing a prescription. Most of the war he'd been away from Emily and she'd been unceasingly busy with her nursing; busy, he saw now, as a way of keeping her madness at bay. When the war had ended, married women weren't allowed to work at the hospital any more, and she'd taken to her bed and not left it since. She hadn't been a wife to him for a long time. But Harry had always refrained from making other arrangements; it was the kind of thing that smelt bad to him. He could make an arrangement in this place if he wanted, for little more than the price of a couple of drinks. But he didn't want an arrangement. He wanted Aisling. And sending her away just made him want her more.

Ryan was at the door. He'd never seen him before, but he knew it was Ryan, because his clothes were clean and he was well fed, even a little on the paunchy side, and because he had his collar turned up and his hat pulled down to stop anyone recognising him. He looked around the room until his eyes met Harry's. He gave one discreet nod, and came to his table.

'Mr Ryan?' said Harry.

'And you're Mr Evans. Or so you've led me to believe.'

'What will you drink?'

'One half of porter only. I'm not a big drinker, you know. I'm a man of good habits.'

'Is that so?' said Harry. He got the porter and returned to the table, making sure he was sitting with his back to the wall, watching the room, watching the door.

'How much?' said Ryan, keeping his eyes and his voice low.

'How much what?'

'Come on, Mr Evans, we're both men of business. Let's not waste our time. Let's not stay in this godforsaken hell hole longer than we have to. We both know why we're here. How much do you want?'

'It's not money I'm after, Mr Ryan.'

'Well what then? Revenge? The girl's father is paying you? He'll not pay you much.'

'Not that either. Rather, I want you to help us. Help the people I represent. But in the process you'll be helping a member of your family. One who has gone astray.'

'You're not wearing a collar, so don't talk like a priest. Just tell me how much.'

He patted his pocket, and lowered his voice to a whisper.

'I've money on me now.'

'Thomas Byrne,' said Harry. 'When did you last see him?'

Ryan flinched as if he'd been hit.

'Never heard of the man.'

'Not a very good uncle, are you? What would your sister Marie say if she could hear you?'

Ryan gave a deep sigh and looked into his porter.

'Jesus, Mary and Joseph. You've done your homework.'

'Tom's gone to the bad. Thrown his lot in with a gang of Fenian murderers. We want to get him back.'

'Who's we, Mr Evans?'

'Any right thinking person. Anyone who wants to see murder stamped out.'

'You work for the Castle, right?'

'I'm on the side of law and order.'

Ryan turned and looked at the door, as if he was thinking about escaping. He fumbled in his pocket for a cigarette, lit it, and turned back to Harry. He shook his head.

'All right. You know about Tom. The poor lad. It's not his fault, you know. It was the fault of that bastard father of his. Everything's his fault, in the end. I told Marie he was trouble. I told her and told her, right up to the day of the wedding. He did nothing for her, and nothing for the lads, except to drink and piss away their money and knock them around. He's dead now, but they all bear the scars still. I give Marie money, but she's lost her confidence. And none of the lads have come to anything. It doesn't surprise me Tom's in with them Fenians. But we've not heard from him in a year. That's God's honest truth. I'm sorry, Mr Evans, but I can do nothing more for you. Now would you return my letter? It's still my property until the addressee is in receipt of it.'

'What would you do if Tom told you he wanted to leave the Fenians?'

'Give him a box round the ears for having run his Mam ragged, and then try and fix him up with a proper job.'

'Leaving the Irish Republican Army isn't like resigning a clerkship, Mr Ryan. There will be ruthless, dangerous men after him, men with guns. He'd be lucky to live a week outside of the IRA. But we can help him. Help him to start a new life.'

'Turn him into a tout, you mean?'

'We can keep him safe.'

Ryan dragged on his cigarette greedily, and looked at the ceiling. He rubbed his forehead with the back of his hand. Harry remained calm and still as he always did. He'd done this many times before. He knew Ryan would tell him soon. He knew he had him where he wanted him. It was all working out as it should. He should feel relieved and proud, but instead he felt a little sick.

'What if I tell you to mind your own business?' said Ryan at last.

'You're a man of honour, Mr Ryan. A man of integrity. You're well respected for it. That's why your practice has no shortage of clients. But precious few people would want their legal affairs managed by a man who got his maid pregnant and then threw her out of the house. And if your clients didn't reject you, your partners would. They've been itching for an excuse for a while now.'

'Mr Evans. You're a Protestant, right? You've a Protestant accent. Do you know how many solicitors in Dublin are Catholics? Five. Do you know how many solicitors there are in the whole of Dublin? One hundred and forty-seven are on the roll. Does going to Mass send the law out of your head? I've had to fight every day of my life to get where I am. I'm not a man who gives up easily.'

Ryan leaned over the table and stared at Harry, up close to his face. Harry could smell whiskey on his breath. For all he'd said about not drinking, he'd come to the meeting fortified against his nerves. It gave Harry an advantage.

'Come on, give me the letter. It's my property. I know the law, you know.'

'I don't have the letter with me. Where is Tom?'

'Give me the letter.'

'You've done well for yourself. It helps you to support your sister. But you couldn't support her any more with no profession to call on. You couldn't support your wife either. If she didn't go back to her mother in Limerick when she found out. This is a lonely city for a man with no wife and no job and no reputation. I don't want any money off you, Mr Ryan. All I want is the truth.'

Ryan drew on his cigarette. Then he stubbed it out and spread his hands out on the table, looking down at them as if he was consulting important papers. He waited a while. Harry waited, too. He could afford to.

'You say you want the truth, Mr Evans. All right. This is the truth for you. I don't love my wife. I never have done. I married her because she was expecting our first. I put in the hours at the office to get away from her. I've strayed since then, more than once. But what happened between me and Sinead was not a man having some fun with a servant and then getting rid of her. It was true. Truer than true. I truly loved her and she truly loved me, and I miss her every day. And I miss my son too. The son I've never seen. I worry about her and I worry about him, and if I could take myself off to County Cork to be with them without ruining myself I'd do it tomorrow. But as it is, I make enough money to send some every month. She tells her parents she married a sailor in Dublin and then he was called to the sea and she gets the money from him. So far they've fallen for it. But every sailor has to come home from the sea one day and I worry sick about what will happen to her and the lad when they find out.'

He'd got Ryan to open up. The whiskey had helped. Now Ryan was ready, ripe for the picking. Normally, Harry relished this moment; it felt like sending the batsman's stumps flying had when he'd played cricket at school. But tonight he hated himself.

'Not all sailors come home from the sea, Mr Ryan. If Sinead receives a letter – on official, Royal Navy notepaper – informing her of the death of her brave husband in a tragic accident while in the service of His Majesty's Navy, she will receive sympathy, not suspicion. And she will also receive a pension that will keep her and her child for the rest of her life. Who knows, she might even be able one day to love again. To provide a father for her child.'

Ryan looked up.

'Would you do that for me?' he said.

'It depends on what you do for us.'

Ryan studied Harry's face as if reading through a contract, line by line.

'Will you look after Tom? He's a good lad under it all. If anything happened to him, it would break Marie's heart. And he was always my favourite. I was more of a father to him than that bastard Dermot ever was.'

'We'll give him a new life.'

'Keep him safe from the Fenian guns?'

'We saw off the Germans. We can see off the Fenians.'

Ryan looked a bit longer. He turned away, looking at the door again. Then he said, to the door, 'Tom's meeting his brother for a pint in Mulligan's on Henry Street Friday night,' and stood up, put on his hat, and walked out.

Harry watched him go, waited a minute, then swallowed his drink and left. It was cold, but it was a clear night. He leaned against the wall outside O'Hea's and looked up at the moon, just visible in a crack between the overhanging houses.

Tom would be taken in to the Castle and tortured. When the last drop had been squeezed out of him, he'd be shot while trying to escape. Sinead would carry on bringing up her bastard child on her own in her little village in County Cork, spinning out occasional remittances from Ryan, besieged by whispers and looks, unsupported by a navy pension. And Ryan would do nothing about it, because they would keep his intercepted letter to Sinead.

Good work, Lovegrove. He could go off duty for the night now. He could get drunk if he wanted to. He could celebrate. If there was anything to celebrate. A whore on the other side of the street called to him.

'You're looking upset, my dear. Is it cheering up you want?'

She was young. She still looked pretty. She could have beautiful children.

'No thank you,' he said. 'I'm going home.'

'What, is there someone at home waiting for you? Someone who'll put a smile on your face? Someone who'll love you? Someone who'll make you happy?'

'Yes,' said Harry. 'Yes, as a matter of fact, there is.'

CHAPTER EIGHTEEN

When Aisling woke at last it was dark and cold. She had no idea how long she had been sleeping. It seemed like a long time. She realised she was still fully dressed. She scrambled out of her clothes and into the nightdress she kept folded up under her pillow. But she didn't feel like going back to sleep yet. She reached for the box of matches on the table by her bed and lit her candle. She looked round her room in the sudden burst of light. A small, solid wardrobe, containing a winter dress, a summer dress, a Sunday dress, two plain pairs of shoes. An apologetic little chest of drawers, not even filled, her underwear and her monthly cloths huddling together inside it for warmth, underneath them the money she'd saved from her wages. A chair onto which she'd folded her day clothes. Thin curtains keeping the wind out. One tentative rug by her bed. Mam's rosary hanging off the bedpost. No pictures of her parents or prints of her home town like the Major had. That was it. That was her lot. She didn't have a home town any more. It had been burnt to the ground by the English. Everything she owned in the world could be put in the suitcase she kept under the bed. And so it would be as soon as the Major had bullied someone into giving her a job. If he even bothered to do that.

Well, if he was throwing her out, she'd get something off him first. Something that would save dozens of men's lives and get back at his lot for Clifden. She pulled on her dressing gown, picked up the candle and left her room.

She listened outside the door to his bedroom. Normally he wheezed a little in his sleep, but there was no sound. He wasn't back yet. She pushed the door open slowly. By the light of her candle, she saw that his sheets were still folded down, neatly, just as she'd left them. She set the candle down on the table by his side of the bed, next to the photograph of his mother and the Kipling book. She opened his wardrobe. His jackets seemed to hang stiffly to attention, as if they were leading a parade. His trousers lined up behind them, like junior officers. She stroked the sleeve of one of his jackets, held it to her face. The cloth was a little coarse, but she liked its touch of roughness; it felt like the thick hair on his arms. It seemed to smell of his skin, too, that smelt like leather that had been left out in the sun. She looked at the hook on the door of the wardrobe. It was empty. She ran her hands over each of his jackets, down each of his trousers. One after another, they gave easily to her touch. At last she felt something small and hard in the side pocket of one of his jackets, one that he wore on Sundays. She reached in and put her hand round a pair of cuff links. Six pairs of shoes were lined up in the bottom of the wardrobe. She tipped them up one by one and shook them, making the laces flap. Then she opened each of the drawers in the wardrobe. She felt his crisp shirts, sliding her hands into and under and through them, feeling as if she was running her hands over his chest as he wore them. But there was nothing. No response. She rummaged amongst his socks; she thrust her fingers into the thick wool of his underwear, her breath quickening as she did. Beneath his underwear, she found an envelope. She took it out. In the envelope were some banknotes. She counted twenty pound notes. She caught her breath. She put them back in the envelope carefully, all face up, and replaced them in the underwear drawer. She let her hand linger in the drawer a little while. She felt both very close to him and painfully distant at the same time. She straightened and smoothed everything and closed the wardrobe door as quietly as she could, even though she knew she was alone in the house. Next, she turned to the bed. She prodded the mattress a couple of times, stretched her hand under the sheets. She lifted up the pillow. Pyjamas, neatly folded. He was always neat; like her. Except when he'd let the house go to ruin, but that was as if he'd caught whatever Mrs Lovegrove had. His pyjamas were soft to her touch, like his face when she'd wiped away his tears. That leathery smell was on them, too. She replaced the pillow.

She didn't want to walk back up the stairs in the cold and the dark, to get back into her bed, on her own. She wanted to stay here, to be in his room. She buried her face in his pillow. It smelt of the sweet tobacco he smoked, that he must have breathed on to it. The stale smell of Mrs Lovegrove was gone from the bed now. Her unused clothes were still in her wardrobe, she supposed, but it was closed tight shut. It felt as if she might never have been here; as if he might be a bachelor. She climbed into what was now his bed alone and pulled the sheets over her, right over her head. She'd always slept like that, ever since she'd been a little girl. It made her feel as if no one could touch her. The warmth came up over her body. She felt sleep tugging her down. She could do nothing to stop it.

'Don't move an inch. I have you covered with my gun. So much as a twitch, and I will fire and keep firing until I kill you.'

She had never heard this voice of his before. It wasn't hard, so much as sharp. Sharp like a new knife. But it didn't cut her. It made her feel strangely safe. She knew he wouldn't hurt her. She stayed still under the sheets, slowly sliding out of sleep, holding her breath, waiting for him. She heard him walk towards her across the room, slowly, deliberately, long paces. He was standing over her. He snatched the sheets back, in one large movement.

She could make out the shape of his body. Her candle had burnt down, staining the bedside table with thick gobbets of wax, but the dark of the room was a little tinged with moonlight. In his left hand he held the sheets, which he had pulled full from the bed. In his right hand he held a gun. His arm was stretched out rigidly and the gun was maybe a foot away from her chest. Still, she didn't feel afraid.

'Sir? It's me.'

'Aisling. Good God.'

He lowered his arm, and sat down on the end of the bed, all the tension gone out of him, his head slumped forward, his legs splayed open, his arms hanging between his open legs and the gun dangling on the end of one hand.

'Who did you think I was, sir?'

'I thought you were someone come to kill me.'

Aisling pulled herself up and sat on her haunches next to him. She could smell the tobacco on him, mingling with the smell of his skin. It had a sweet, tangy smell. It made her feel at home.

'Why would they do that, sir?'

'Because I'm the enemy. That's what happens when you're a soldier. You're surrounded by people who want to kill you. And you have to kill them before they kill you. Except... When I was in France... it was different. There, we could see the enemy. The Germans were in their set of trenches, and we were in ours. We shot at each other, we tried to kill each other but - but it was fair. It was open. They wore a uniform, for God's sake. Here, every man I pass in the street could have a gun in his pocket and be waiting to put a bullet in my head. And I have to slink around pubs and brothels trying to find them out. Find them out through lies and cheating and deception. No wonder your people want to kill me. I expect you want to kill me, don't you, Aisling?'

If he'd asked her a few hours before, when he was shouting at her in the hall, telling her to go, she might have said yes. But not now. Not when he was sitting slumped and defeated on the edge of the bed. Not when the man needed comforting. Needed looking after.

'I don't want to kill you, sir.'

She was stroking his hair. It was full and thick, and felt warm to the touch on this cold night. She wanted him to stay sitting next to her like this, didn't want him to go. In the moonlight she saw him looking at her.

'This ought to be somewhere I'm safe,' he was saying. 'This house. If they ever got in here...'

'I'll stop them, sir. I won't let anything happen to you.'

She meant that too. She'd have other Englishmen killed, but not this one.

'You don't have to leave, Aisling,' he said. 'I don't want you to leave. I'm not going to London. Colonel Brind hasn't got me a posting there. I'm staying in Dublin, and Emily is staying in the home in Kingstown. It was all a lie. I was thinking about it all the way home. I made my mind up. I decided I'd had enough of lies. I was going to tell you in the morning. I don't want you to go, Aisling. Do you know why? Because I love you. That's why.'

He pulled her towards him and kissed her. She didn't resist. Soon they were kissing deep and hard, reaching into each other hungrily, like starving people. She heard a sharp metallic clunk as his gun fell to the floor. The wind gusted again, shaking the panes angrily. The cold was all around them, as big as the house, but they warmed each other against it. The wind nudged a cloud across the moon, and it fell dark. In the dark, no one could see them, not God, not Mam, not Da, not Mrs Lovegrove, not Patrick. What they were going to do in the dark would be for them alone, and would have no past and no future. He pulled at her dressing gown, she unbuttoned his jacket, he lifted her nightdress, she fumbled with the belt of his trousers as if it was an enemy they were fighting together. Together they struggled and tussled with their clothes, till his trousers and shirt and socks and shoes and thick woollen underwear and her nightdress and dressing gown all lay defeated, slumped and mingled in a pile on the floor, and they stood facing each other, shivering a little. Then they reached for each other, running their hands from one place to another, wanting to touch everything at once. He took her by the shoulders and pushed her back on the bed, and eased her legs apart and entered her, and it hurt, as Mam had told her it would, and she felt herself hurting and him not hurting, heard him groaning with pleasure, and then it didn't hurt any more, and he pushed into her again, and again, and again, and she wanted him to go on and on and on, and while he did she wasn't in his room or in Dublin or in Ireland, she was somewhere that was everywhere and nowhere that she had ever been; and then he was finished. She felt his heart on top of her, beating fast, as if it was running away from something. He reached for the sheets and pulled them over her. He held her, keeping her warm. They didn't say anything for a long time.

At last he broke the silence.

'Aisling. Thank you.'

Just like he said it when she served him his dinner. Aisling didn't know what to say. She felt as if she was in a foreign country where she didn't speak the language. This soreness between her legs, but also this warm thrumming under her skin that made her feel more alive than she had ever felt before. This holding him close, his skin on hers, his breath mingling with hers, nothing between them now.

'I know what you're thinking,' he said. 'That this is what happens to servants. The master of the house takes advantage of them. Has his fun and leaves them.'

That was what she'd tried to tell herself. But she knew now it wasn't true.

'You didn't take advantage of me, sir. I took advantage of you. I was in your bed, wasn't I?'

'Why were you in my bed?'

'I... it seemed the right thing to do, sir.'

'It was, Aisling. You belong here.'

'But sir. Someone else belongs here. Mrs Lovegrove.'

'No. She doesn't belong here. My marriage is a lie. I've done with lies. This is the truth. I've loved you for a long time. From the first day. I just lied to myself about it. And don't call me sir. No more sir. No more Major Lovegrove. From now on, I'm just Harry.'

He was holding her close, their faces next to each other on the pillow, so close he hardly needed to lift his voice at all. She tried the name out in her mouth, as if it was the first word she had learnt in the language of this foreign country.

'Harry.'

'Aisling.'

It felt as if they had sealed something with their names. She kissed him this time; she touched him, she stroked him into life, she guided him, but when he entered her she hardly knew it; it was as if he had been there all along, as if he was meant to be nowhere else but there. He was inside her a long time, and at the end something gripped her, making her shake and tremble and gasp like a sweet fever, so sweet it made her shout out without realising it. Then they held each other close, listening to their breathing subsiding slowly, and sank into a deep sleep together.

When she woke it was light. The wind had stopped, but there was a little light rain. He was sleeping next to her, breathing softly. She looked at the ruins of their clothes on the floor. The house was cold; the fires needed lighting. When he woke he would need breakfast. The work of the house still had to go on. Whatever had happened, she still had her duty. It would help her to forget what she had done in the night while she decided what to do next. She put on her nightdress and her dressing gown, went up to her room, and washed and dressed. She came downstairs. She passed through the hall on the way to the kitchen, picked the post up and put it on the side table, like she always did. There were four letters, three from England and one from Dublin that looked like a bill. Underneath them was an envelope with no stamp on. It was marked 'Personal and private: for the attention of Major Harry Lovegrove Esq.'. She looked at it for a bit. She remembered what Patrick had said. *Watch everything. Remember everything. Tell me everything.* She opened it. There was just one sheet of paper inside. On it was written, in a hurried hand:

Your maid is spying on you. Get rid of her however you have to, or she will be the death of you. Collins has told me everything. It will happen on Sunday. You are on the list. Meet me at Reilly's on Grafton Street half past eleven today. I know what is going to happen and I will tell you. Burn this. Patrick.

Oh dear God. She remembered the sergeant's gun pointed at her the night Da died, and how she'd made an act of contrition, certain that she was going to die. That was how it felt now; only then she'd felt proud and certain that she'd die a blessed martyr for Ireland. If she died now, it would be with mortal sin and treachery smeared all across her soul. She looked at the clock that hung on the wall over the table for the post. It was five past eleven. She could still put things right; but only if she ran.

CHAPTER NINETEEN

Standing by the pond on the Green, Patrick turned the collar of his trenchcoat up against the rain, which was blustering more strongly now. A stray leaf, one of the last of autumn, blew up into his face, and he brushed it aside. He glanced at his watch. Ten past eleven. Ah well, a woman had to be late. He looked up, and he saw Aisling at the other side of the pond, a shawl wrapped round her, half running. When she reached him, she was breathless, and her face was tight with tension.

'I'm sorry I'm late.'

'Well you're here now. It's good to see you.'

It was. He wanted to kiss her, with a warm, welcoming kiss. The sense that they were both there on business stopped him. That, and the unexplained panic in her face.

He studied her for a long time as the rain thickened and her breath slowed.

'I'm glad you're still here,' she said.

'I wasn't going anywhere.'

'Should we... go indoors somewhere?'

'The more it rains the safer we are.'

She looked down, then she looked up at him. She swallowed deeply, as if reaching inside herself for words that would not come out. She said:

'I've been a fool. Such a fool, God forgive me. I've let you down. Let myself down. Let Ireland down.'

He was glad she was confessing to him, felt closer to her for it. But he worried about what she might be confessing.

'Why? What have you done?'

'I've... God knows what I've done. Let's leave it with Him for now. But I want you to read this.'

From under her shawl she pulled out an envelope and thrust it at Patrick's face. He took out the piece of paper inside. He held it close as he read, protecting it from the rain with the rim of his hat. He read it a second time, and then a third time. It felt like reading the news of someone's death. Except it was about someone who was still alive.

'Jesus, Mary and Joseph,' he said at last. 'Himself.'

'Did you write that, Patrick?'

'I did not.'

'Do you know who did?'

'I do.'

'Who?'

He didn't want to say. He didn't want to say it. And yet he did; he wanted to tell Aisling, because he wanted to tell Aisling everything, just as he wanted her to tell him everything.

'My brother. If it is his hand. But I'd know it anywhere. My own brother's only a traitor.'

'Well sure there's another one standing here.'

'What do you mean?'

She turned her back on him. What was she doing? Was this a double cross?

'Aisling. Are you working for Lovegrove?'

'You know I am.'

Still the back turned.

'Doing what, exactly?'

'Cooking. Washing. Cleaning. Running his house.'

'Is that all?'

She started walking fast round the pond, past a group of ducks huddling together in a bedraggled bunch. He called after her. 'Aisling!' She went on walking, over the bridge into the middle of the Green, the circular area where the flowerbeds were in spring and summer. He thought that if he didn't catch her now, he would never see her again. He started to run. She was walking fast, but she didn't run; she let him catch her up. He overtook her when she was twenty yards from the gate onto the street. He spun round in front of her and held his arms out, blocking her from going any further. He was swallowing his breath in thick gulps and the rain was dripping from the brim of his hat.

'Aisling. Tell me what you mean. This isn't a game.'

'Ah, you don't want to know.'

'I do, so.'

'You don't want to know me any more, Patrick Kelly.'

'I do, I tell you.'

He was gripping her by the arms. He was strong. He wasn't going to let her go.

'I've got a little money saved,' she said. 'I'll get on a boat to England. I won't be the first. Let me go. I'm not wanted here.'

'What do you mean, you're not wanted?'

He wanted her. He didn't want her to go. The thought filled him with panic.

'You've got what you need from me. Shoot your brother. Shoot who you need to shoot on Sunday. Just... spare Major Lovegrove, would you? He's a decent man, for all he did to your friends. He doesn't deserve it. Nor does his wife. Apart from that, do whatever Collins tells you to. Follow your orders. Set Ireland free. But leave me alone.'

He knew he shouldn't say it. He knew he was meant to be a soldier. He knew Mick had told him not to, not till Ireland was free. But he couldn't stop himself. He'd lost his brother. He wasn't going to lose her.

'Aisling! Don't you understand? I don't want to leave you alone. Not even if you never bring me another scrap from Lovegrove. Jesus, not even if you're a traitor. I love you, Aisling.'

'No you don't.'

'I do.'

'How could you? Last time we met I said I wasn't a whore. Well I am. How could you love a whore? How could you love a woman who's gone with a married man whose wife's locked up in a madhouse? Who's gone with your enemy? When all the while she's spying on him?'

His arms fell to his side. She could have got away now, but she stayed where she was, her head lowered in the driving rain, her face twisted. Jesus. That bastard. That murdering whoring English bastard. He wanted to walk round to Mount Street this minute and put a bullet in his head.

'You... went to bed with Lovegrove?'

'Yes.'

'Did he make you? Did he force himself on you? Because that's what the English will do, with -'

'No, Patrick. He didn't make me. I let him. I encouraged him. I told you a lie last time we met. He didn't kiss me. I kissed him first. And last night... last night I wanted it.'

He didn't want to believe her. But he could see in her eyes that she was telling the truth.

'Why, Aisling? Why?'

She lifted her head, looked at him straight, defiant, angry even.

'Ah, you told me to, so. You told me to get into his trousers.'

'That's not what I meant.'

'I know it isn't. Look, I'm sorry, Patrick. I've given you the note. You don't need me any more. Let's not see each other again.'

She mustn't go. In spite of it all, she mustn't go, or he'd never see her again.

'No. Are you truly sorry for what you've done?'

'You sound like a priest.'

'Well maybe it's a priest you need to be talking to.'

'I will. I will when I'm ready.'

'So you know it was wrong?'

'Oh, I know that all right.'

Thank God. Then there was still hope. He hadn't lost her yet. But Sean. There was still Sean to think of. He whipped out his watch, glanced at it, cursed under his breath. It was time to be a soldier now. The other thing he could work out later.

'Look, Aisling. There's something you can do for me. Something very important. Something that might make the difference between life and death to my brother. And maybe many more. Will you just do one more thing for me? One more thing?'

Her face relaxed. She gave a little smile, and nodded slowly, and he squeezed her shoulder, and she let him, and it felt like forgiveness.

Aisling had never been in a pub before. The only women who went into pubs were whores. So maybe it was the right time for her to be going into one. Reilly's was halfway down Grafton Street. When she opened the door, she found a dark little room, made up of shadows and smoke and the lingering smell of slopped stout. The only sounds were the clink of glasses and the slapping of coins on the counter and the barely audible rumble of conversation going on continuously like a nagging pain.

She looked around the room, scanning the faces of the men. Yes. There in the corner. The same chiselled face, the same angular, lithe body, only even thinner than Patrick. He was on his own. He had a pint in front of him, but he wasn't drinking it. He looked uncomfortable, as if he wasn't at home in pubs; the sort of man who was often on his own, and didn't like it much.

'Miss?' said the barman, from across the room.

'Oh, I'm sorry. I'm sorry to disturb you, so. Only I'm looking for my father. I... haven't seen him in five days. My mother's worried sick. He's been gone like this before, but never for so long. He's not in any of his usual pubs, so I'm looking in all of them.'

'Do you see him here?'

'No. No, I don't.'

'What does he look like?'

'He looks like me.'

'You don't sound like a Dubliner.'

'No. We just moved here two years ago. He could find no work in Connemara, but he misses the old place. He's not a man for the city. It's that that sent him to the drink.'

'Well I wish you luck, Miss. I hope you find your father soon.'

'Thank you.'

As she left, she felt a little ache of sadness that she would never see her Da again. She could do with him now, all right.

Patrick looked in the window of Doyle's as he waited for her, but he didn't see any suits. He saw the reflections of people walking past. He wondered who'd betray him next. Even if she'd wanted it, he still wanted to kill Lovegrove. *Keep calm, Kelly. You've a job to do.* Still the rain was running down his neck. He'd been looking in the window for too long. People would be noticing. Then he felt her standing next to him. In spite of what had happened, and in spite of the rain, he felt warm and safe with her next to him. He didn't turn round.

'Well?' he said.

'It's him,' said Aisling.

'You're sure?'

'He's the dead spit of you. Curly hair and all.'

He felt as if he'd been kicked in the stomach. There was no going back now.

'Why? Why, Aisling?'

The same question he'd asked her about her and Lovegrove.

'Let's walk,' she said. 'People are looking at us.'

They set off down Grafton Street, kicking up the water in the puddles. Aisling walked close to him, as if his hat could shield her from the rain. She tucked her arm in his. He put his hand on hers, and drew her closer.

'What will you do now?' she asked him.

'I have no choice. I have to tell Mick.'

'Mick Collins?'

'Himself.'

'What will Mick do?'

'There's the thing. He'll have Sean shot. He'll have to.'

'So you'd have your brother shot?'

Have his brother shot. Well, he hadn't told Mick yet. Just as Sean decided who Patrick would shoot and who he wouldn't, now Patrick could decide whether to have Sean shot or not. He could crumple up the note, toss it in the gutter, forget he'd ever seen it. But there was no choice, at the end of it.

'This... whatever's going to happen on Sunday,' he said at last. 'There might be fifty men involved. Maybe women too. Blow it to the English and they'll all – including me – be rounded up. After the Rising, they sentenced ninety men to death. In the end, they only executed fifteen. But they won't be so merciful this time around.' He held up his thumb and finger an inch apart. Aisling squinted at them through the rain. 'We're that close to war, all-out war. This Sunday will decide it. Fifty men, and a nation – or one man. Which would you sacrifice?'

He needed to know. He needed to know she was on his side. A thunderclap came, so loud it sounded as if Dublin was being bombarded. Patrick looked ahead at the rain. It was blowing harder now, and it was hitting his face. A couple passed them, the man's face covered with a beard and a scarf and a hat, the woman's face blown pink and raw, her hair streaming behind her, their arms tightly interlocked and thrust into each other's pockets. The couple barely seemed to walk; it was as if they were propelled forwards by the wind. He and Aisling, though, were walking with their heads down against the rain, face into it, feeling it fire into them like bullets. Still she didn't say anything.

'If you're going to be a soldier, Aisling,' he said, 'if you're going to fight for Ireland, then you've got to give up everything, you know. Everything. Do you understand what I'm saying?'

You liar, Kelly. It's not that you care about Ireland. You only want her to give up Lovegrove so that you can have her. She looked away from him.

'I understand all right,' she said. 'But it's one thing understanding something. It's another thing doing it.'

She took her arm out of his. He wanted to grab her back, spin her round, hold her close, beg with her and plead with her. But there was no time for any of that. It would have to wait. He pulled himself to attention.

'All right,' he said. 'We'll talk some more later, so. You'll see how things are, soon enough.' He looked over his shoulder quickly, and pulled up his collar higher. 'But there are things you can do now. That you need to do now. Where was Lovegrove when you left him?'

'Asleep.'

'So he could be at home, or he could be in the Castle. Sean won't risk the Castle. But he might try the house. You get home now, and make sure it's you who answers the door to Sean. You tell him your man's not at home, he's gone out, you don't know where. If he recognises you, you don't deny being the lass who was looking for her Da in the pub. That all fits in. Meanwhile, I need to find Mick.'

'So you're going to do it?'

They were at the end of Grafton Street, where the shops parted, spilling people over Merrion Row onto St Stephen's Green. Not that anyone was going there in this weather. Patrick felt a great chasm opening up in front of him. He had to jump over it, or he'd fall in it.

'Like I said. I don't have a choice, do I?'

'And you're sending me back to Harry... to Major Lovegrove? A married man? After what happened? Did you never hear about an occasion of sin?'

Patrick looked at her. He could see she wanted to go back to Lovegrove, and she was fighting it. Wanted to go back to his filthy English groping hands. But if he let Sean get to Lovegrove, he was a dead man and so were fifty others.

'It'd be a sin not to. You'll be saving fifty lives. You'll be turning something evil into something good. Just promise me one thing, Aisling.'

'What?'

'Don't let the bastard lay a finger on you.'

'You don't understand, do you? You still think it's him laying a finger on me.'

There was nothing more he could do. He had to let her go. He had to get to Vaughan's and find Liam and get to Mick. But still he couldn't give up altogether.

'Tomorrow morning. In the Cairo. At nine, good and early. Things'll be clearer by then. You'll see sense. You'll see who Lovegrove is. We'll talk some more then.'

And he turned and set off north up Grafton Street, the rain and the wind behind him, propelling him on to what he was going to do; what he had to do. He turned round once, and saw Aisling still rooted to the spot in the midst of the rain, trapped between two worlds.

CHAPTER TWENTY

Liam was straight down. Patrick had barely sat with his stout in the front bar at Vaughan's when he came in. He walked across the room in that way he had, in long angular strides, without taking his arms from his side. They shook hands wordlessly.

'Mick told me you might be coming. You're one of Sean's boys?'

'I am.'

'You've got something off Lovegrove's maid?'

'I have.'

'Is it big?'

'Too big.'

'Is it Mick you need to see?'

'It is.'

'And only Mick?'

'It has to be him.'

'Is it urgent?'

'Very.'

'All right.'

Liam looked at his shoes and tapped his teeth.

'Mick said...' began Patrick.

'Yes, I know what Mick said.' Liam looked out of the window. 'Come with me. Leave your drink.'

They strode out together, battling against the rain side by side, collars up and hats down. Liam was as unbending as ever, moving his legs quickly, as if walking was a regrettable necessity to be got over with as fast as possible. They strode past shoppers holding their packages to their chests as if they were nursing a baby, past a pair of nuns, their wimples flapping in the wind, past a boy in shorts running and screaming and holding a newspaper over his head, past half a dozen British soldiers batting the rain aside like the troublesome Irish thing it was. They strode past Rutland Square where Patrick had sat all night at gunpoint after the Rising failed, knee to knee with a hundred more men, the stench of urine coming up from the grass. They strode down Sackville Street, right in front of the GPO, looking up at its shattered, lonely facade, under the window where Patrick had lain with his gun, the window from where he'd shot a man on the other side of the street. They strode over the very paving slabs where Pearse had stood and read the Proclamation, they strode past the Independence Hotel, that four and a half years before had illuminated the night sky as it burnt, set on fire by English shells. Patrick's whole fighting life seemed to have been lined up to parade before him, as if to say goodbye. When they reached Sackville Bridge, Liam wheeled sharply to the right, and took Patrick down Bachelor's Walk, where Patrick and Aisling had walked the day before, and where Patrick had killed Casey the day before that. Patrick saw a Mass card for the dead man tied to the railings right by the spot where he'd done it, twisted and bent and dripping in the rain. Under a black cross and a photograph of a tightly groomed man in a police uniform, it said *Of your charity pray for the soul of Francis Xavier Casey,, murdered in Dublin, November 15th, 1920*. R.I.P, There was a broad purple smudge still on the pavement where Casey's brains had come out, not yet washed away by the rain, though it would be soon enough.

They strode over the curved metal back of the Ha'penny Bridge and saw the rain pock the Liffey like gunfire. To their left bent over people scuttered across Sackville Bridge, to their right the Four Courts loomed proud and grey. They strode into Temple Bar, and doubled back into Crow Street. Still neither of them said a word. That was Liam's way. His conversation was as thin and angular as his body. That suited Patrick just now. Silence helped him to summon all his courage together like a scattered band of soldiers that needed bringing under discipline. He would need it if he was going to condemn his brother to death.

They turned into Number 3, under a sign for the Irish Products Company. A man was sitting on a chair by the front door in a trenchcoat with a bulge in the pocket. He nodded to Liam and Liam nodded back, quickly, sharply, with the minimum of effort.

'Is he upstairs, Vic?' Liam asked the man.

'No. They're meeting.' Vic nodded at a door off the entrance hall.

'Who?'

'The usual.'

'Well I need to see him.'

'He won't like it. Take him out of that room and God alone knows what Cathal might do.'

Liam turned to Patrick.

'Is it as urgent as you said?'

'It is.'

'How urgent?'

'If I don't see him there could be fifty of our men dead in a week. There, I've already said too much.'

'If you're stringing him along, there'll be hell to pay, you know that?'

'I do.'

'All right.'

Liam knocked tentatively at the door. Patrick could hear a man saying loudly and clearly 'You say delay will cost lives. I say action will cost lives.' Liam knocked again, harder, and opened the door. Six men were sitting round a large table. In front of them were overflowing ashtrays and piles of closely typed papers held together by treasury tags in the corners. The room was thick with smoke. At the head of the table was Mick. A smaller man with a tense, taut face, was jabbing at Mick with his cigarette and saying, 'Now is not the time, Michael. Now is not the time. Our first duty is to defend our people.' Mick sat sullen and silent, scrunching up his face as if at a bad smell. Then he saw Liam, and said, 'There's strangers here, boys. To what do we owe the pleasure, Mr Tobin?'

'I need a word, Mick. Or rather, this man does,' said Liam, jerking his thumb at Patrick.

Mick looked steadily at Patrick.

'Can it wait an hour?'

'No,' said Patrick. 'It can wait barely a minute.'

'All right,' said Mick. 'I propose we adjourn this meeting forthwith. To resume in thirty minutes.'

The small man held up a hand like a priest about to bless them, and in his other hand picked up a pamphlet which lay in the middle of the table. He thumbed through it till he found the page he wanted.

'Point of order, Mr Chairman,' he said, very slowly, very quietly. 'Executive committee may only be adjourned before the conclusion of the agenda in the event of enemy action or the reasonable apprehension thereof. Are you suggesting that Mr Tobin and / or his friend constitute the enemy?'

Mick glared at him. Patrick saw him clench his fist.

'I'm suggesting, Cathal, that I need to talk to this gentleman. On an urgent intelligence matter.'

'Are you prepared to share with us what that matter may be, Michael?'

'I am not. Partly because it is a matter of the greatest secrecy. And partly because I don't know what it is till I've spoken to him.'

Cathal turned to Patrick, and raised his left eyebrow.

'Perhaps he can tell us,' he said.

'No he fucking well can't,' said Mick. 'He can tell me, upstairs. Because I'm the fucking Director of Intelligence, and every minute you sit here fiddling with your rule book, men's lives are in danger. Meeting adjourned, by order of the Chair. And, by order of the Chair, you can all stay in this room till I'm ready for you again. You can pass the time giving each other little quizzes on points of order.'

With that, he stubbed out his cigarette, shoved back his chair, and walked round the table towards Patrick and Liam, not looking any of the committee in the eye. Cathal sighed deeply, shook his head, and began to ruffle through the book he had picked up.

Mick closed the door behind him.

'Fucking Cathal,' he said. 'If he had his way, we'd sit around all day scratching our bollocks and waiting for the English to attack. I know he was a hero in the Rising and all – the Cuchulain of our day, the man they couldn't kill, all that – but now he's only interested in his rule book. If I didn't know better, I'd think he was an English agent, the time he wastes.'

He put his right arm round Patrick and his left round Liam, and pulled them into an embrace. Patrick felt a wave of gratitude, in spite of everything.

'Good on you for coming,' he said. 'You found Liam at Vaughan's?'

'I did,' said Patrick.

'Wait down here,' said Mick to Liam. 'I may need you later. And don't let those buggers escape,' he added, jerking his thumb at the committee room.

They went upstairs. Mick fumbled in his pocket and pulled out a bunch of keys. With one of them, he opened a door.

'No one sets foot in here but me,' he said.

Along one wall were half a dozen shelves, filled with box files carefully labelled and arranged in alphabetical order. There was a desk with an empty in-tray, an empty ashtray, a pen and a card index box. Under the desk was a waste paper basket, also empty. Patrick half wanted to genuflect when Mick showed him in.

'If anyone asks, this is the Head Office of the Irish Products Company, and I'm its managing director,' said Mick. 'There's fuck all in those files up there and there always will be. If the Tans come here all they'll find is my farts. That's how it should be.' He sat behind the desk, and waved Patrick to a chair opposite. 'This better be good. If you've made me lose my rag with Cathal for nothing, I'll rip your bollocks off.'

Patrick reached in his pocket and pulled out Sean's note. He smoothed it on the table and pushed it across the desk. Mick scanned it quickly.

'Where did you get this?'

'Aisling – Lovegrove's maid – picked it off the mat this morning.'

'Did she see who delivered it?'

'No.'

'It could be any one of those men downstairs. Jesus, if it's Cathal... I know he hates me, but this...'

'It isn't Cathal, Mick.'

'How do you know?'

'I recognise the writing.'

'Who is it then?'

Patrick breathed deeply. He had to do it now.

'Sean.'

'Your brother Sean?'

'Himself.'

'Christ. Of course. I briefed him after you left yesterday. He's meant to be leading you. Now I know why he didn't want you seeing that girl. But Sean? Sean's fucking brilliant. He's a bastard, but he's a brilliant bastard. He'll kill the English like other people eat their breakfast. I'd never let him do what Liam does, because the men hate him too much, but I never had him down for a traitor. A fucking maniac, yes, but not a traitor. Ah, you fool, Collins.'

Mick put his head in his hands. For a moment, he looked broken, vulnerable. Patrick felt a little scared to see him like that. Then he looked up, the decisiveness back in his face.

'Pat. I read dozens of reports every day, before I burn them. Handwriting's a slippery thing. It can be forged and faked and hidden. I teach men to do it. Who's to say that couldn't have been turned against us?'

'I know it's him, Mick. Aisling went to Reilly's. She pretended to be looking for her Da. Sean was in there, on his own.'

'The man who never set foot in a pub from one day to the next. Right. Where is he now?'

'Aisling has gone back to Lovegrove's... in case Sean turns up there.'

'Lovegrove's at home still?'

'He was sleeping when she... when she left him.' An image of Aisling in bed with Lovegrove flashed before him, making him clench his fist. 'At eleven, it was.'

Mick glanced up at the big clock on the opposite wall. It said twenty to two.

'They're lazy buggers, the English. But they're not that lazy. What's to prevent him going out, meeting Sean in the street, or even at the Castle? Can your Aisling stop him leaving his own house?'

Patrick winced. Jealousy shot through him like a jab from a hot poker.

'Aisling... Aisling has a grip on him, Mick.'

Mick looked at Patrick for a moment without saying anything. Then he nodded.

'Right. She must love Ireland, that girl. I'll see she gets a medal when this is all over. And you, too. Now, we've no time to waste. Sean'll have spoken to the boys at half twelve. Minus you. He'll have noticed that. Then he'll have gone back to his lodgings for his dinner. He's got no more meetings today, and he doesn't go out, unless he has to. He's a man with no friends, except for a cup of tea and his right hand. We'll have to pray to God he hasn't had time to get to Lovegrove yet. I need to get down to Abbey Street now. I'll get Rory and Vinnie to do the job, because Rory hates Sean almost as much as he hates you. Well, Rory hates everyone. And Vinnie'll do what he's told.'

Mick looked at Patrick, his eyes like a gun pointed at him.

'Christ. You know what you've just done? You've sentenced your own brother to death.'

As if he was about to die himself, Patrick began to think very fast. He saw Casey holding Siobhan to him the moment before he pulled the trigger. He saw some of the sixteen other men he'd killed: his first, the young policeman who'd fallen on the steps of his mother's house and splattered her front door with blood; the barman at Vaughan's, who'd been listening in and reporting back to the Castle, and who'd brought down half a dozen bottles of stout with him when Patrick had shot him in the chest behind his own bar; the hero of the Somme he'd finished off as he came out of the Protestant cathedral one Sunday morning, who'd fallen into the arms of his screaming wife, the blood running onto his medals; the two young soldiers who didn't look old enough to be out of school and who'd come staggering out of the pub arm in arm and into the barrel of his gun – he was only meant to get one of them, but they were too drunk to separate. He felt Sean clinging to him, retching tears, unable to stand, suddenly the weak one, as they looked down together into their mother's grave. If Patrick hadn't held on to him, Sean would have fallen into the grave with her.

Patrick doubled up as if he had been punched in the stomach. He felt his long ago breakfast surge up to his throat. He pulled out the waste paper basket and vomited into it in five short, sharp bursts. The stench rose up to him. He saw some undigested gobbets of egg on the top. Mick stood and came round the desk and took the waste paper basket off him and offered him his handkerchief. Patrick wiped his mouth with it.

'Keep it,' said Mick.

Patrick put it in his pocket. Mick went to the door and stood with one hand on the knob and one hand holding the waste paper basket.

'Go out for a walk,' he said. 'Get some fresh air. Go to a pub, or a church, or a whorehouse, or wherever'll make you feel better. Then report back to me here at three. It'll be done by then. And know this, Patrick Kelly. You're the biggest fucking hero Ireland's ever seen, and when Ireland's free I'll make sure you're remembered.'

Outside, it had stopped raining at last, and the sun had come out. People walked now more slowly and more at ease, all of them standing up straight, relief on their faces as if a truce had just been declared in a long war. Puddles littered the streets. Patrick leant over Sackville Bridge and looked down at the restless waters of the Liffey, going out towards the sea and towards England, forever. He put his hand in his pocket and felt Mick's handkerchief. When Mick had recruited him for the Squad he'd warned him that every day of his life from now on might be his last; that a Black and Tan bullet or an English rope could finish him before he'd got started on work and wife and family and all the things other men took for granted. He'd told Mick that was fine by him. He'd rather die young doing something good than die old regretting that he'd never lived – or regretting that he'd ever lived. What mattered to him was to do the right thing, whatever it cost. But what was the right thing to do now?

He straightened up. He saw a boy looking in at the window of Reiss's, where he and Aisling had stood a few days before. The boy had a curious look on his face, as if he could not understand what jewellery was for. His trousers were three sizes too big for him and were torn around the crotch. He had on just one thin shirt – not enough, even in the sun. His face was patched with filth and his hair was sticking up. He looked as if he was hungry, but wouldn't admit it. Patrick walked over to him.

'What's your name, boy?'

'Patrick.'

Patrick smiled.

'Sure, that's my name too. Patrick, would you take a message? For a shilling? With sixpence from the man when you give it to him?'

'I would, Mister. Thank you, Mister.'

'Wait here.'

Patrick took out his notebook and pencil from his pocket. Sean insisted on them all carrying them everywhere, on the understanding that they didn't tell Mick. Sean loved writing things down as much as Mick hated it. Patrick leant the notebook on the window of the jeweller's and wrote fast.

Sean,

God knows I have reason enough to hate you, all the more now I know you are a traitor. But you are my brother still, and the only family I have left. There has been too much blood spilt already in this war and I am sick of it now and I do not want the next blood spilt to be blood of mine.

Mick knows about you and the English spy. He has sent Rory and Vinnie to kill you. Get out now to England or America or anywhere and never come back. When you get there have a Mass said for Mam and Da and pray that they and God may forgive you for all you've done.

Burn this, or it'll be my death warrant. I'm risking my life for you, brother. Christ knows why.

Patrick

P.S. Give the boy sixpence.

He folded the paper three times and wrote Sean's name and address on the folded part.

'Can you read, Patrick?'

'No, Mister.'

'Take this to Mr Sean Kelly at Number 15 Mountjoy Street. You know where Mountjoy Street is at least?'

'Yes, Mister. Two streets past Rutland Square.'

'Number 15. The number on the door'll look like this number I've written here. You see?

'Yes, mister.'

'Run as fast as you can. When I say it's a matter of life and death, I'm not joking. Will you do that for me, Patrick?'

'Yes, Mister.'

'Good lad.'

Patrick put the note and a shilling in the boy's hand.

'When you give this to your man, ask him for sixpence. He'll give it to you. Off you go, now. Run.'

The boy sprinted down Sackville Street like a young whippet, dodging this way and that, in and out of surprised people who turned and followed him with their eyes. As Patrick watched him go, he felt utterly alone.

CHAPTER TWENTY-ONE

After Patrick had turned on his heel and left her, Aisling stood still in the rain for a good three minutes. There were two more claps of thunder during this time. Her shawl was over her head, but the rain ran down the edge of it and dripped onto her chest. Her dress was soaked, and her stockings and her shoes were invaded with water. She knew people were looking at her as they scuttled past. When it was raining like this you were supposed to keep moving until you found some shelter. Still she couldn't move. Moving meant knowing where she was going and what she was going to do next. For those three minutes she could no more move than she could fly.

When she moved at last, it was back up Grafton Street, to buy something, to give her a reason for having gone out. She bought a loaf of bread and some eggs and some butter at McGrath's. She remembered that they did need some butter. McGrath himself remarked on the rain and that it was a harsh one, even for Dublin, though it would be stopping soon enough, for sure. Aisling found a smile and said that she hoped he was right. Then McGrath leaned forward and whispered that he was sorry to hear of Mrs Lovegrove's trouble and that he hoped she'd be better soon and would she tell the Major that. Aisling said that she would. McGrath noticed that she didn't have her usual wicker bag. Aisling explained that she'd gone out to post a letter and had just then remembered the bread and the eggs and the butter. McGrath looked at her dripping clothes and offered to lend her an umbrella. She said thanks but no it was only a step back to Mount Street and she couldn't get any wetter now. McGrath nodded wisely and told her to keep the paper bags well under her shawl, as they'd fall apart in this rain. Aisling said that she would.

She went home past St Stephen's Green. An hour and a half before, she'd run there, desperate to undo what she'd done the night before. Now she was walking slowly, trying to hold the bread and the eggs and the butter together under her shawl, and not at all sure she didn't want to do it all over again. She let herself in the front door.

The letters were gone from the hall table. She was about to call Harry's name, to see if he was at home, like Mam used to do with Da. She stopped herself. Servants didn't call their masters. They slipped discreetly into the house and got on with their work and waited to be called. She saw that his coat was gone from the stand; he was out. She gasped with relief, and then straight after felt a shooting pain of loneliness. She took the bread and the eggs and the butter into the kitchen. She tore the soggy paper off them. Then she took off her shawl, shook it, and hung it over a peg in the kitchen. The kedgeree from last night sat in its pan, cold and untouched. Aisling sighed. The sight of it made her feel sad. She would leave it for him. He could heat it up himself on the stove for his dinner later.

The rain beat against the window of the kitchen for a couple more minutes, and then it stopped. The sun came out with great suddenness. There seemed to be a strange silence over the city. She felt a silence inside her as well. She cut two slices of bread, smeared them with butter, added some cheese, and sat and ate at the little table she had for her meals. The kitchen was warmed by the stove and her clothes were slowly drying. While she ate she listened to the silence in the house. She was used to Harry's noises: his brisk military step on the stair, his firm way of opening and closing doors, his little impatient sniffs as he came across a knot in his paperwork. She missed them.

She finished her bread and cheese. Harry must have gone to the Castle. There would be nothing out of the ordinary about him going in late; he often did that, because of his working at night. She knew now it was working, and not a woman; she was glad of that, at least, that he didn't have a woman. She looked at the clock. It was one exactly. He would be home at six. He always was. She needed to stay here in case Sean tried to bring any messages. But Patrick was on his way to find Mick, perhaps had found him already. To find Mick and to tell him about Sean. To tell him about his own brother. When he had told Mick, Mick would have Sean shot. She'd never had a brother. She wondered what she would have done if she'd found out Da was a traitor. She didn't think she could have had him shot.

How long would it take Mick to find Sean? Not long, surely. 'He has the whole of Dublin in his pocket,' Patrick had told her. If Sean hadn't come to the house by three, she decided, he must have been shot and would no longer be a danger. At three, she could leave. She could leave well before Harry came home.

In the last twelve hours two men had told her that they loved her. One of them was married, with a sick wife, and had had men shot in their beds. The other was on his way to have his own brother shot, and must have killed a good few other men himself. She hadn't told either of them that she loved them; not yet. But something had changed in the last twelve hours. Though she hated herself for what she'd done, she realised now that she had never before felt so alive as she had in Harry's bed last night. Never. It was as if she had been locked in a darkened room all her life and someone had thrown open the door and had bundled her out into the light and the air, and she wanted to go on walking forever, barefoot on the grass, smelling the flowers, feeling the sun on her face. She didn't want to go back into that darkened room.

But she had to leave. She knew she had to leave. Leave these men. Leave these men to their killing. They wanted to kill each other, these two men who loved her. First a little thrill went through her stomach at the thought, then a choking disgust. She had to leave at three and not come back. Not come back to Dublin, or even to Ireland. She had to get on the boat to England, and start over again, just as she'd done when she'd left Clifden. Liverpool was full of Irish, they said, was nothing more than a suburb of Dublin. She'd take a train to London, where no one would know her. She'd find a Catholic church there and make her confession, scrub out her sin. She'd work in a hotel or somewhere that she wouldn't be on her own, and after a bit she'd find herself an unmarried man who didn't kill people. But she would keep, always, the last twelve hours locked in her memory like the one precious piece of jewellery that a bankrupt woman can't bring herself to sell.

She washed up her plate in the sink, and put the butter and the eggs and the remainder of the bread in the pantry. She went up to Harry's bedroom. The blankets were thrown back from the bed. Harry's clothes were no longer on the floor. She saw a patch of blood in the middle of the bed, mingled with Harry's semen. First she remembered how it had hurt and then she remembered how it had felt to have him inside her. She stood with the thought for a while, feeling warm and damp between her legs, wishing she could stop the feeling and loving it at the same time. Then she ripped the sheets off the bed, and took them down to the scullery. She did not want whoever took over from her knowing what had happened in Harry's bed. She washed the sheets in the sink in the scullery, pounding and pummelling them, scrubbing away at the blood and the semen with a brush until it was all gone, watching it run down the plughole. Then she wrung the water out of the sheets and hung them over the maiden to dry. Before she left the scullery she ran her hands over the damp sheets as if she was saying goodbye.

She took clean sheets from the cupboard and brought them up to Harry's bedroom. When she had made his bed, she opened his wardrobe. The key to his desk was not hanging there, nor was it in any of his clothes, but the envelope with the money in was still there at the bottom of his underwear drawer. She took it out and counted it. Still twenty pounds. She could live on that for a month. No. She wouldn't steal from him. She had her own money now, put aside, in the bottom of her drawer. She'd had precious little to spend it on. She put the money back and closed the wardrobe. She went into his study and checked his roll top desk, but it was still locked, as she expected.

She went up to her room. She took out the suitcase from under her bed. In it, she folded up the two dresses she wasn't wearing, made neat piles of her underwear and monthly cloths, and put her spare shoes in upside down. It wasn't big, and was full to bursting, but it was not heavy to carry. She remembered snatching it from under her bed in her burning house in Clifden. She wondered who was still alive in the town. Lastly, she took the money she had saved out of the drawer she had kept it in. She counted it. Five pounds ten shillings and sixpence. It would be enough to get her to London and keep her there for a week or so. She'd heard with all the men that had been killed in the war there were women taking men's jobs there. She would find something.

She took the suitcase down to the kitchen. It was just past two o'clock. She checked in the hall. Sean had not left any messages. She did not think he would call. He was probably dead by now. Poor man. He'd seemed nervous and lonely when she'd seen him in the pub, the sort of fella who wouldn't have too many friends, would wish he had more, and would never understand why he didn't. She went back to the kitchen. Her shawl was nearly dry in the heat off the stove. She took out her notebook and pencil from her pinny and sat down at the table and wrote.

Friday, 19th November 1920

Dear Major Lovegrove,

I am writing to tender my resignation from your employment with immediate effect.

I am aware that we agreed a notice period of a month on either side, but I hope that you will understand that under the present circumstances I wish to waive that requirement, and I hope that you will forgive me for doing so without consulting you. I do not require a reference. It is my intention to take myself to England. I do not know where or how, so I am unable to leave you a forwarding address.

I want you to know that I am very grateful to you for all the kindness you have shown me during my time in your service. No servant could hope for a better master than you. But about what happened last night, it is better for both of us to forget it. You have a sick wife to care for, and I have my life to make. We are from different countries and religions and stations in life and there are some things that cannot be. This does not mean that I will not keep that night in my heart always as the sweetest of memories.

I am sorry to leave you without a servant. I hope you will find another girl soon. I have striven to give you and Mrs Lovegrove the best of service, and I hope I leave the house in good order. Please God Mrs Lovegrove will find her health again soon.

Aisling O'Flaherty

She put down her pencil and looked out of the kitchen window, now filled with bright sunshine. She felt tears well up. They seemed to come from her chest up through her throat into her eyes. She rubbed her eyes with her hands to stop the tears falling on the paper. She saw Harry as he was when he had sat opposite her in the dining room in the morning, praising her fruit pie. She swallowed and tapped her pencil on the table a few times. Then she wrote some more.

P.S. I know that your work is dangerous, but there is one day when you will face special danger. Do not be in Dublin this

Sunday. I cannot tell you how I know this. My people have reason enough to hate the English but you are a good man and you do not deserve what is going to happen.

She tore the page out of the notebook, folded the paper over and wrote *For the attention of Major Harry Lovegrove: Private and Personal* on it. She took it into the dining room and put it on the table at the place he always sat at. She sat down in the place opposite that she would sit at when they were discussing menus and looked at his empty chair for a while. She hoped he'd survive Sunday. Then she went back into the kitchen. Quarter past two. Forty five minutes left. Then it would be time to go.

She had to do something. She couldn't sit still all that time. It had been three weeks since she had polished the silver. She took all the silverware out of all of the cupboards, spread it out on a newspaper on the kitchen table, and began attacking it with polish, piece by piece, as if she was interrogating it for dirt.

She had done all the cutlery and was on the fourth candlestick out of six when she heard the front door open. She froze for a moment, a candlestick in one hand and a cloth in the other. She listened. She heard Harry pause in the hall, then make his way steadily upstairs. She looked at the clock. Ten to three.

He was in the house. He was upstairs, probably working in his study. He would have taken the key out of his trouser pocket and opened up the roll top desk. He would be writing in his little black leather notebook; the one she had copied out of for Patrick. She saw him crouched over the desk, frowning a little, just as she had seen him in the middle of the night, writing slowly and carefully, in his neat, precise hand.

She put down the candlestick and the cloth and took off her pinny. She looked at the silverware all laid out on the newspaper. She didn't like leaving a job undone; she never had. She liked to do things thoroughly. That was one thing Mam had taught her. But she knew that if she spoke to Harry or saw him or was in the same room as him, she would not be able to leave.

She threw her shawl over her shoulders, picked up her suitcase, and walked out of the kitchen and into the hall. She had her hand on the door knob when she heard his voice.

'Aisling. Where are you going?'

She turned and saw him at the top of the stairs. She kept hold of the suitcase. Though it wasn't at all heavy, its weight seemed to anchor her. She thought that if she let go of it she would run up the stairs and embrace him.

'Sir. I'm sorry.'

He came down the stairs, and sat down on the bottom step. He looked down at his shoes, then up at her.

'It's me that should be sorry, Aisling. It was terribly bad manners of me to sleep in like that. I do have to work late, it's true, and I've not slept at all well lately, but even so. But do you know, I don't think I've ever slept as well as I did last night. Not one dream of France. That hasn't happened in a while. I thought you'd gone this morning. When you weren't there when I woke. Well, I thought. That'll teach you, Lovegrove. You'll have to get yourself a new maid on top of everything else. I got dressed, went into work, tried to get on with things, tried to put my little folly behind me. But I couldn't. Because it wasn't a little folly, Aisling. Quite the reverse. Quite the reverse.'

Aisling gripped her bag to her more tightly. She wanted to leave, but she couldn't.

'I could do no work. I had too much to think about. I spoke to Colonel Brind. Told him I had matters to deal with, to do with Emily. He said I could go home, provided I put in an extra shift on Saturday morning. I agreed, and came home. I looked in your room, and, as I thought had happened, your things were gone, all packed up. I was about to write to you. Then I realised I had no address for you. But now I don't have to write; now I can say what I have to say. And I have to say it. It's easy to say now that you're here, in front of me, easier than writing would have been.'

The tears were welling up in her eyes again. She could hardly get the words out.

'Please don't say it, sir.'

'What happened to Harry?'

She pointed to the door.

'Sir, I have to –'

'Is it Clifden you were going to?'

'How could I?' she said, with a little flash of anger. 'There's no Clifden left. It's burnt to the ground. By the English.'

'Of course. I'm sorry. Stupid of me. Where then?'

'I... I don't know. I don't know where I want to go. I don't know what's right and what isn't any more.'

She put her suitcase on the floor, but didn't let go of it. Just as when she had been out in the rain earlier, she felt frozen to the spot.

'I think I know what is right, Aisling. Much of my work is... is finding out the difference between truth and lies. I've got very good at it. Except in my own life. I've been living a kind of lie for the last six years. A man shouldn't live by lies. Nor should a woman, come to that.'

He stood up, walked over to her, and pulled her towards him. Instantly, her whole body softened and relaxed. She dropped her suitcase. He pushed at her shawl, and she let it fall to the ground. He kissed her first, but then she was kissing him back. She felt him grow hard against her. She didn't want to stop. It felt right, right, right, righter than anything to be in his arms, to be in his house. To be in their house.

She felt a sudden surge of energy. She pulled herself away from him for a moment. She picked up the suitcase, swung her arm back, and threw it down the hall towards the kitchen. When it landed on the floor, it skidded from the hall into the kitchen, and hit a leg of the table the silverware was on. A candlestick fell to the floor with a sharp clatter. Harry looked down the hall, his mouth open. She grinned with triumph. The world seemed to expand around her. She took him in her arms.

'Go on with you, Harry Lovegrove,' she said. 'Why would I want to be leaving you now?'

CHAPTER TWENTY-TWO

After he'd given the lad the note, Patrick went straight into the DBC on Sackville Street Lower. He'd seen it burn in the Rising, heard its great glass roof crash in. It had been rebuilt since then, along with the rest of the street, except for the Post Office, which the English had wanted to leave in ruins, just to rub their noses in it. He went up to the second floor restaurant. It was swamped with sunlight, which seemed to inject colour and energy into the customers and staff. It was far bigger than the Cairo, several dozen tables, and the waitresses rushed in and out of the overflowing pot plants and the overloud customers as if they were being chased, while a pianist played relentlessly upbeat music hall numbers. The conversation was noisier and faster than the Cairo, people banged their cups down harder, and there was less smoke in the air because everyone was talking at once. It suited Patrick. He wanted to be somewhere that the noise would drown out his thoughts, and where he'd be ignored. The two tables next to his didn't hold a friendly crowd. There was a gaggle of Englishwomen at one table who'd been shopping, braying over their bags and complaining about their servants, and at another, there were a couple of Tans bragging to each other in harsh accents from the north of England about a house they'd smashed up. But Patrick found he couldn't hate any of them. He couldn't feel anything, except empty. It was as if he had spewed all his anger into Mick's waste paper bin. He sat with a tea and a cigarette. He thought about Sean. If his anger had gone, Sean's never would. He'd been angry since the day he was born. In England or America he'd find someone or something else to be angry with. Please God he'd make it to the boat; and please God he'd burn the paper. Mick had told them all often enough to burn everything, made them carry matches everywhere even when they were out of fags. Patrick saw Mam with Sean on her knee, when they were little, and happy, before she got sick and Da started drinking. 'It's like cuddling a lump of wood, so it is, Sean Kelly. Will you never relax now? Will you be like this in your grave?' Mam was always on at them not to fight. Jesus, Mam, I'm risking my life for my brother now – is that enough for you?

He ground out his cigarette and lit another straight away. One of the Englishwomen said, 'The fact is they're more savage than the blacks. My husband was in India and he said the natives were better behaved there.' The Tans fell into an awkward quiet, having run out of violence. An older waitress shouted to a younger one to pick her feet up, for the love of God. The pianist banged out 'Molly Malone' for the third time that afternoon, his head swaying from side to side and his pink face grinning complacently. Patrick thought of Aisling. The way her body seemed to flow like water when she walked. Her face breaking into a smile, her head at one side. Her arm in his down Grafton Street. And only a few hours before she'd been in the bed of an English officer. For sure she'd meant what she'd said. She'd enjoyed it. Was there the slightest chance he could ever get her back now?

'Patrick Kelly, as I live and breathe.'

He started, and reached in his pocket for the gun that wasn't there. She was standing by his table clutching a handbag and smiling at him. She'd grown her hair longer, and she'd put on some weight; she was fuller in the face and in the body. She looked like a woman now; before it was like she was pretending to be a man. But that nervousness, that fear that she would say or do the wrong thing that had always seemed to propel her onwards, that had meant she was never quiet, that was still there.

'Dear God. Molly. It's only yourself, so it is.'

Suddenly, the last four and a half years vanished. The last time he'd seen Molly had been three days before the Rising. He'd hinted at what was coming to impress her, but he hadn't been able to tell her everything. And yet somehow he hadn't wanted to. He'd wanted the Rising to be something he kept to himself; had looked forward to a few days or weeks away from her and her incessant chatter. Then he hadn't written from Frongoch, and in the end she'd written to him of her marriage, and he'd thought that was the end of it; the end of something that would have ended anyway, even if it hadn't been for the Rising. And now here she was in front of him.

He stood awkwardly, almost knocking over the chair. He didn't know whether to kiss her or not. She helped him by holding out her hand. He shook it.

'It is. Molly Delaney as was. Molly McGarry as is.'

'Won't you take a seat?'

They sat down, and neither said anything for a moment as they sized each other up.

'So what are you doing in Dublin, Molly? Is it family you're visiting?'

'I don't have any family in Dublin, Patrick. You know that.'

'Your husband's family?'

'I don't have a husband either.'

'But... you wrote to me.'

'I had a husband. He was like you.'

She clutched her handbag tighter. Did she hold a candle for him still, even as she married the other man?

'He fought for Ireland. Back in Kilkenny. One night they went after a policeman. When they got to his house, half a dozen Tans were waiting. Someone had spoken. At his wake, they kept the coffin closed. They told me he had no face left to speak of.'

Her skin was tight and her lips were trembling.

'Jesus, Molly, I had no idea.'

'Why would you? So I came back here. I work at Bewley's. It's all right. I'm in a house on Baggot Street Lower – a Mrs Maloney's - with two other girls. Well, one now. The other's got married and gone to London. We have a vacancy.'

She gave a nervous laugh.

'And I get Friday afternoons off. What are you doing now, Patrick?'

'I work for a carpenter's in Abbey Street,' he said, a little too quickly.

'Have you given up on Ireland since the Rising, and the prison?'

'Not yet. Not quite yet.'

Apart from letting a traitor go, he thought to himself.

'I've... I've done nothing since Dermot. They tried to recruit me, said I should carry on his fight. I couldn't do it. One reason for coming here. To get away from his pals lecturing me. Start again. But now... I'm starting to think I should do something. Ireland's more than Dermot.'

Patrick looked across at the next table. The Tans had livened up again, and were shouting at each other about women. He lowered his voice.

'Ireland's more than any of us.'

This was the sort of thing they had said to each other in the old days. It was coming back to him now.

'How is Sean?'

'Ah, he's all right. We work together... at the carpenter's. Family business; cousin of ours. But you know Sean. Never content. He'll be moving on soon.'

They grinned at each other's shoes for a bit. Patrick looked at his watch. Ten to three. Jesus. He'd have to run. The Big Fella didn't like being kept waiting. And the last thing he wanted now was to arouse his suspicions.

'I have to go back. My boss is waiting.'

He stood, relieved to be active again.

'Patrick.'

'What?'

'Do you have a sweetheart?'

She'd always been straight. Had none of the tricks and turns of most women.

'Kind of.'

'Kind of?'

'We've... had a difference.'

'What about?'

'It's to do with the English.'

'Politics, is it? Well, you and me always saw things the same way, didn't we? About politics.'

'That we did.'

'It's here I come on a Friday afternoon. If you have Friday afternoons off too. It looks like you do. We could talk some more. It's a long time since I talked to anyone about politics. It's not the favourite topic of waitresses at Bewley's. I miss it.'

He jammed on his hat and tightened his trenchcoat round him. The last thing he needed now was an old flame trying to fan him into life.

'I'll maybe be seeing you,' he said. 'Dublin's not such a big city. I'm sorry about your husband and all. I hope they got the tout who did for him.'

She looked away and didn't say anything. He ran down the stairs, taking them three at a time. Outside, the sky had cleared completely. But it could still rain any time. You couldn't count on anything. Sackville Street lay wide and lazy, dividing the Irish and the English. They and their girls walked on the west side, the Irish walked on the east side. Which side was Aisling walking on now? He made to cross into Middle Abbey Street, but there was a tram passing. He felt something bang into his leg, and spun round.

'Mister.'

It was the lad he'd given the message to. Holding his trousers and pleading up at him like a hungry dog.

'What?'

'I've been waiting for you. By the jeweller's. He didn't give it to me.'

'Didn't give you what?'

'The sixpence.'

Ah, Sean was a tight bastard.

'Did you give him the note?'

'I tried to. But the other man took it.'

'What other man?'

'There was two of them. One with big ears, one with a moustache.'

Jesus.

'The one with the moustache took the note.'

'Did you get your man's name?'

'His friend called him Rory.'

Jesus fucking Christ.

'Did he read it?'

'Yes.'

'Did your other man read it? Mr Kelly?'

'The one who looks like you?'

'Himself.'

'No. The Rory man wouldn't let him. I'm sorry, Mister. He made me give it to him. He had a gun. I told him you'd sent me, asked him for the sixpence, but he said he wouldn't do what you said. Said you was a traitor. Is you a traitor, Mister?'

Patrick looked up at the piercing blue sky, and swallowed. If only the boy knew.

'Christ knows, when it comes down to it, we're all traitors, to something or someone.'

'Only he pointed the gun at me and made me go away and didn't give me the sixpence. And there's five bairns younger than me at home and we're all hungry and me Da's gone. And I did take the note for you and I tried to give it to him. Only the other man took it off me. Only he had a gun.'

Another tram went rattling by. A man was standing on the platform, holding out some flowers to a girl, making her laugh. Patrick felt in his pocket and pulled out his money. He had three pounds and a shilling left. He gave the boy the shilling.

'Here. If anyone asks you anything about any of this, you never saw or heard anything.'

'All right, Mister. Thank you, Mister.'

'There's men with guns on every street and one of them'll have you if you blab. You understand? Whatever you say, say nothing.'

'Yes, Mister.'

'Now go home. Look after your family. There's trouble coming soon.'

The boy thrust the shilling into his pocket and skipped away. Patrick turned back in through the big doors of the DBC, pulled up the collar of his coat even though it was warm indoors, and strode up the stairs. The pianist was singing now, about Irish eyes and smiling, and one of the English women had her head tipped back in laughter as if she was swallowing the sun. The Tans had gone. Molly was still sitting where he'd left her. She was clutching her handbag to her stomach as if she was in pain, and her head was lowered. He sat down next to her.

'Molly.'

He took her right hand and clasped it in both his hands. He hated himself for what he was going to do, but he had no choice.

'Molly, I want to talk to you.'

As she looked up, he saw she had been crying.

'I need you. I need you now. For old time's sake. And for Ireland. I want you to do something. Do something, for me, and for Ireland.'

CHAPTER TWENTY-THREE

Going to bed with Harry was different this time, Aisling found. They both had their eyes open, and daylight was still coming in through the windows of the bedroom, though the sun was dipping down and preparing to set. They could see everything. They undressed slowly, almost reverently, smiling at each other, relishing each touch. Aisling was no longer afraid, or anxious, or carried away. She took charge of him, and she took her pleasure like she might take a long nourishing meal after days without eating. God still sat in her suitcase where it had skidded across the kitchen floor, His accusing cry of pain coming from the crucifix at the end of Mam's rosary, wrapped inside her nightdress; Mrs Lovegrove still lingered in her heavy thick winter dresses hanging in the wardrobe. But for that half of an hour, God and Mrs Lovegrove were silent, and the world was silent, and there was nothing but the two of them.

Afterwards, he lay with his head on her breast and she stroked his hair. It was lovely thick hair. Outside it was growing dark.

'Thank you for staying, Aisling. I don't know what I would have done if you'd left. I don't ever want to be separated from you.'

Aisling ran her fingers through his hair a few more times, but said nothing. His breath was warm and soft on her tender breasts. His leg was hooked around hers and his arm lay lazy, defeated, across her chest. She heard something that sounded like a shot, but was only a car backfiring. He twitched a little at the sound, and held her tighter. In all her twenty years in Clifden she'd never seen a car. In Dublin you could barely walk down a street without seeing one.

He'd said he didn't want to live by lies, although it was his job. She didn't want to live by lies, either. But she'd started living by lies the moment she'd taken that notebook and pencil and sat at his desk. She'd done it – for what? For Ireland? For Da? For Patrick? For Patrick's dead friends? She didn't know now. And here she was in bed with the man she'd spied on; spied on for another man who'd have him shot in two days' time. All the while his wife locked up in a lunatic asylum in Kingstown. But by God she wanted the weight of him on her, pushing into her, again. Father Garvey used to teach them Bible stories when he visited the National School. He'd told them the story of the garden and Adam and Eve. 'What did the fruit taste like, Father?' she'd asked. 'Was it nice to eat?' 'Oh, it was the sweetest fruit in the world,' he'd said. 'Just one bite and you'd want to go on eating it forever. That's why God didn't want Adam and Eve to have any. Because He knew that just one bite and He'd go clean out of their heads forever.'

It was no good. This couldn't go on. She had to stop it now. She lifted Harry off her, and climbed out of his bed. The cold of the unheated room slapped at her like a punishment.

'That silverware needs finishing,' she said.

After Aisling had got up and got dressed, Harry lay in bed and looked up at the ceiling. He thought of the way Aisling had thrown her suitcase down the hall. He'd found it exciting. It was so unlike her. She was so neat and careful normally. As was he, come to that. But then neither of them was being very neat and careful at the moment. What had come after, when she'd taken charge, had surprised him as well. He felt himself stirring at the thought.

But then she'd suddenly got up and gone. He'd asked her to come back, but she had said nothing, just got dressed and gone downstairs. He thought she looked guilty. Those damned Catholic priests got inside their heads; it was their way of controlling them. Everyone said that. There was no cheerful Church of England hypocrisy over here.

He realised he needed, physically, to be in the same room as her. It wasn't enough any more just to be in the same house. And he needed to talk to her - quickly. She might try to leave again at any moment. That mustn't happen. He'd made up his mind, walking home from meeting Ryan, and he wasn't going to change it now. He sprang out of bed, as if following an order, and dressed rapidly.

The candlestick had a dent in it, Aisling noticed, from where it had fallen on the floor. It was hardly a dent, really; it was barely more than a scratch. You could easily not notice it. But it was there. Aisling noticed these things; she always noticed them. She was like Mam in that respect. Da had said that once. 'There's nothing gets past you in this house, Aisling. I know I daren't so much as drop a crumb from my toast for fear of you.' Harry had noticed it too. Well, there was nothing to be done about it. It was there and it would be there till doomsday. At least she could make the dent shine. She picked up the cloth, dabbed some polish on it, and attacked the candlestick, biting her lip as she scrubbed. When she'd finished, she held it up to the light, and then she went on to the next one. If she scrubbed hard enough, maybe the answer would come to her. Maybe she would know what to do next.

Although she had her back to the hall, she felt him – she almost smelt him – before he spoke.

'Aisling. Come back to bed.'

She made the circle of her polishing smaller. He walked up behind her. He put his arms round her waist, took the candlestick and the cloth from her hands, and put them down on the table. Then he held her to him. Again the warm shudder from her knees to her breasts; it was no longer strange, it felt at home now.

'Don't touch me.'

'Why? Don't you like it?'

'I like it too much.'

He released himself and went and sat in the chair in the corner, where she would sit to do her mending. He was wearing trousers and a vest, and his shirt was hanging open. She noticed the little knot of hair on his chest, and remembered how it had scratched against her when he was on top of her. He took a cigarette out of the silver case he carried in his pocket. It had a dent in it too, quite a large one. He'd told her once that the dent had come from a ricocheting bullet in France. She shivered a little at the thought that that bullet could easily have killed him. He took out a cigarette, tapped it on the case, and lit it. He took down a saucer from the shelf and put it on the floor in front of him.

He wasn't supposed to come into the kitchen. It was her place.

'How can you like something too much, Aisling?'

'You're a married man.'

'I've told you I don't love my wife any more.'

'You're an Englishman. A Protestant. And you're an officer and a gentleman, and I'm a servant. Wouldn't that be enough to be going on with now?'

He drew on his cigarette and flicked some ash in the saucer. He looked down as he talked.

'Those are the things we... dress ourselves up in. But when we... take those clothes off – we're just two human beings who love each other. Aren't we?'

Love. The word hovered between them like a ghost. Aisling thought of reaching for it, but then she turned her back on him and picked up the candlestick and the cloth again.

'I have to go,' she said. 'I have to go to London. I would have gone to London if you hadn't come home.'

'Why London? Do you know people there?'

'No. I know no one. That's why I have to go there.'

'Listen to me first, Aisling. Put down your work and listen to me. That's an order, Aisling.'

His voice rose a little on that, in a way that hurt her and thrilled her at the same time. She put down the candlestick and the cloth, and went and sat at the chair by the table where she ate. It was at the other end of the kitchen, and she had the table between him and her.

'I'm not one of these socialists, Aisling. I do have that much sense. But war – the war I was in in France, and the war here – does make certain things clearer.'

He pressed his knuckles into his forehead, as he often did when he was thinking. Then he took another pull on his cigarette.

'In France, there was a man called Quinn. An Irishman. From Dublin, in fact. He talked a lot about this city. Meant I knew it pretty well even before I set foot in it on... this latest assignment. Been very useful for me, that. Anyway, Quinn came from one of the tenements, north of Sackville Street' – he made a northward gesture behind his head with his cigarette – 'had a father who drank, went to London to get away from all that. When the war started, he joined the army and rose from the ranks to be an officer, purely on ability and drive, remarkable man. I knew a few like that - this last war threw them up - and I can tell you they were all bloody good officers. That might mean something. But before he joined the army, Quinn had worked in a big house in London, as a chauffeur. Driving all and sundry to parties and balls and whatnot. Well, all and sundry. There was one member of the house in particular. The youngest daughter. If I told you her name – which I won't – you'd know her. At least if you've ever opened a magazine, or read the society columns of a newspaper, you would. He had to take her round all the events of the season, all dolled up in her finery, as if – this was his phrase, not mine – she was a slave on sale at market to the highest bidder. Actually that was her phrase. It was how she felt they treated her, she told Quinn. She didn't feel anything for the suitable young men she was introduced to night after night. In the car, though, she would get talking to Quinn. And they could talk to each other, they found. Then she started sneaking down to his garage during the day, when he was servicing the car, and they talked some more. Before long, they were spending afternoons in his quarters when her parents thought she was out having tea with her girlfriends. Quinn told me all this, one night in the trenches, when we were under heavy bombardment. Boche were going mad that night. We split a bottle of whisky, the two of us. You see, Aisling, war does that to people, it breaks down those walls we put up. When you've got bullets and shells flying past your nose, you depend on the man next to you for your life, and it doesn't matter whether his father is a duke or a dustman. It didn't matter that I came from a farm in Norfolk and he came from a tenement in Dublin. It's there, in the trenches, that you find out the true quality of a man, not from consulting Burke's Peerage. And Quinn was solid gold, I can tell you. Saved my life once, and saved a few other men's lives, too. I would have gone to the ends of the earth for that man, and he would have for me.'

His voice was soft now, softer than she'd ever heard it before, and it rose and fell carefully as he talked. He leant forward, taking occasional puffs between sentences on his cigarette, looking down to flick ash into the saucer, looking up at Aisling. His eyes were a mild grey, a gentle colour. Aisling felt his gaze on her as if he was stroking her with his eyes. He'd never talked to her as long as this, and she wanted to go on listening to him. She shifted in her seat and pushed away from the table a little.

'Do you love her? Does she love you? I asked him straight out, man to man, no time to waste. Yes, to both, more than anything in the world, was the answer. Is she married? Engaged? No, not yet, she'd managed to fob them all off. Well then, man, what are you waiting for? The minute this war's over, you get back to London, and you do what it takes. If her family won't have you, then make her grab all the pearls she can lay her hands on from her jewellery box and get on the boat back to Dublin. Quinn said all that you've just said. Wrong background, wrong religion, wrong everything. Look, Quinn, I said. You're a straight man. I've always admired that in you. If she marries someone else, if you marry someone else, you're living a lie. Don't be a liar. Live by the truth. Then you can look yourself in the face in the morning when you're shaving.'

'So we agreed, there and then, the two of us in that dug-out, Boche trying to blow us to kingdom come, that he was going to do it. He had leave due in a week, and he was going to propose to her. Dawn came up. He was on stand-to. He went out to inspect the men, words of encouragement, made them feel they could face it, like he always did, only he was better than ever that morning, all geed up by what we'd decided. And a bullet, one bullet, from a sniper, caught him in the neck. Fell dead at my feet.'

He ground out his cigarette in the saucer, pressing it down hard, harder than he had to. When he looked up, Aisling saw tears in his eyes. She wanted to get up and walk over to him and brush the tears away and hold his face to her chest.

'That's it, Aisling. That's war. And I'm fighting in another one here. Any day of the week – today, tomorrow – someone could put a bullet in my neck. And when we're dead we'll regret the things we haven't done, not the things we've done. If there is a merciful God in Heaven He'll be giving Quinn a good rollicking right now for not marrying that girl earlier.'

Aisling found she was trembling, though it was warm in the kitchen with the stove. She stood up. She walked over to the table where she had been polishing the silverware. She felt as if she was walking along the edge of a cliff; one slip, and she would fall. And yet she wanted to fall. She picked up the candlesticks and replaced them in the cupboard. Then she put the cutlery back in the drawer. She returned the cloth and the polish to another cupboard, folding the cloth carefully into four. She screwed the newspaper into a bundle, and threw it into the stove. Then she stood in the middle of the kitchen for a few seconds, looking at Harry, who was looking at her, had been looking at her the whole time, following her with his eyes. Those beautiful gentle grey eyes. The way he spoke. What a lucky man Quinn was to have such a friend, who spoke to him so honestly and so truthfully. It was no good. There was nothing she could do. She went out into the dining room, picked up the note she had left by Harry's place, took it back into the kitchen, and threw it in the stove. She removed her pinny and hung it up carefully from the usual hook. Then she took Harry's hands in hers and lifted him out of her mending chair. She gave him a little kiss on the lips, like a wife might give to a husband on his return from work.

'Come on,' she said. 'Let's talk some more upstairs.'

CHAPTER TWENTY-FOUR

Mrs Maloney was always in, Molly told Patrick, and Mr Maloney was always out. 'He works so hard, so he does,' Mrs Maloney would say, 'always at that business of his. Scratching and scraping along, scratching and scraping a living for him and for me, now there's just the two of us, now the girls are all grown up.' The truth was, Molly told Patrick with a little nervous giggle, that Mr Maloney spent more time on a bar stool than behind his desk, and his business was close to collapse. She'd hear him stumbling and falling up and down the stairs when he got back late at night. Mrs Maloney said she rented out the rooms because 'the house is so empty now, with my girls all flown away like birds, I rattle around in it, my dear, and I can't bear the silence,' but it was only their rent kept Mr Maloney from bankruptcy, and most of it went straight into the pockets of J. Arthur Guinness, Esq.

She told Patrick all this as they walked over Sackville Bridge, she eager and wiry and bubbling over with chatter like a schoolgirl walking out with her first boyfriend on a Sunday afternoon, he all eyes, moving fast to make himself a harder target, looking up and down every street, a soldier watchful for the enemy; the enemy who only that morning had been his comrades.

'I always knew you'd do something like this, Patrick,' she said, grinning up at him as if he'd given her the best gift ever. 'Risking your life taking on traitors. They're running the IRA now, you say? Actually running it?'

'We don't talk about it in the street,' he said.

She blushed at the rebuke, but carried on grinning, hugging the secret to herself. Once they were on the other side of the river, he began to feel safer. With the Bank of Ireland, squat, heavy, plump as a well fed financier on one side, and Trinity College, its smooth classical facade breathing carefree privilege on the other, Rory and Vinnie and Mick seemed a little further away. But only because he was a little boy skulking behind the big English. Christ, he hated himself all right.

As they walked, she told him about Bewley's, and Kilkenny, and Dermot, flinging out talk to cover her nervousness. He let her run on, half listening, holding his own thoughts tight. There were some right stuck up English coming into Bewley's. Only last Thursday an English officer had made a suggestion to her that was to do with him paying for her to do something and his friend had roared with laughter right in her face and when she'd said she'd report him to his commanding officer he'd slapped his gun bang on the table. That was it with the English, she said, for all their talk of civilisation, all they could do was bang a gun on the table, and we had to make sure we banged a bigger one. Patrick looked over both shoulders twitchily.

They went down Nassau Street, the playing fields of Trinity a little burst of green on their left, the rugby players surging back and forth like enormous insects. It was good and it was bad, Kilkenny. Sure it was good to be home, and Mam was pleased enough to see her – she'd never wanted her going to Dublin in the first place – but it all seemed small and cramped and the people ignorant after Dublin, with all the meetings and arguments and books and pamphlets you found in the city. You weren't going to be bumping into Patrick Pearse or Mr Yeats in the street in Kilkenny. But there was nothing left for her in Dublin once the Rising failed. Once Patrick was carted off to England. She knew he'd get let out one day; knew Ireland would rise again one day. But patience was never her strong point, was it now, more's the pity. She gave another nervous laugh, and twisted a clump of her hair between the second and third fingers of her right hand, and looked up Kildare Street to the fatherly bulk of the National Library, as if it would give her some comfort. Still Patrick said nothing, kept his head down, his collar up. Already she was annoying him. He fought back his annoyance. It felt like an enemy that could stop him completing his mission. Back in Kilkenny she'd found Dermot again, and found they wanted nothing less than the same thing – freedom for Ireland – and that had brought them together and kept them together. There was a uniformed IRA guard of honour at their wedding, so there was, and they got away with it. The police didn't touch them. He was a feared man in Kilkenny, was Dermot. Nothing fearful about him at home, though, there he was gentle as a mouse, grateful for all she did for him. He loved Ireland, so he did.

But she knew Patrick did too, or he wouldn't be doing what they didn't talk about. She looked up at him on this, and gave his arm a little rub, and he tensed into himself, wanted to push her away, just stopped himself. Losing Dermot, well, maybe God had sent that trial as the price of freedom for Ireland. It was a kind of test for her. One she'd failed at first, abandoning the cause. But maybe it had all been meant to be, to send her back to Dublin, and now God had given her a second chance – meeting Patrick again; that couldn't just be an accident now, could it? Surely they were called to defend Ireland against traitors together, weren't they?

They were at Merrion Square, on the exact spot where Patrick and Aisling had parted the first time they met. It seemed a long time ago. He wished he could go back to that day, and just be a lad making a date with a lass, and they could be boyfriend and girlfriend and no spying and no shooting and him doing an honest trade, being a carpenter for real, and no more war. Aisling was five hundred yards down the street. Doing what? Waiting in for Sean. Well, Sean wouldn't be calling on her now. For a moment, he wanted to dismiss Molly, walk off down Mount Street, bang on Aisling's door. But there was no knowing if Mick might not have sent someone to watch the house.

'Let's go and see Mrs Maloney, shall we?' he said. 'I need to get indoors.'

Mrs Maloney insisted. It was no trouble at all, no trouble at all, and the least she could do in the sad circumstances. You poor man, you must be parched and starved, parched and starved after such a journey. Patrick said that Kilkenny was not Timbuktu, now, and gave her a flirtatious lift of his eyebrow, and she waved her hand across her face and said that that was the truth, to be sure, but that she would die of shame if she let him, a bereaved man, pass through her living room without partaking of a slice of her ginger cake and a good pot of strong tea. This was not a hotel, she said, it was a home, and her young ladies – and now her young gentleman – were no more than paying guests, and should be treated as such.

'An uncle, you say, Mr Delaney,' said Mrs Maloney, pouring a thick stream of tea into Patrick's cup.

'That's right, Mrs Maloney,' said Patrick. He was sunk into one cushion of the sofa, and Molly was sunk into the other. Molly held her hands demurely in her lap.

'Well I'm sorry for your trouble, so I am. And Molly here hasn't said a word about him?'

Molly shifted nervously.

'The truth is, Mrs Maloney,' said Patrick, 'he was a man who kept himself to himself, if you know what I mean. He never married, now. There was talk in the family that he'd been for a priest when he was younger, but that then he went to the bad. He was a little too fond of the drink, you know, and it'll be that that carried him off in the end, for he wasn't of a great age.'

Molly shot a sharp look at Patrick, but Mrs Maloney went on pouring Molly's tea.

'Ah, that can happen in families. I thank the Lord that our own has been spared that particular curse, though Lord knows we've had our trials. Cake?'

'Thank you, Mrs Maloney. The fact is, my address was the only one his landlady could find amongst his papers.

He'd not been good at keeping up with his family. I think there was some shame there at what he'd become. So naturally I jumped on the first train I could find – no time to pack or anything – because, although she's the only one of us that lives in the city, I didn't think it fair to leave it to Molly here.'

He patted Molly's hand. Molly took hold of it, making him wince inside himself.

'There's a special bond between cousins, I've always said. Sometimes stronger than brother and sister,' said Mrs Maloney. 'And when is the funeral to be?'

Patrick released his hand.

'Well, that's what I've to arrange. Turns out, Mrs Maloney, there's quite a lot to arrange. He left things in some disorder. Papers all over the place. And I'm not a man to rush a job. Not as important a one as seeing to the affairs of family. Family's the rock and stone of it all, isn't it Mrs Maloney?'

'Oh, it is that, Mr Delaney,' said Mrs Maloney, settling back complacently in her armchair, her teacup balanced perilously on the borders between her bosom and her stomach.

'So when Molly told me you had a room to spare, naturally I jumped at the chance.'

'Stay as long as you need, Mr Delaney. Just pay me day by day. Make yourself at home. You sound like a Dubliner already.'

Molly breathed in sharply. Patrick took a sip of his tea.

'I spent my first ten years here till a death took us back to Kilkenny. I've never quite been able to shake off the Dub way of talking.'

'And why should you, Mr Delaney, why should you?' laughed Mrs Maloney, slopping her tea into the saucer as her bosom shook.

'I see you have a small table up there?'

'I do.'

'That'll be grand, as there's much for me to work through before everything's settled. If you find me shut away in my room morning to night, that's what I'll be doing. Getting it done as soon as I can. I've not come to Dublin to gallivant in pubs the night through.'

'My husband's the same. He as good as lives in that office of his. I sometimes beg him to step out for half an hour, just to take a drink with an old friend. A man needs to relax once in a while, Mr Delaney. It's not good for his health otherwise.'

'It's when I'm home I'll relax, Mrs Maloney.'

He realised Molly was looking up at him adoringly. He wished she wouldn't. She would blow the cover as much as anything else.

'They're understanding at your work now? Back in Kilkenny?'

'It's a family business. A carpenter's. They're grateful that I'm seeing to the family.'

'Family's the greatest gift the Lord can give us. I thank Him daily for Mr Maloney and all he's brought me. Now you and Molly must have stories galore of when you were nippers. I'm betting Molly was a handful.'

Molly laughed and leaned her head against Patrick's shoulder, letting her hair brush against his neck. Again she took his hand, and this time held it so tight he could not get it free. Patrick wondered if he'd ever be able to get rid of her.

Alone at last in his room that night, Patrick inspected what he had left. He had his coat and his hat, which he hung up in Mrs Maloney's echoing wardrobe, his cheap suit, fraying at the edges, his thick knitted sweater, his shirt, his socks, his shoes, his underpants and a packet of cigarettes with thirteen left, his notebook and pencil, and a box of matches and two pounds and seventeen shillings after he'd paid Mrs Maloney for the first two days. Mrs Maloney had said one and sixpence a day if he wanted all his meals, just pay her for the first two. He counted on his fingers. He could afford to stay forty days. Like Jesus in the wilderness. He'd have more food than Jesus, but by God he'd stink to high heaven after forty days in the same clothes.

It wasn't a bad room. The bed was good and hard, it was a quiet street, and she kept it clean. There was a rug by his bed, and flowers on the chest of drawers. He could even walk up and down in it a bit. She'd had gas lighting put in so he could at least pretend to work at night. The lamp flickered and hissed. It was a sound he'd hardly heard before, but it was a kind of company. The bathroom was right next door. He wouldn't have Vinnie's feet in his face any more. As prison cells went, he could do worse.

He lit one of his thirteen cigarettes and sat down at the table opposite a pale faced Madonna who looked like she hadn't been sleeping too good, holding a plump, red faced Jesus. He couldn't stay in Dublin forever. Mick would find him. Mick always found his man. He could go inland. But he knew no one outside Dublin. And Mick's men would be there, too. He could go to America. He had a cousin in New York, like everyone else. No – two pounds and seventeen shillings wouldn't get him to America. He had another cousin in London, though. Jim had left two years ago, as soon as the war with Germany had finished. He'd gathered his pals in Reilly's the night before he sailed; it had been a desperate, drink-soaked evening, Jim fighting his nerves, the rest of them fighting their envy. 'I'll be picking up the leavings of the war;' he'd told Patrick. 'the English jobs, the English money, the English women.' He'd done all right, though. He'd written last Christmas to say he had a lease on a pub in Hammersmith called The Wild Goose. It looked over the River Thames, and if Patrick ever needed to get out of Ireland in a hurry he'd have a job waiting for him there behind the bar. So England it would have to be. England, the home of the frustrated and the hopeful and the disappointed Irish. He laughed, and blew a cloud of smoke in the Madonna's face. All those years fighting against the English, Kelly, and you end up being one of them.

England. On his own. No. He wouldn't go on his own. If he got anything out of this sorry mess, if he could get anything out of this sorry mess, it would be Aisling. He would not go there – or anywhere – without her. Again, the physical urge to stand up at that moment and walk the two streets to Mount Street Lower and drag her out of the house. *Never act on your feelings*, Sean used to say. *Use your brain, make a plan, then stick to it.* For all he was a traitor and all, and a bastard and all, his brother had been a bloody good soldier. Even Mick acknowledged that. He'd wait until morning; wait for their date at the Cairo. If she turned up, she was still interested; if she didn't, he'd have to leave without her. Though at the thought of leaving without her he wondered if he wouldn't rather just stay here and be shot.

There was a shy tap on the door.

'Come in.'

Molly came in and put a cup of tea next to him.

'She kept saying you must be parched working on your own. I said I'd bring another one up to you.'

'Thank you.'

She stood behind him. He went on looking at the Madonna. He wanted her to go.

'She likes you, you know.'

'I know.'

'You're good at making people like you. You're a natural at it.'

'Molly. Thank you. Thank you for saving my life.'

'It's a life that's worth saving, Patrick. I'm only sorry I didn't know that sooner. When you were taken away. I should have waited. But I was so angry you didn't write. Other women got letters.'

'I can't stay here long, you know. It's not safe.'

Molly put her hands on his shoulders. He tensed a little. Again, that wanting her to go.

'Jesus, you're a brave man, Patrick.'

'I'm going to have to leave very soon, Molly. There's someone I have to see tomorrow morning. Depending on the plans we make, I'll like as not be on my way after that. Tell Mrs Maloney she can keep the money for the extra day. Tell her another cousin popped up and insisted on me staying. Go out to Mass one morning and pretend it was the funeral. I can't tell you where I'm going. For your own safety.'

Molly moved her hands down to his chest and pulled Patrick towards her. She pressed her cheek against his.

Despite himself, he felt desire stirring. It had been a long time since he'd had a woman.

'Mrs Maloney's in bed by ten, on the floor above,' she said. 'She snores when she's sleeping. Mr Maloney'll be staggering up the stairs just after eleven, when the pub shuts. He's out dead when he's drunk. Which is every night. And Maeve's away at her cousin's wedding in Donegal. There's a clock on the landing strikes the hours. Myself, I'm a light sleeper. I'm always awake to hear it strike midnight. There, in my room, just past the bathroom. All by myself.'

CHAPTER TWENTY-FIVE

Aisling and Harry went on talking as it got dark, holding each other, side by side now, their faces close, their legs wrapped around each other, their breath and their warmth mingling. Although Aisling missed seeing Harry's face after the light had gone, she loved to touch him, and touch seemed to sound louder in the dark. She listened to him talk. He told her about Norfolk and his early days in the army and how he'd met Emily. He'd really loved her at first, it seemed. He told her about how she'd got ill after the end of the war, and how he'd realised he didn't love her any more. Aisling felt a sharp shard of guilt shoot through her at the thought of Emily in her nursing home, and she shifted and wriggled a little in his arms, but then he was talking about the war with Germany, about the mud and the filth and the rats and the shells going all the time, and then he got onto seeing his pals' heads blown off in front of him, lads, some of them, he'd known since he'd been a lad himself, and he was shaking and after a bit he started crying and he couldn't stop. She held him to her breast and let him cry until he stopped and then she wiped his face dry with her hand, breathing in the leathery smell of his skin deep into herself as if it was a drug. She could feel him looking up at her in the dark.

'Thank you, Aisling,' he said. 'I have never been able to talk about that. To anyone. Nor have I wept like that. Does it make me less of a man to weep?'

Da never wept after Mam died. Maybe he should have. Maybe he wouldn't have got so angry with the English if he had. Maybe he'd still be alive.

'No,' she said. 'It makes you more of a man,' she said, and she meant it. She felt very close to him then. She wanted to go on holding him and not let him go. She wanted to stay like this forever; her head on his chest, his arm round her, his breath on her face, his smell in her smell.

'Do you want to go on being a soldier?' she asked him.

'Not here. Not the way I have to be a soldier here. Creeping round pubs and brothels, picking up scraps of gossip and half-truth like rotting food that's been swept off the table. Lying to people, cheating them. Looking over my shoulder every time I walk down the street.'

She thought of how she'd broken into his desk when he was out and copied out his secrets and given them to another man. Well, they were both deep in lies. Maybe that was what war did to you. A time would come when they would have to be completely honest with each other.

'Sometimes I think -' he went on, '- and this is not something I would ever say out loud, or that you should repeat. But sometimes I think we should just leave Ireland to the Irish.'

'Not say it out loud? I'd say it's common bloody sense.'

He laughed, making her head bounce on his chest. When he had stopped laughing, he said,

'Would you fight for your country, then, Aisling?'

She thought of his notebook: the regimented writing, the carefully composed sentences; secrets snapped up tight under the black leather cover. Secrets that fired bullets into the heads of sleeping men; Irish men. Suddenly she felt a surge of disgust. She didn't want to talk any more. And yet she didn't want to leave him, not even leave his bed. She didn't know what she wanted to do. It hurt, this confusion in her mind. Well, what's tangled at night is straight in the morning, Mam used to say.

'I'm tired,' she said. 'Let's go to sleep.'

She turned away from him and closed her eyes. Please God Mam would be right. She wondered what Mam would have her do. Though she pretended to be asleep, she was awake for hours wondering.

Mrs Maloney always served bacon for breakfast. It was one thing she didn't stint on, she told Patrick. Mr Maloney, a thin, ghostly man who ate as if food was a punishment he reluctantly accepted, had one rasher. Molly had two and Mrs Maloney had four, to start with at least. She insisted on eating with her guests, as if pretending that they were not paying her. They all ate jammed up together round an oval table covered with an embroidered tablecloth. Unused silverware jostled for position on a side table.

She ladled three rashers onto Patrick's plate. 'A good fry in the morning, Mr Delaney, is the best start to the day a man can have. Is that not a fact, Maloney?' she added, raising her voice as if Maloney was deaf. Mr Maloney waved his fork in the air above *The Irish Times* in assent.

'Sure, the hours Maloney works he needs it,' she added.

'We all need it, Mrs Maloney,' said Patrick. 'And I can tell you that your bacon is none but the finest.'

Across the table, Molly grinned at him. He saw triumph written on her face. A little after midnight, Molly had taken the initiative. Patrick had been half awake, half dozing, half in bed by himself, half in bed with Aisling, twisted and stretched with lust, thinking of reaching for himself, when Molly had crept his door open, closed it silently behind her, slipped her nightdress over her head and let it float to the floor, and climbed in with him. 'Molly,' he'd grunted, but she'd closed his mouth with a kiss, and let her hands and her arms and her legs loose on his body. Patrick had felt as if he was tumbling down a hill, gathering speed, and couldn't stop himself. Afterwards, he had felt a great release and had fallen straight asleep, Molly holding him, covering him, warming him. The next thing he had known was the sound of Mrs Maloney clattering with her pans in the kitchen, and Molly whispering in his ear, 'I'm going to wash and dress now, and then I'll see you at breakfast.'

'Do you have any plans today, Mr Delaney?' asked Mrs Maloney, spearing a whole rasher on her fork.

'I do indeed, Mrs Maloney,' said Patrick. 'As soon as I've finished this excellent breakfast, I'll be off and out. I've someone I need to see about my late uncle's business –'

'- *our* late uncle,' interrupted Molly.

' – our late uncle indeed. His affairs'll keep me very busy today.'

'Ah, it's a good man you are, Mr Delaney, sacrificing yourself for family so,' said Mrs Maloney.

'He's always been like that,' said Molly, leaning back in her chair and looking at him admiringly, 'always thinking of others.'

'Will you be back for tea, though?' said Mrs Maloney.

'That depends, now,' said Patrick. 'It depends on my business. My business may take me away from Dublin for a while.'

'There's the funeral, Patrick,' said Molly. 'You won't want to miss that.'

'Of course I won't. But there's no date been fixed.'

'You'll be sleeping here tonight, anyway,' said Mrs Maloney. 'We agreed that much.' Her back was turned as she sneaked her fifth rasher, and Mr Maloney was still behind his newspaper. Molly stretched out a leg and stroked the inside of Patrick's thigh with her foot. He jerked his leg away and bent over his plate, shoving the last rasher in whole, with an uncomfortable violence.

'If my plans change, I'll see you know,' he said as soon as the rasher was down. 'What time is it you have to be at Bewley's, Molly?'

'Ten till four. So we've time for a wee walk, if you want? Let your cousin show you Dublin. You'll find it changed a lot since you were a nipper.'

'No, no, thank you, but no. The man I have to see, I've an appointment with him at nine.' Patrick wiped his mouth roughly with his napkin, and stood. 'So I'd better be going. Thank you, Mrs Maloney, for a wonderful fry. It's set me up for the day, so it has.'

'Ah, you're very welcome, Mr Delaney. I wish you the luck of your day.' Patrick jammed his hat on and headed for the front door, desperate to leave. The thought that Aisling might be at the Cairo was so sharp it almost cut him. He wondered if she would be able to forgive him for last night with Molly; if he could forgive her for her night with Lovegrove. Ah, he was talking as if they were as good as engaged. But maybe, just maybe, they might be by the end of the day. Or maybe that was madness to think. But he was going to think it anyway, he couldn't help himself. 'Let me know your plans, now,' called Mrs Maloney after him. 'I don't want good food going to waste.'

'And it's a grand lunch they serve at Bewley's, don't forget,' called Molly, her voice shaking a little with fragile hope.

Mam was wrong. Things were no straighter for Aisling when she woke and saw the wintry sun shining low through the window onto Harry's sleeping face. It was madness, surely, going to bed with her boss, going to bed with her enemy, going to bed with one of them that had killed Da. Going to bed with a married man, condemning herself to mortal sin. Looking down at him, she felt a sickness in her stomach. She remembered one day in their tenth summer when she and Sinead had dared each other to walk along the high wall by the church, teetering, waiting to fall, knowing how much it would hurt when she did. That was how she felt now. And yet she wanted to fall; wanted to jump. She wanted to kiss him awake, and run her hands over his chest and his legs and his arms and his face and take him inside her and make love to him again.

She had to get out of this room. And she had to talk to someone. It was the only way she could work out what she felt. But who could she talk to? Patrick. She had no one else. She had no one else in the world. Patrick had said to meet her in the Cairo at nine. She picked up Harry's watch from the bedside table. Just gone eight. She'd go to the Cairo. She'd talk to Patrick. She'd tell him Sean had never turned up. She'd find out what had happened to Sean, if he knew. And then she'd tell him her story; she'd lay it all before him, see what he said, see what she felt as she told it. And after she'd said it all to him she'd know, for sure, one way or another.

Harry's eyes opened.

'We need bacon,' she said. 'There's none left.'

'What about that kedgeree you made me?' he said.

'No. Not this morning. I fancy bacon for breakfast.'

'Will you be eating your breakfast with me then?'

'Wait for me till I come back.'

Patrick got to the Cairo well before nine and sat in his usual corner seat where he could watch the door. He nursed his usual tea, his usual paper in front of him. Nothing too different; nothing to arouse suspicion. Just no Englishmen to watch this morning. None of the Castle men were in. The cafe was bustling with women hunched over steaming cups of coffee shrieking laughter at each other or urgently consulting in hushed voices, but Baggally and Fitzgerald and all the rest were out riding or playing golf or at the races or lying in bed. They had weekends off, unless there was an emergency. Well, by God there would be an emergency tomorrow morning, thought Patrick. He wondered who would die and who would live. Once he would have loved nothing more than to be there when it was all happening, to be killing the English, to be winning the war for Mick. But since he'd met Aisling, he realised now, all that had been fading away. He wasn't a killer any more. He'd lost the hunger. He just wanted to be on a boat out of the city before it happened. He would tell Aisling it wasn't safe, that there was going to be a war, that she needed to get out now. Surely he could talk her into it; surely once she was away from that bastard Lovegrove she would see sense, see who he was. He scanned the runners and riders for Limerick, but he found he was taking nothing in.

Aisling picked her way through the frost on the pavements, fearful of slipping, but glad to be out in the fresh air, to see her breath turn into steam in front of her, to have the cold pinch her awake. The sky was nothing but blue. She went across St Stephen's Green. It was the long way round, but she wanted to be somewhere open, under the blue sky, with the pond and the ducks and the empty flowerbeds to herself, maybe even take a turn or two round the pond, to get things straight in her head before she saw Patrick, to think about what she should say to him, how she should say it. There were never many people on the Green at that time of the morning. It was as bare as the trees, stripped for winter. Which was, she realised when she had time to think about it, why they chose the Green to catch up with her.

She was on the bridge going over the pond, looking down at the ducks, who were circling each other warily. One of the two men, the one with a moustache, walked past her, fast, unafraid of the frost, then turned, and tipped his trilby at her.

'Miss O'Flaherty?' he said.

The other one, the one with the big ears, had stopped dead behind her. The bridge was narrow. They could stop her getting past them in either direction simply by stretching out their arms.

'Who are you?' she said.

'I'm a friend of Patrick Kelly's. As I believe are you. A little more than a friend, so I've heard.'

'What do you want?'

'We want you to help us. You see, Patrick's gone missing. We were wondering if you might know where he is.'

'I've not seen him since yesterday morning.'

The man pushed both his hands deep into his pockets and narrowed his eyes at Aisling.

'Is that a fact, Miss O'Flaherty?' he said.

'It is. Now would you let me go? I've a man's breakfast to get.'

'An Englishman's breakfast, is that, Miss O'Flaherty?'

'They have to eat too, you know.'

'Sure they do. Where else would they be getting their strength from to be killing Irishmen?'

'I've a job to do. Would you let me go?'

She tried to get past him, but he stretched out his arm.

'I wouldn't do that if I were you, Miss,' he said.

She knew it was no good. She knew he wouldn't let her go. She'd managed not to show her fear, but it was a mighty effort not to shake and cry and scream. She turned her back on him and saw the other man. He had a gun in his hand and was pointing it at her.

'That's why I wouldn't do that, Miss,' said the first man.

'What do you want with Patrick?'

'He's a traitor. We want to do with him what we do with traitors.'

So he'd decided. He'd switched sides. He'd loved his brother more than Ireland. In fact, he'd done what she'd told him to. They were traitors both now. They were in it together. And these men were after killing him. Did they know about her and Harry? Who knew but they wouldn't be after killing her and all. She'd escaped the English in Clifden, and now it was the Irish in Dublin who were after her. And wasn't there a bit of her that thought they'd be in the right to kill her, if they'd only let her be confessed first?

'Where is he?' said the man with the moustache.

Two ducks had started an argument. One was pecking at another, till the pecked duck flew squawking away, just past her head.

'I said, where is he?'

She didn't want Patrick killed. He was a good man. He'd been right to let his brother go. There'd been enough killing. Altogether too much. Killing more men wouldn't bring Da back. Enough of the men killing each other.

'I'm sorry, sir. I can't help you. I have no idea where he lives. And I have no idea where he is now. I last saw him yesterday morning and that's all I can tell you.'

'If you won't say anything, you're coming with us,' said the man. 'Them's our orders.'

'As I said, I've to get back to work. I can't help you, I'm afraid.'

'You can tell that to Mick.'

'Why don't you tell it to Mick?'

'Just come with us, Miss, would you,' said the other man, 'I don't like shooting women.'

'Would you do it?' said Aisling.

'If he didn't, I would,' said the first man, thrusting his hand into his pocket and letting her see the shape of a gun. 'You'll come with us. Vinnie here'll walk with you, arm in arm, like you're a courting couple. I understand you're used to walking out with a triggerman, so that should be easy enough for you. He'll take you to our friend Annie's. I hope you're not too houseproud, as she lives in a slum of her own making. I'll walk behind you, to make sure you get there. My gun's in my pocket. If you even look like you might run, your brains'll be on the street.'

Vinnie took Aisling's arm. They started walking, Vinnie leading her towards Grafton Street, the other man a few paces behind. Aisling walked as fast as she could. Movement kept her fear at bay. She felt Vinnie getting breathless, finding it hard to keep up, though he wouldn't tell her to slow down.

CHAPTER TWENTY-SIX

Harry sat at the long table in the dining room, washed, dressed, shaved, ready for breakfast. Breakfast with Aisling. Sitting opposite her. Looking into her strong beautiful face. Sitting at the same table for the first time. It felt almost as shocking and as exciting as sleeping in the same bed. But last night had changed everything. He'd never felt as close to anyone as he had to Aisling. He'd never told anyone about the war like he had told her. He'd never told Emily; he'd never been able to tell Emily. He'd never cried like that, either. Now that he had, he felt refreshed, cleansed, a new man. He wanted to go on talking to Aisling; he would have gone on all night if she hadn't gone to sleep. He felt he could tell her anything. And yet he felt there was something she was holding back. He didn't know what.

He wondered where she was. Why had she gone for bacon? He'd have preferred the kedgeree, and she knew it. Well, it must be some whim of hers. He'd have to leave at nine. He had a meeting with Colonel Brind at half past nine, rescheduled from yesterday afternoon, when he'd told Brind he had to go home to deal with urgent matters related to Emily, when he'd really only wanted to see Aisling. It would not do to be late, especially as he had specifically disobeyed Brind's orders by not dismissing her. That would need solving. A lot of things would need solving; but after last night, they were worth solving.

Where was she? He looked at his watch. Nine, on the dot. He would have to go. He couldn't afford to anger Brind. If he wanted to regularise an irregular situation, he would need him on his side. He took out his notebook, wrote a quick note, and left it by his place at the table. *Had to go into work. Will be back this afternoon. Harry.* He looked at it for a moment, and then, with uncharacteristic impulsiveness, added three words. *I love you.*

He opened the front door and the *Irish Times*, propped against it, fell onto his shoes. He'd forgotten about the newspaper. Normally, he read it over breakfast. 'Read the *Irish Times* every day,' Brind had told them. 'You need to know what's going on in this bloody awful country.' He should glance it at, in case there was anything to discuss with Brind. He picked it up. More shootings in Cork. A pronouncement from a bishop. Then, on the second page, halfway down the third column, he saw:

MAN GUNNED DOWN IN MOUNTJOY STREET

Killer walks away whistling

Mr Sean Kelly, 28, of 15 Mountjoy Street, Dublin was shot once in the chest and twice in the head by two men yesterday afternoon at about three o'clock, on the steps of his residence. The shots were heard by his landlady, Mrs Eileen Murphy, who rushed to his assistance, but was too late to save him. She saw two men walking away, who she believed to be guilty of the crime. One of them, she said, was whistling.

Mr Kelly was briefly imprisoned for his part in the Easter Week rebellion, but was released shortly afterwards. It is thought likely that the killing was prompted by an internal dispute amongst rebels of the kind that is very common. As long as they are killing each other they are not killing us, and for that we must be grateful.

Above the article was a prison photo, taken just after the Rebellion. Sean Kelly looked straight at the camera, unshaven, untidy, defiant, bitter. It was him all right. It was the man who had called himself Patrick. They had discovered his treachery.

Across the road, a woman was pushing a pram, singing to her baby in Irish. Harry cricked his neck back and looked up at the sky. It was such a brilliant blue that it hurt his eyes. Who could have betrayed this Sean? He wasn't the nicest man you could hope to meet, but he wasn't stupid. He obviously knew how to look after himself. He wouldn't have risen so high in the rebels if he hadn't been pretty smart. He'd written nothing down, except for the note he'd pushed through Harry's door. He'd said he'd do it again when he had anything. There was no one else in the house who could read the note. Emily was too ill... Oh dear God. It must be. There was no other explanation. It was Aisling. Aisling had been spying on him, and had turned Sean in to his comrades. Aisling, the woman he shared his house with, the woman he'd shared his bed with, the woman he loved, who he'd believed loved him back, had betrayed him. Had she got into his bed in order to betray him to the Fenians? Would they be coming after him now, now they had got Sean? Was that why she had left this morning? Was that what she had been holding back?

The woman's song faded as she disappeared round the corner at the end of the street. Harry saw the vicar of the English church, a red faced, anxious man, who liked to share urgent facts about his parishioners in a short, sharp voice, bustling up the pavement towards him. Harry didn't want to talk to him. He went back into the house, the paper in his hand, closed the door behind him, and leaned against it. It was here, right here, that he and Aisling had kissed, for the second time. That she'd thrown down her suitcase, abandoned her departure. When had she done it? How had she done it? Had Sean been sending notes regularly, and she'd intercepted them all? Why? He knew what had happened to her father. That sort of story was common enough in rebel propaganda, but it was real for her. Or was Brind right, and she had a rebel boyfriend? If he found the boyfriend, he'd have him shot. Though that wouldn't bring Aisling back. Brind had been right to tell him to dismiss her. He would have to have someone come to the house and arrest her; have her taken into the Castle. He knew what happened at the Castle. He'd taken part in interrogations himself. He'd been the one telling Winter to go easy, that breaking teeth and bones wouldn't bring the truth, that persuasion was better. Which was probably why they'd taken him off interrogations. What would they do to a woman? Might it be worse? Might they even...? Oh, dear God.

Had it all been a set up, had she been told by her handlers to get him into bed so she could get into his secrets? She'd never told him she loved him. She'd tried to leave. She'd used him. She'd seen he was weak and vulnerable because of Emily, and she'd jumped in and used him. He was a pawn in the Fenians' grubby little game. You fool, Lovegrove, you bloody love struck fool. Briefly, he felt his fists clenching, saw her in a cell in the Castle, was ready to slap her himself.

She'd been very quick to get out of bed this morning. Bacon. No bacon; she was meeting her handler. And, foolishly, taking too long about it. 'Never trust an Irishman. Or an Irishwoman, come to that,' Brind had said. 'Charm your trousers off you and walk away wearing them themselves, and you'll walk down the street showing everyone your arse and be none the wiser. Famous bloody Irish charm. More dangerous than a hundred guns.' But it wasn't just charm. There was more to it than that. He'd written the truth on that note. He loved her. He really, really loved her.

He thought of tearing up the note he'd left. No, best to leave it. It might keep her here till... till they came for her. He winced, feeling the blows they would land on her as if they were happening to him. But there was nothing for it. He'd betrayed Emily, and now he'd been betrayed. He had to face the music.

Come on, Lovegrove, he said to himself. If she's let you down, you've still got your duty. He had to see Brind and make a clean breast of it. Nothing else to be done. If he was lucky, he might get away with a reduction to the ranks and a boat back to England. Perhaps what had happened to Emily might be taken in mitigation. It would be the end, one way or another. But the truth was that he'd had enough of this stinking, sloping, hole in corner war. He'd be glad to be out of it. He'd take Emily back to Norfolk, put her in a home there, take over the family farm, live out his days in peace, and forget this bloody awful country and everyone in it.

Except that he knew he could never, would never, forget Aisling. A cutting, searing pain washed through him at the thought of her. Tears came to his eyes; he'd rather she'd had him killed than betrayed him.

He forced the tears away with his fist. He tucked the newspaper under his arm, pulled the front door open decisively, and set off for the Castle, at the double, looking round him at every step, feeling as if he was once again in France, walking steadily into the raking hail of bullets.

Sitting in the Cafe Cairo, Patrick looked up from his paper as he heard the door go. A woman walked in and started signalling to her friend on the other side of the room like a tic-tac man at the races. The clock behind the counter said ten past nine. He'd wait. If a woman could be late for her wedding, she could be late for running away too. It was cold today, no rain. The window wasn't steamed up. He looked out of it. He saw Aisling.

She was walking fast. She always walked fast, like she had no time to waste. It was one of the things he loved about her; she was a woman who knew what she was doing. But she was arm in arm. And not with Lovegrove. With Vinnie. Vinnie, skinny, jug eared Vinnie, for Christ's sake, who a woman wouldn't look at if she'd spent the last twenty years in a convent. She was looking straight ahead, lips pursed, holding a tight grin. Trying not to look terrified. As she passed the window of the cafe she threw in a glance, like a drowning woman far from the shore reaching for land. He caught her eye. He made to stand up, but she shook her head, briefly, instantly, no more than a twitch. He wanted to run out and punch Vinnie in the face and embrace her there and then, in the middle of Grafton Street. But he had no gun and he knew by the expression on her face that Vinnie did. He was still enough of a soldier not to get himself killed. He sat down again. As he sat down, Rory passed the window, hand in his pocket, looking straight ahead, eyes on Aisling's back. They were going north. Jesus. They were taking her to Annie's. She'd spied for them, she'd risked her life for them, and they were taking her to Annie's. He watched Rory's bitter, angry tread disappear up the street. Then he thought of what had passed between him and Molly in the early hours of that morning, and he had an idea.

CHAPTER TWENTY-SEVEN

Mick was leaning against the bed in the room in Annie's house, his long legs stretched out in front of him. He hadn't bothered to take off his coat or his hat. He'd let Aisling have the armchair, a small courtesy she'd found herself appreciating in spite of her fear, or perhaps because of it. There was a tall, broad back to it, and it had three plump squashy cushions. Each of the three cushions had a tear in them and stuffing coming out. The bed was high, with scratchy blankets on it. There were no holy pictures on the wall; instead there was a frame inside which mass cards for the men who had been shot after the Easter Rising had been stuck, as if they were the saints. A thin coating of dust covered everything like sin. A smell of grease seemed to hang in the stale air of the room.

There was a wardrobe, with the door half falling off. Aisling had nothing to put in it, as she had only the clothes she had dressed in when she had gone out to meet Patrick. Outside, on the landing, Vinnie was sitting on a rickety kitchen chair with a gun on his lap. There was a toilet at the end of the landing. The bowl was encrusted light brown and the chain was rusty and there were shameless patches of filth on every surface. When Aisling had had to use it, she had called to Vinnie and he had unlocked the door and watched her down the landing with the gun still in his hand, not pointed at her but ready to use. There was just one small window in the toilet up high. Vinnie sat directly opposite the toilet, so he could have shot her through the door if he'd wanted. The toilet hadn't flushed properly, and Vinnie had had to take his chair in and stand on it and fiddle with the ballcock. Altogether, this house was a kind of hell of untidiness and filth and chaos. She wondered if that was part of the punishment; if they thought she'd say anything or do anything to get out of here.

'Where is he?' said Mick.

He was staring at Aisling. His stares were like another man's blows. Aisling could see why Patrick was half in love with him. She sat very still in the armchair. It was hard to sit still, because the cushions were so squashy. They were covered with patches of grease. She didn't want to sink back into them, for fear it would anger Mick, and because she couldn't bear to be touching the grease. She wanted to throw the cushions on the floor, but she didn't dare.

'I don't know,' she said. 'I've no more idea than you.'

'I need to know where he is,' he said, his voice softening a little. 'Lives may be at stake. Dozens of lives.'

Exactly what Patrick had said to her.

'I saw him yesterday morning. In Grafton Street, in the rain. That was the last I saw of him.'

She shouldn't have looked into the window of the cafe. She should have kept her gaze ahead, but she couldn't stop herself. He'd looked as if he was going to run out of the cafe into the street. If he had, they would have killed him and maybe killed her too. She'd risked both their lives shaking her head like that but thank God it hadn't been noticed and thank God he'd sat down. When she'd shook her head she'd meant No, don't come out, don't follow me, don't think of me, forget me, get out now.

Mick looked at his shoes.

'Right. And what had you done just before this sad parting?'

'I handed him a note, addressed to... to my employer.'

'Major Lovegrove?'

'Himself. It was from a man who called himself Patrick. He told the captain he knew all about Sunday and would meet him at Reilly's. Also told him to get rid of me. Because I was spying on him. For you, Mr Collins, remember?'

'I do remember. And very useful your reports were too. They showed us the blood on your man Lovegrove's hands.'

'Are you going to have Harry... Major Lovegrove shot tomorrow?'

'What's it to you?'

Mick looked back up at Aisling and it was as if he had slapped her across the face. She swallowed, and felt her face burning. She thought of Harry being shot. She wondered if it would look like Da being shot. She didn't think she could bear seeing that twice. She reached behind her and took out one of the cushions and put it on the floor in front of her.

'I said, what's it to you?'

'Ah, nothing. I just wondered.'

'Well, you can stop wondering. Wondering gets you a bullet in the neck these days in Ireland. Now, what did Patrick say when you gave him the note?'

'He said it was his brother's writing. But he wanted to check. So he sent me in to Reilly's at the appointed time.

I pretended I was looking for my Da, out on a batter. Sure enough, there was a man there who was the dead spit of Patrick.'

'You told Patrick that?'

'I did.'

'How did he take it?'

'It was hard. Finding out his own brother was a traitor.'

'Sure, it was hard. A bit too hard, maybe.'

'What do you mean?'

'I told you not to wonder. Patrick's sweet on you, right?'

'Perhaps a little.'

'More than a little, Miss O'Flaherty. He's deep into it up to his neck. I know Pat. I saw that.'

'But we quarrelled.'

'What about?'

'I had to tell him I wasn't as sweet on him as he was on me. That there was someone else.'

'Someone in Dublin?'

'A boy back home. So he said that was that. He didn't want to see me any more. Never again. That was it.'

She'd tried too hard, out of fear; she could see the disbelief on Mick's face. Sure he was going to kill her now. But she had to keep her head. *If they capture you, never let them see you're afraid*, Flanagan used to say, back in Clifden. Now she'd been captured by one of her own. Mick thrust his hands into the pockets of his trenchcoat and looked at the Easter martyrs, as if he was consulting his junior officers.

'Are you going to let me go?' said Aisling. 'I've been three hours buying six rashers of bacon from Connolly's. I think Major Lovegrove might be suspecting something.'

'You can't go back to him. You've got to stay here.'

'Are you going to shoot me? After I risked my job, maybe my life, spying on Lovegrove for you?'

'No. You're no use to us dead.'

'I'm hungry.'

'I'll have Annie bring you up something on a tray. But you stay in this room. It stays locked. Vinnie stays outside.'

'Why?'

'I told you. Not to wonder.'

And Mick was gone, sweeping by her, not looking her in the eye now, rapping on the door. She caught a glimpse of Vinnie, his sallow face and his jutting out ears, as he unlocked and opened it. Vinnie closed the door, avoiding Aisling's eyes. She heard the key turn. Through the door she heard Vinnie. He had a whining, nasal voice.

'Mick. Sean said me and Rory's doing Lovegrove tomorrow. Is all that still on, with Sean gone and all?'

Then, in Mick's rasping whisper,

'Yes. But for fuck's sake don't talk about it.'

Aisling sank deep into the armchair. She clutched at her stomach as if she had been shot herself. The room seemed to spin round her. *Doing Lovegrove.* Doing Harry. They were going to kill him. They were going to kill him like Da was killed. They were going to fire bullets into his beautiful, gentle body. She couldn't bear to think of it. Then, suddenly, she had a strange sense of relief. Everything that had been muddled and confused in her mind since the night she had first kissed Harry at last became clear.

CHAPTER TWENTY-EIGHT

Harry turned into Dame Street and saw the Castle loom up at him. He'd never hesitated – never even thought of hesitating - in France, but now a sick feeling of dread at his own stripping naked by Aisling's treachery invaded him. Oh Jesus. What had he done?

Sergeant Wallace, who was always on the gate in the mornings, snapped to attention and saluted briskly, trying to keep warm. Harry felt a wave of relief and gratitude at his simple soldierliness.

'Morning, Wallace.'

'Morning, sir. Working Saturday, are we?'

'Needs must, Wallace. The enemy doesn't take weekends.'

'Indeed he doesn't, sir. And nor do those of us who are billeted here. We can't hardly go out now. Them Fenians waiting in every pub with a revolver behind the bar.'

'But you're due for leave soon, aren't you, Wallace?'

'I am, sir. Sailing on Monday morning.'

'Family?'

'Wife in Rochester. And a daughter. Six weeks old. Never set eyes on her.'

Wallace blushed, and half stood back to attention to hide his embarrassment.

'Good for you, Wallace. Children are a wonderful thing.'

'Any of your own, sir?'

Harry briefly saw a boy and a girl chasing each other from rock to rock on a Norfolk beach, and himself sitting on a blanket, Aisling in his arms, watching them. He slapped the thought away.

'None yet, Wallace. Is Colonel Brind expecting me?'

The sergeant picked up a clipboard.

'He is, sir. There's another gentleman with him. An Irish gentleman. Didn't know him, sir.'

'Really?'

It would be a potential agent. Damn. Bloody nuisance. Well, he would have to go through the motions and then ask for a private word.

Harry saluted, and Wallace saluted back, glad to return to formality. As Harry walked across the wide cobbled courtyard of the Castle, he took several deep cold breaths, sending out clouds of steam that wreathed him like gunsmoke.

The Irishman Sergeant Wallace had announced was sitting in one of the chairs facing Brind's desk. He was leaning forward as far as he could go without falling off the chair and his hands were together in his lap. When Harry came in, both he and Brind stood. Harry saluted, and Brind saluted back, and the Irishman smiled weakly and twisted his hands.

'Thank you for coming in, Lovegrove,' said Brind.

'Of course, sir. I'm grateful to you for agreeing to postpone yesterday.'

'Consider it repostponed. Something else we need to talk about.'

'That's much what I was going to say to you, sir.'

'Later.'

'With respect, sir...'

'Major Lovegrove – Mr Grady. Sit. Won't leave you to it if you don't mind because there are operational implications. Need to know the lot. Sorry. When you're ready, Grady.'

Grady leant forward again and held his hands open to Harry as if trying to catch something. He coughed, sniffed and sighed. Harry wanted him to finish what he'd come for and go away. He couldn't bear to wait a minute longer to make his confession.

'Spit it out, Grady. Major's not a fool,' said the Colonel.

'The thing is, Major Lovegrove,' said Grady, 'Mr O'Connor has an elderly mother.'

'Mr O'Connor?' said Harry.

'In Cork. She may not be spared much longer. It's a long way to go, but he insists. Every weekend. I admire him for it, Major Lovegrove. I've no doubt you'd do the same yourself. The train leaves at six on a Friday.'

'What are you talking about?'

'Grady's 2 i/c,' interrupted Brind. 'Explaining the compassionate leave policy.'

'You met Mr O'Connor, I believe. Earlier this week. Myself you haven't met. Mr O'Connor would have wanted to tell you himself, I'm sure, if it hadn't been for his mother. As it was, I took the decision you should know immediately.'

'Quite right, Grady,' said Brind.

'I drove. So as not to waste time.'

'Parked in the yard,' said Brind. 'Gave permission.'

'Of course, I went to your house first, but there was no one at home. Your maid was out somewhere. So I came here, knowing this to be your place of work. I must have only just missed you at home, as it happens; I probably passed you in my own car as you were walking to work. Well, I got here, I explained my business, and the Colonel was highly understanding, and said that as it happened he had a meeting with you himself at half nine, and that as like as not you'd be on your way to it at that moment, as it was your habit to walk to work, and that I was most welcome to wait for you here. So it's all worked out very nicely.'

'Get on with it, Grady,' said Brind.

Again, Grady sighed, stretched out his hands and closed them.

'It's about your wife, Major Lovegrove. I'm afraid I have bad news.'

Harry felt the muscles in his stomach tense.

'Emily? What do you – That O'Connor. You're from St Mary's?'

'2 i/c,' confirmed the Colonel.

'She was found this morning. By a man walking his dog. Washed up, on the beach. We checked her room. There's a nurse on duty all the night through, only a step down the corridor. She'd got out the window. It was open. We can't put a lock on the windows, Major Lovegrove, we can't, the poor women would suffocate in the summer.'

'Washed up? Is she –'

Grady blessed himself and bent in prayer a moment.

'Drowned, the poor soul, drowned. I've no authority for saying this, Major Lovegrove, but myself, I'm convinced that the Lord has mercy on those poor souls whose minds are disturbed. He won't condemn her.'

'Dear God,' said Harry. A shiver ran through him. He clutched onto the sides of the chair. Poor Emily. Poor sick mad Emily. He'd almost forgotten he had a wife. And now he didn't have a wife any more. No, he did have a wife. A dead wife. A wife who'd killed herself. A much greater burden than a live wife, no matter how sick. A dead wife he'd betrayed with a woman who'd betrayed him.

'Thank you for coming in, Grady,' said Brind. 'Anything else?'

'She's been taken to the morgue. In Store Street. If you don't mind, sir... I can take you in my car, though it's only a step... it will have to be you. To identify her.'

He'd have to look her in the eye. And with no chance now to tell her the truth about him and Aisling. Or the truth about how it had ended. So much he could have said, should have said. Too late now.

'Straight there, Lovegrove,' said Colonel Brind. 'Take the rest of the day off. And Monday. Long as you need. Man can't work at a time like this. If you'd been in France you'd have been sent home. Soon as the inquest is done, take her home. Lay her to rest in... Norfolk, isn't it?'

'Yes, sir.'

Norfolk. The home of his happy childhood. But he couldn't go back there. Everyone in the village would be whispering behind his back about Emily Where would he go? His brother had gone to India. A lot of men had done that after the war, unable to cope with England any more. Maybe he would follow his brother.

'Of course. Stafford's daughter,' said the Colonel. 'Blow for Stafford. Lost a son on the Somme, too, I heard. Like a lot of men.'

Harry tried to stand, found he couldn't, found his legs were weak under him.

'You don't look well, Lovegrove,' said the Colonel. 'Hardly surprising. Take three weeks leave.'

'Sir, if you don't mind...'

'No, insist. Need it. Deserve it. We've got murder by the throat here.'

He made a strangling gesture with his hands.

'When you come back, there'll be nothing left to do. Done your bit. Deserve a rest.'

He had to tell him. He had to tell him now or he'd never be able to.

'Sir, there is just one thing...'

'Leave it. Didn't you hear the man? Wife's waiting for you. Need to be with her.'

'It is of some urgency...'

'Can't be. Leave it till Monday.'

'Sir...'

'Monday. That's an order, Lovegrove.'

The Colonel stood. Grady stood. Harry hauled himself up, and took Grady's outstretched arm. He couldn't disobey an order. It would have to wait till Monday. In any case, he no longer felt strong enough to talk about Aisling to anyone.

The kaleidoscope of stained glass in the windows of Bewley's softened the sharp winter sunlight. It was always a little dark in here, even on a bright day. A vortex of chatter and cigarette smoke and the chink and clink of knives on plates gathered on the ground floor, swirled and drifted up to the floors above. It reminded Patrick a little of a noisier version of the Cathedral, what with the glass and the dark and the smoke and the people coming and going all day. The waitresses in their white and black were like women priests, flitting on busy errands amongst their people, guiding, directing, serving them. Saturday was their Sunday, when they were busiest. Patrick stood by the door, scanning the women's faces. After a couple of minutes, he saw Molly balancing a bowl of soup and a plate of sausages and mash, weaving her way diagonally across the room away from him. She delivered her burden to a stout, imposing man whose beard nearly reached down to his waistcoat and his little bird of a wife, who was barely four foot six. Patrick was surprised to see she was having the bangers and mash and he was having the soup. The man nodded gravely and the woman tossed Molly a smile. Molly half curtseyed. She turned, wiped her forehead with the back of her hand and pushed her hair back with the same gesture. Then she caught sight of Patrick. Triumph passed over her face. She walked towards him much more slowly than she had walked towards her customers.

'And what can I do for you, Mr Kelly?' she said, standing very close to him, talking very low. 'Is it a table you're after? Or something more?'

'Is there somewhere we can talk?'

'Did your man let you down after all?'

'It's that I want to talk about.'

Molly looked around the room, still keeping very close to him.

'Ah, if I'm seen talking to a man on duty, I'll be out, and there goes my rent. Take a table. There, that one, where your man's just getting up, that's one of mine. And I'll come and take your order. I like to see to it that my customers have satisfaction,' she finished, cocking an eyebrow and brushing her shoulder against his as she headed for the kitchen. Despite himself, desire stirred a little in Patrick. She was not such a bad looking woman when you thought of it; her looks had improved with marriage and widowhood.

He sat at the table, pushed a dirty teacup to one side, and swept a few crumbs off the table and into his hand, tipping them into the cup. He disliked disorder; it reminded him too much of home after Mam died. He also felt exposed in the midst of all these people. He'd not known any of the Squad to come in to Bewley's; it was too public, too well known. But you never knew. And Mick would go anywhere. Mick hid in plain sight. Always had done.

Molly bent over him, flicked her hair back, and took out a notebook, a pencil and a smile.

'Sir? What is it you'll be having today?'

'Listen carefully, Molly. I need you to do another thing. For me and for Ireland. Like when you got me into Mrs Maloney's. Only this is bigger. More important. More dangerous. Are you ready for some danger?'

'It's always been on the menu round here. It's one of my favourite dishes, only I never get to try it.'

'Good. Well listen, and, if you need to, write it down on that pad of yours. Only swallow the paper if you look like getting caught.'

Molly held her pencil to attention.

'You remember what I told you yesterday? About the sell-outs? The traitors within? The ones who are after shooting me because I won't kow tow to the English?'

Molly nodded. Patrick looked around the room.

'Well they're that close,' he said, holding up his finger and thumb an inch apart. 'That close to destroying the IRA. And with it any chance of freedom for Ireland.'

'What would you have me do? You know I'd die for Ireland. And for you.'

'I don't want you to die, Molly.'

A blush sprouted on Molly's face, and spread to her chest. She shifted on her feet, then stood even more attentive. It was working.

'Now. The man I was trying to see this morning. He's one of us. I can't tell you his name. I'd put you in danger if I did. But I need to make contact with him. Once he and I get together, there's hope. Hope for Ireland. They know that. That's why they've taken him.'

'Where?'

'You remember Annie McCarthy?'

Molly tossed her head back a little and laughed.

'Of course I do! Her and her messy house, all full of books. Oh, we had grand nights there, didn't we, the two of us, talking and talking and talking with her and her husband, till he dropped dead. She must have poisoned him; I never saw her wash up a cup.' Her face tensed. 'Is she still with us? Or is she with the sell-outs?'

He had her. There was not a shadow of doubt on her face.

'After the Rising, she worked for us. She was doing a good job, which I helped her with, running a safe house. She's perfect cover, because she's so slatternly and unmilitary like that no one would suspect her. The neighbours just think she's a mad woman. Now she's gone over to the other side, like so many. But she'll be doing the house still, and it's ten to one they'll have taken our man there. It's the number one safe house in Dublin.'

'You want me to get him out?'

'She'll have an armed man sitting outside his room, and the room locked. I know, because I've been that armed man. I can't go there, because they'll know me. Which is where you come in. As soon as you get off here, you go there. You tell her the truth, that you've just come back to town, since you were widowed and all. You have a good long chat about old times. But you say nothing – nothing – about me. You've not seen me since the Rising. And you say even less about your man upstairs. Look out for the carriage clock on the mantelpiece. When Annie goes into the kitchen to make you some tea or something, look behind it. She keeps the key to the bedroom there. Mick made her put it there, and there only, because she kept losing it. One man was nearly taken by the English because of her scatterbrain. Now, you pocket the key. After you've had your tea and your craic, you tell her you need the lavatory. It's upstairs, remember?'

'I remember. It was filthy.'

'It's even filthier now. The room where our man is kept is on that landing. There'll be one of the boys sitting outside it with a gun. You say hello. Be friendly like. You use the lavatory. Drink enough tea so you'll have to.'

Molly blushed again.

'Patrick Kelly!'

'Only the chain. Remember the chain?'

'Always getting stuck. She never had it fixed.'

'Still hasn't. So you come out, very coy, very embarrassed, tell your man the chain's stuck, would he give it a go? Make him want to be all gallant like. Then while he's in the bathroom, you put the key in this, and push it under the door of the room.'

Patrick reached in the pocket of his coat, and drew out a fat envelope. It had no writing on it. It had not been sealed. He pushed it into the pocket of Molly's apron. She lowered her hands to cover it, and briefly their hands touched. When he felt the pressure of her hands desire stirred again. He slapped it down.

'It contains orders. Orders for the defence of Ireland. You must absolutely swear in the name of God and all His saints not to open it or to read what is in it.'

'In the name of God and all His saints.'

'Then, when you're done, thank your man for the chain, thank Annie for the tea, and skedaddle. And thank God for what you've been able to do for Ireland.'

Molly was breathing hard. Patches of red had appeared on her throat.

'Thank you, Patrick. Thank you for trusting me.'

Patrick said nothing, just nodded. He couldn't look her in the face. He was good at lying, but not that good.

'Will I see you tonight? At Mrs Maloney's?'

'Of course you will. I'll be wanting a full report, won't I?'

'And will we...'

A woman from the table behind reached out and almost tugged at Molly.

'Miss? Are you going to be there all day? Only I'm parched for a tea.'

'So what was that, sir?' said Molly, lifting her pencil.

'Something quick,' said Patrick. 'A ham sandwich and a glass of milk.' He pulled his newspaper out of the pocket of his coat, snapped it open, and turned to the racing page. Molly wrote down his order, gave a little bob, and hurried off to the kitchen.

CHAPTER TWENTY-NINE

Harry leaned on Grady all the way to the morgue, because otherwise he might have fallen in the street. Grady had sense enough not to make him talk. Harry had seen men drowned in the mud in France and he knew what they looked and smelt like; bloated and blotched and blue and already stinking of decay. He felt sick in the stomach at the thought of seeing Emily like that. When they got to the morgue, he found it was an orange sandstone building, with crenellations like a castle, and a slab of a front door like a prison. It looked like the sort of building no one could get into and no one could get out of. Grady heaved at the front door, and held it open for Harry. The floor of the hall shone with polish, as if to keep out the stench of death. There was a desk at the end of the hall, and behind it, a neat, dapper little man with a moustache, a heavy book and a pen.

'Morning, Mr Grady,' said the man.

'Morning, Mr McConnell,' said Grady.

'You know each other?' said Harry.

'Only very slightly,' said Grady. 'It's been a long time, hasn't it, Mr McConnell.'

'Too long. That is, not long enough,' said McConnell. 'It's about the lady you've come?'

'I have, Mr McConnell.'

'You've timed it well. It's just a quarter of an hour she's been here. The boys have just taken her downstairs.'

'This unfortunate gentleman here is her husband.'

McConnell put down his pen, stood, and shook Harry's hand, patting the back of it with his other hand.

'Well, I'm sorry for your trouble, sir, so I am.'

So it had come to this. The Irish carrying him down the street and stroking his hand like a sick old woman.

'Thank you.'

'May the Lord have mercy on her soul,' said McConnell, blessing himself.

'As He surely will,' added Grady, also blessing himself.

'Should I not see the body?' asked Harry.

'Of course, sir. If you'd follow me.'

McConnell led them down winding stone steps to the basement and opened a pair of heavy double doors into a long, cold room, lit by slanting light from high windows. It was like a hospital where no one got better. Trolleys neatly lined up, men on one side, women on the other. Bodies and faces covered, labels tagged on their feet. Harry realised that the twins he'd had shot must have come here. Did they lie next to each other, as if they were back in their childhood bedroom? Sean Kelly, who he'd called Patrick, might still be here - if he went up and down the line of men, pulling back the sheets, perhaps he could look into his eyes one last time. But then Sean had never looked him in the eyes. And most likely he wouldn't have a face, or eyes, to look into any more.

'This is her, sir,' said McConnell, pointing to the trolley nearest them. He picked up a bucket from the corner, and placed it discreetly under the trolley. 'Some men find they need this, sir. It's no cause of shame.' With brisk, neat movements, he rolled back the sheet.

Emily looked nothing like the drowned men in France. Her face was undamaged, and the soft complexion she had always had, the girlish openness that had first attracted him on the lawn at her father's house, was still there. Her thin blonde hair had been dried, or had dried of its own accord, and spread itself generously on the pillow and around her swan-like neck as it used to do when she slept. They said the dead looked peaceful. Emily didn't look peaceful. But nor did she look troubled. She was devoid of all emotion, all movement. She would never again twitch and tremble and weep and cry uncontrollably. She would never again mutter to herself in the night. She would never again turn away from him and bundle up in a ball and screech in fear when he came to her naked and erect. She would never again lie all day in bed, staring at the ceiling, impenetrably silent. And she would never again laugh without restraint like a little girl, or thrash him at tennis, or let him chase her round a lake, or skip from rock to rock on a Norfolk beach, or tell him breathlessly of how she and her brothers fought the Spanish Armada in the shallows all through a childhood day soaked in the light and sun of the first summer of the new century, before she grew up, before the war, before everything. Harry reached out and stroked first one cheek, then another, with the back of his hand. 'I'm sorry, Emily,' he said quietly. 'I'm sorry you couldn't be happier. I'm sorry

I wasn't a better husband to you.' Then he turned back to McConnell.

'That's her, Mr McConnell. That's my wife.'

'Thank you, Major Lovegrove,' said McConnell. 'Now, if you could just come back upstairs with me.' He replaced the sheet as tidily as he had unrolled it, and led them back through the double doors, and up the stone steps. Now that he'd seen her, now that he'd looked the worst in the face, Harry found he could walk without Grady's help.

'There are papers to sign,' went on McConnell. 'And there'll be the inquest. Colonel Brind has already telephoned. I understand he's anxious to deal with matters swiftly, to let you take Mrs Lovegrove home. And to let yourself have a rest from your duties. We've a slot on Monday, and if all goes as it should, which I've no reason to doubt, you should be in a position to sail with her as early as Monday night.'

'We couldn't lock the windows, sir,' said Grady. 'What if there'd been a fire, now? Of course we thought of it, but –'

'Please don't worry, Mr Grady,' said Harry. 'It would have happened anyway. One way or another.'

Lying on the scratchy blanket in the bedroom in Annie's house, coughing and wheezing a little with the dust, Aisling felt strangely happy now that she knew, knew the truth at last. The truth, the honest truth before God, was that she loved Harry. She wanted to be with him and never be parted from him. For all he was English and married and had killed Patrick's friends and all that, she loved that man, loved him more than her life. Nothing else mattered. Now, when he would be dead in a matter of hours and she would never see him again, it was clear at last, the clearest thing there had ever been in her whole life.

She could hear voices from downstairs. Annie had a friend round, another woman. They sounded like they hadn't seen each other in a while; they were having a good old gas. Outside the sky was turning red. It must be about half past four. Eight hours since she'd gone out to buy bacon, and she hadn't come back. Harry would be worrying about her, she hoped. Could he have any idea where she was? She wondered how that woman Annie could have such a filthy house and not die of shame. She'd made herself eat the toast and eggs Annie had brought her, trying not to touch the grease on the bottom of the plate, but only because she was half fainting with hunger.

She heard steps on the stair. The strange woman's voice.

'Good afternoon to you.'

A grunt from Vinnie. The woman walked to the toilet. Aisling heard her using it. Heard her struggling with the clanking chain, just as she had, humiliatingly.

'Oh, excuse me, sir.' The woman again. 'Only I can't get the chain to work. I think you know the workings of the house better than me. Would you be so kind?'

Another grunt from Vinnie. His steps. Then a scratching sound, like a mouse. It was coming from the door. Aisling looked over. An envelope was nudging its way under the door, little by little. It was struggling because there was something thick and hard inside it. One last push, and it was in, sliding across the floor to her.

The toilet flushed. Vinnie came back.

'Thank you, sir. You're a true gentleman, so you are. I'd have done it myself, only...'

Again, a grunt. Vinnie couldn't talk to women, she could tell. The woman's steps, down the stairs. She waited until she had heard the competitive exchange of goodbyes with Annie, then climbed down from the high bed, went over to the door and picked up the envelope.

There was no name or address on it, and it was not sealed. Inside there were two sheets of paper, tightly written over, and a key on a piece of string. If she knelt on the bed and held it up to the window, there was just enough light for her to read the writing. It was oddly like the writing on the letter she had picked up from Harry's mat.

Saturday 20th November, 1920

Dear Aisling,

By rights I ought to be on a boat to England by now, and starting a new life. I am staying in Ireland for one reason and one reason only. That reason is you. I love you, Aisling, like life itself. And my life is truly in danger. I sent Sean a note at the last minute warning him to get out because I would not have my own brother shot, traitor though he was. Mick's boys found the note and shot Sean and now they would have me shot. I need to get out. I will get out. But I want to get out with you.

Inside this envelope you will find the key to the room where they are keeping you. I know where it is kept because I used to do the guard duty in Annie's house. I have asked an old friend to find the key and pass you this envelope as a favour to me. Tomorrow morning I believe there will be no guard because every man Jack is needed for a big operation, in which I would myself have taken part. I will not do so, because I have had enough of killing. I am a killer no more. I will be at the docks outside the ticket booth for sailings to England. I will be there at eight o'clock, and will wait for you. If you do not come, I will get on the quarter to nine boat to England and try to forget you. But if you come, I will buy your ticket too and we can sail together. When we get to England we can be married. My cousin Jim has a pub called The Wild Goose in Hammersmith in London and he will give me a job and I will have enough to keep the two of us. I swear I will do all I can to make you the happiest woman that ever lived. If you cannot return my love, I pray to God that you will get out of Annie's house safe and sound and live happy and blessed all your days.

I am a man of action not words but I could not go to England or my grave or wherever I am bound without telling you how dearly and deeply I love you. Please God you will be able to get out and come tomorrow. I will be waiting for you.

Patrick

She folded the letter once, twice, and put it back in the envelope. She pressed the envelope down on her lap with her left hand, and made a fist with her right hand, clutching the key so tight it dug into her. She looked out of the window and saw night come down over the city. She was glad to be in the dark alone, to think. Though she had already decided what she was going to do, even before she got to the end of Patrick's letter.

CHAPTER THIRTY

Harry walked home, refusing Grady's offer of a lift, his tread slow, his eyes cast down, his head full of Emily's vacant face in the morgue, not noticing the cold, not noticing the other people on the street, the spy no more. He understood why Brind wanted to send him back to England. He was no use to anyone here. When he got back to Lower Mount Street, he walked up the front steps, put his key in the lock, and pushed open the front door. He closed the door behind him, and leant back on it. Though the house was empty, it seemed to be full of a great weight pressing against him, stopping him from moving.

There was a letter on the mat for Emily, addressed in her mother's handwriting. She still wrote dutifully, brisk briefings on small movements in the parish council and the War Widows' League. Harry always read them out to Emily. He would have to telegraph her parents. No, better to write. He had a feeling they would not be surprised. The church where they had married for the funeral, a quiet service, and then the family vault. He could put it about that it was an accident; a fall from her window into the sea. There would be the inquest's verdict of course, but that would be in Dublin, and he'd be gone. Perhaps for good. Enough of Ireland; enough of this skulking war. Maybe enough of England, too. He might join his brother in India. He imagined himself sitting on a veranda in shimmering heat, the sun glaring at him off the dust, and felt a brief little thrill of elation. But then he looked down the hall into the empty kitchen, and thought of Aisling, realised he missed her, realised he loved her, and realised he would never see her again. He screwed up his eyes tight and, feeling two warm tears run down his face, clenched his fist and banged it against the door once, twice; three times. *Oh, Aisling, come back now. I forgive you. I hate this bloody war between our countries. I was fighting for mine and you were fighting for yours, but let's stop now, and let's make peace, between us two at least. Let's get on a boat to India together. Let's start over again.*

Come on, Lovegrove. You're talking nonsense. Things to do. If there was to be a sailing on Monday, for him and for Emily, he had two days to turn around a full decamp. Notice to be given. Bills to be paid. Matters to be disposed of. Packing to be done. Her kit, his kit. He pushed himself away from the door, and ran up the stairs, taking them two at a time. He strode into the bedroom, flung open the door of her wardrobe, and wrenched out first one of Emily's many unused dresses, then another, then another, then another, throwing them on to the bed like prisoners being rendered immobile.

For all the long talks with Molly and Annie and all the others and all the books that Molly had pressed into his hands, Patrick was not a reading man. When he was on his own, he had nothing to do but smoke and think. He lay on his bed smoking and thinking by the gas light in his bedroom at Mrs Maloney's after dinner that night. Jim would give him a good welcome in London, he knew. He'd always had good craic with Jim. According to Jim, the Irish stuck together in London; it was as good as Dublin-by-the-Thames. Work in a bar would be all right. It would be sociable work, a welcome change from the boredom and loneliness of the Squad. It wouldn't be such a bad life, even without Aisling. He tried not to think of Aisling not coming tomorrow, to wish away the thought. Molly knocked again.

'Come in.'

She was carrying a cup of tea.

'Mrs Maloney insisted. As last night. He's working so hard up there. As you aren't. She's half in love with you, Patrick Kelly. Did you not see the way she was looking at you all through dinner? You want to watch yourself.'

'I will.'

She put the tea on the table by Patrick's bed, and pulled up the chair from the desk and sat on it next to him.

'So. Do you not want to hear what I got up to this afternoon?'

Patrick stubbed out his cigarette and sat up on the bed. He felt tensed and ready for action, although all he had to do was listen.

'I do.'

'Annie didn't suspect a thing. Or didn't show it if she did. I told her the story we agreed. We had a good old talk about times past. The fallen heroes. And her crazy ideas for the future. She's going to be President of Ireland, would you believe? She could start by taking charge of her house before she takes charge of the country. It's filthier than ever. I had to hold my nose going to the toilet.'

'But you went?'

'I did. And I found the key too, just where you said it was. I put it in the envelope. And under the door while your man was in the lav. All according to plan. Mission accomplished.'

She gave a little mock salute. Patrick felt a surge of relief.

'Grand. That's absolutely grand. Good lass, Molly. You've done your bit for Ireland, and no mistake.'

Molly blushed.

'I didn't do it for Ireland. I did it for you.'

'It's Ireland that'll benefit.'

'Good, well I'm happy for Ireland. But as far as I'm concerned, at the moment it's us that matters more. Patrick, I wanted to say –'

Patrick reached over and put his hand on her wrist. He steeled himself, as if he was going into battle.

'Stop there, Molly. I have something to tell you first. Tomorrow morning, I have to leave early. I have every hope the prisoner will escape, and I have to make a rendezvous with him. And then he and I have to go into hiding for a long time. I've paid Mrs Maloney for two days. Explain to her I was called away suddenly back home. You'll finish up with our uncle.'

'Patrick, I want you to –'

'I won't be coming back here, Molly. You won't be seeing me again. I'm a dead man if I stay in Dublin. And you'll be a dead woman if you stay with me.'

He could feel her hand shaking under his, and he saw tears forming in her eyes. He tried to blank her out, like Sean used to say to do with a man you were shooting.

'But last night...'

'For your sake – for your own personal safety – try to forget last night, Molly.'

She snatched her hand away suddenly, and made it into a fist, which she rubbed hard and quick with her other hand.

'But why did you...'

He lay on the bed and turned his face to the wall. He couldn't look at her any more.

'I don't know, Molly. I really don't know. Let's just say... oh, I don't know why. I'm sorry, Molly.'

Now she was sobbing and swallowing hard.

'You bastard, Patrick Kelly. You absolute fucking bastard. I hope they do find you, and they do shoot you, and I hope you burn in Hell afterwards.'

'Don't you go saying anything to anyone, now, Molly, or they'll shoot you too. You know that. I'm sorry, Molly. I'm so sorry. This is what a soldier has to do. You need to stop falling in love with soldiers.'

'Well fuck all soldiers then.'

She stood up, turned her back on him, and walked out, still sobbing. He turned to watch her go and then he punched the pillow, very hard. 'I'm sorry, Molly,' he said to the door. Then he reached over, turned out the gas light, and flopped on to his back on the bed in the dark. Molly was right. He was a fucking bastard. He did deserve to burn in hell. He'd been a traitor to Ireland, a traitor to his brother and a traitor to Molly. Aisling was all he had left. And, like as not, she'd be a traitor to him. He lay on his bed for a long time thinking about Aisling, imagining London with her, imagining London without her, trying to block out the sound of Molly's weeping from the room above, until he fell asleep in his clothes.

CHAPTER THIRTY-ONE

Harry worked through the night in a fury, whirling from one room to another, using up half a dozen candles, lighting one from the stub of another, ripping up papers, stacking shirts, counting cuff links, packing trunks, addressing envelopes, marshalling his life in all its fragments. He found the note he had written to Aisling and left on the dining room table, and he screwed it up and threw it in the stove. He sat at his desk and for three hours straight wrote letters and lists, looking up only to dip his pen in the ink. All the while he felt panic looming, looking just over his shoulder, waiting to pounce. The only way to keep it away was to keep active. It was like when he worked in the night to keep away the nightmares of France, only much, much worse. Just before dawn, his head swirling with sleeplessness, he pushed open the door to Aisling's room, forgetting it was hers. He stood for a moment and looked at the rosary hanging off the bedpost and the sad single bed. Then, at last, the tears came, and he doubled up on the floor, next to his candle, and sobbed loud and long for a good half hour, remembering what had been and what might have been, until the candle was burnt out and he was empty. After that, he went back to his study, wrote one last letter, his eyes so red and raw he could hardly see to write, tucked four five pound notes in the envelope, and put it on the hall table with the rest. Exhaustion crashed over him like a wave. He changed into his pyjamas, got into bed, and fell asleep straight away. He didn't hear the bells for early Mass.

Aisling was woken by the bells for early Mass; there was a church right next door to Annie's house. For all it was a scratchy bed and she was sleeping in her clothes, she had slept better than she had all week. She felt calm, resolved, just as she had done when the Tans had woken her. She knew exactly what she had to do. She clutched the key to her room tight in her hand, and in her other hand she held her purse and the front door key for number 23, Lower Mount Street. She could still hear Vinnie snoring outside. The Mass bells slowed to a toll and stopped. She heard Annie come down the stairs from her room.

'Vinnie?'

A grunt.

'Vinnie?'

She was whispering as if she did not want Aisling to hear.

'Vinnie. It's time for you to wake up. Time for you to go now. Mick said. You know what to do? Where to go?'

'I do. Thank you, Miss Annie. Thank you for your... hospitality. I'll be going now, but I'll be back soon. I should be back by ten, God willing. Wish me luck, now.'

'That I will. God bless you, and God bless Ireland.'

'Amen.'

Aisling heard Vinnie's chair creak; heard his heavy steps down the stairs. She heard Annie use the toilet, and struggle with the chain, like everyone else. Jesus, did the woman never think of getting it fixed? Then she heard Annie go back up the stairs to her room. Oh, thanks be to God, she was a long sleeper; she was one for lying in on Sundays. Aisling waited until the Mass bells had stopped, to be sure, then she climbed out of bed and unlocked the door. She opened the door a crack and looked up and down the landing. No one. Nothing. She slipped out of the door through as narrow a crack as she could manage and walked with soft steps down the stairs and out of the front door, closing it behind her so gently she was almost stroking it. She felt excited and terrified in equal measure. She wrapped her shawl round her and turned left down Hill Street past the high Georgian houses, onto Great Britain Street past the shuttered shops, onto Sackville Street past the burnt out Post Office, past two girls arm in arm hurrying late to early Mass at the Cathedral, past a British soldier finishing off a dirty joke to his friend who laughed and slapped him on the back, past Reiss's jewellers where Patrick had held up her hand and picked out a ring for her three days before. She felt time pressing down on her as if it was chasing her. If only she could be in time, please God, if only she could get there in time.

When she got to Sackville Bridge she threw one glance east down the Liffey to the docks, and gave a brief smile, as if acknowledging a compliment from a stranger. *Thank you, Patrick*, she said softly to herself. *God bless you for your kindness.* Then she took a deep breath and walked forwards over the bridge, fast. She would have run, except that a woman running in the street was liable to be stopped by a soldier or a policeman or just a concerned man, and the last thing she wanted now was to be stopped.

Patrick had heard the Mass bells roll down the Liffey, carried out towards the sea by the wind from the west, as he stood by the door to the ticket office of the Dublin Steam Packet Company, catching the early morning sun. He'd woken early, still in his clothes, as he knew he would; he never needed a call or an alarm. He'd taken off his shoes as he walked down the stairs of Mrs Maloney's house to be sure not to wake her. Maloney's drunken snores came from their bedroom down the landing. He'd been relieved not to see Molly. He wrote out a note on the back of one of Mrs Maloney's shopping lists, and left it on the breakfast table. He couldn't trust Molly to tell his story.

It was a mild day. He was wearing his three days' clothes; his only clothes. He had eight cigarettes left. He'd had one on his way here, walking through the early morning streets, as the sun came up, his collar turned high, his head down, and another when he'd got here. He'd bought his ticket from a man with a tight little moustache behind a grille like a confessional.

'What is it takes you to England?' the man had said.

'Ah, sure, I'm hoping I'll find some work there. I've a cousin runs a pub in London says there's always a space for me behind the bar.'

'You could be better off there than here. Them shootings in the street are still going on.'

If only you knew what's going to happen this morning, thought Patrick. If you only knew.

He looked at his watch. Twenty to nine. Still no Aisling. He remembered what Mick had said, when he'd first spoken to them about today; about the knockout blow they'd be giving the English. 'If we do it, we'll need to show those whores, the English, that the Irish can be on time,' Mick had said. 'We'll strike at nine exactly. All across the city.' In twenty minutes his rival for Aisling's love would be dead. But Aisling wasn't here. Where was she?

The *S.S. Mersey Queen* sounded its hooter. It looked restless and uncomfortable, outsized in the narrow little river dock, eager to be off. A sailor called from the top of the gangplank.

'Are you coming aboard or not? Last chance to go to England.'

Well, that was it. She wasn't coming. Maybe Mick had kept the guard on her room; or maybe she'd got out, but decided she didn't want to go with him. That was the end of it, one way or another. Now he had no money, no job, no family, no one to love him. He was still in love with Aisling all right, though, and he always would be. He could have made a life with her; a home, children, doing a proper job. He could have done it, could have been like other men. He felt bitterly disappointed. Now all that was gone, and he wouldn't be surprised if he didn't go the way of his Da, getting married to the bottle. Especially working in Jim's pub. He'd have to watch that. He wasn't in love with fighting any more, though. He wouldn't miss the Squad. It was a dirty, vicious business, shooting men in their beds, no longer the heroic sacrifice he'd signed up for at Easter 1916. He wanted to be on the high seas and away before it all happened, not least because he had a hunch that the English would as good as burn down Dublin afterwards in their anger. Come on, Kelly, he told himself. This is where you start again. London's your city now. You have to try and forget her.

He threw down his cigarette, ground it under his heel, and strode up the gangplank. He hoped the boys would do the job properly with Lovegrove. And please God they'd spare Aisling.

CHAPTER THIRTY-TWO

Now Aisling was in Merrion Square, sweeping past the big white houses, feeling as if she was flying. *Please God please God please God let him be there, let him be safe. Holy Mary and all the saints watch over him.* Would they have shot him yet? Would he be waiting for her? Would he be gone? Would he throw her out for playing cat and mouse with him like she had? She turned into Lower Mount Street, counting the houses off as she passed them, flicking one last look over her shoulder to check no one was following her. The street was empty. She took the front steps in two leaps, and put her key in the door.

In the hall there was a large trunk, sealed with a thick leather belt. On top of the trunk were three suitcases stacked on top of each other, the largest on the bottom and the smallest on the top. He was getting ready to leave. He must know it was going to happen. But he didn't know it was going to happen this morning, or he'd have been gone already. On the hall table, evenly spaced in a neat column, were envelopes addressed to the butcher, the draper, the baker, Colonel and Mrs W.J. Stafford of Norfolk, Colonel G.C.J. Brind of Dublin Castle, and, at the bottom, Miss Aisling O'Flaherty.

Aisling picked up the envelope addressed to her. She felt the crinkle of notes inside it. She thrust it into the band of her dress. There would be time to open it later. In any case, she didn't want his money. She wanted him. And she wanted him alive.

She ran up the stairs three at a time and pushed open the door to his room. He was curled up, fast asleep, holding his pillow. The doors of the wardrobe were swinging open, and it was stripped empty. There was nothing on either bedside table. He looked utterly exhausted.

'Harry,' she called to him from the door. He stirred, turned, and went on sleeping. She walked towards the bed. She felt strangely nervous, not wanting to disturb him when he was so peaceful, so calm, so oblivious of what was going to happen. She knelt by the bed. 'Harry,' she said. Still he slept. She stroked his face, his soft, kind face, first with the back of her hand, then with the front. She caught the leathery tang of his skin again. 'Harry, it's me. Aisling. I've come back.'

He opened his eyes.

'Aisling. Good God. I thought you'd gone. Gone for good.'

'Well I'm here.'

She leaned over and kissed him, long and deep. She wanted to go on kissing him, to climb into bed with him, to make love to him slowly and carefully, to savour every touch. But there was no time.

'It's not safe for you to stay here a minute longer,' she said. 'I've come to tell you. And also to tell you that I love you.'

'Thank you, Aisling. I love you too.' He took her hands, pulled her towards him, and kissed her, and then he lay back and looked at her, still holding her hands. She knew then. She knew from his face that what he said was true, that he loved her, that he would never leave her.

He sat up, rubbed his eyes, looked around him.

'Aisling. Emily's dead.'

Had he killed his wife? Was she always to be surrounded by killing?

'Oh dear God. How?'

'She drowned herself.'

Aisling gave a little gasp of relief, then felt a twinge of shame.

'She got out of the window and into the sea. She finished what she started last Saturday night.'

'Oh Mother of God. May she rest in peace. She was a good lady, a kind lady. But is it a judgement on us, do you think?'

Now she feared he might be slipping away from her, that he might turn away from her in his guilt and his shame. But he took her hands in his.

'No, Aisling. My wife was a very sick woman. It wasn't your fault. It wasn't my fault. We both did our best for her. And now we must do our best for ourselves. Why did you go? Why didn't you come back yesterday?'

'I was taken.'

'Who by?'

'The IRA.'

'Why?'

'They're after someone I know. But I escaped. I escaped and came back to you. Because I love you, Harry. I didn't know that. Or I did know it, but I didn't want to know it, because I was afraid of what I felt. But I know it now. I knew it as soon as I heard they were going to kill you.'

There were tears in his eyes. She wiped them away with her fingers, gently. She put her fingers in her mouth, tasting the salt of his tears. She knew they had to get out of the house, but she didn't want to leave. She wanted to be here forever with him, didn't want this moment to stop.

'That's a soldier's life, Aisling. People trying to kill you. People spying on you. You spied on me, didn't you, Aisling?'

Again she feared he would slip from her when he said that. She held onto his hands tightly as if this would keep him. But she didn't want to lie to him.

'Yes. Yes, I did. I broke into your desk and copied out your notebook.'

'Why?'

'To get back at the bastards who killed my father. Is that enough reason?'

'You betrayed Sean Kelly. You cost a man his life.'

'Ah. They killed him, so?'

'They did.'

'But I had fewer men killed than you did. It's a war, isn't it? That's what it is. Your country against mine. Traitors have to be punished in a war. And I'm a traitor. I've fallen in love with my enemy. I've fallen in love with one of the bastards who killed my Da.'

'And I've fallen in love with one of the people who would kill me. I should be calling the police now and having you arrested. Instead, I'm giving you that – ' he pointed to the envelope tucked into the band of her dress – 'to start a new life somewhere else.'

'I want to start a new life somewhere else, but with you, Harry. That's why you need to get dressed now and get out, because they're coming for you, for you and all the others, this morning, any minute –'

'They're here.'

It was Rory who spoke. He stood in the doorway with his gun out. Vinnie was just behind him, with a sledgehammer in his hand.

'Nice of you to leave the door open for us. Vinnie didn't need the hammer after all. Put it down, Vinnie, you need both hands for a killing.'

Vinnie placed the sledgehammer carefully on the floor, came to stand next to Rory, and held his gun out with both hands. Aisling climbed into bed with Harry and put her arms tight round his neck. He put his arms round her and held her to him. In spite of the two guns pointed at her, she felt safe. She felt that she could come to no harm, and neither would he, as long as he held on to her. She would be happy enough if they shot them both now. She couldn't imagine ever being any happier.

'Shall we kill the bitch, Vinnie?' asked Rory.

'Our orders are only for Lovegrove, Rory. Only for him,' said Vinnie. 'She's one of ours, for all she escaped. We'll take her back to Annie's and deal with her there.'

Aisling held tighter to Harry. She did not feel like one of theirs. She felt like his, and he felt like hers.

'She's fucking an Englishman. She's a traitor,' said Rory.

'I'm not going anywhere,' she said. 'Kill him, you kill me.'

'I'm killing yous both,' said Rory.

'You're not, Rory,' said Vinnie. 'You'll answer to Mick if you do. We're taking her back to Annie's.'

Rory pointed his gun directly at Aisling.

'I'm after killing the bitch,' he said. 'Fuck Mick.'

It happened very quickly then. Vinnie dropped his gun, darted across the room, circled his hands round Aisling's waist, and pulled at her. Harry held on to her as tight as he could, but he was lying down and Vinnie was standing. Vinnie dragged her back across the room, her feet scraping on the floor. Harry started to get out of the bed. Rory opened fire. The first bullet hit Harry in the chest, and sent him flat on his back on the bed. The second also hit him in the chest, and made him buckle and twitch. Then Rory walked up to him and fired into his face, and the pillow was all smeared with blood and bone and brain.

Vinnie held on to Aisling through all this. She twisted and squirmed and screamed as she watched Harry die, feeling each bullet as if it was firing into herself. She wanted to snatch the gun off Rory and put it in her mouth and blow out her own brains and lie there on the bed with Harry and never leave him. After the last shot, she turned from the sight and buried her face in Vinnie's chest and beat her fists against his shoulders, hating him for saving her.

'Let me go,' she sobbed into him. 'Let me go. I want to die. I want to die like him.' 'I'm sorry, Miss,' said Vinnie. 'I know you done good work for us. Now let's get you back to Annie's.'

'I'm still after shooting her,' said Rory. 'We can tell Mick she was caught in the crossfire.'

'Go on!' said Aisling. 'Shoot me! You'd be doing me a favour, you cowardly bastard, but I don't think you've got the balls.'

Splintered Cockney shouts came up from the street.

'Auxies,' said Vinnie, picking up his sledgehammer. 'Come on, Rory, let's get out. Leave the woman now. There's no time. There's a door to the backyard through the kitchen. We can climb over the wall to the alley from there – safer than the front door. We've done our work. You get out of Ireland, Miss, if you know what's good for you.'

'We'll find you,' said Rory. 'Even if you go to the ends of the earth we'll find you.'

'Come on, Rory. The Auxies'll be here any minute.'

'We'll find you,' said Rory.

'Rory, come on,' said Vinnie, tugging at him by the arm. Aisling heard them go down the stairs and through the kitchen and out the back door, into the little yard.

She couldn't bear to look at Harry's beautiful face all ruined and shattered on the pillow. And yet she needed to hold him. She ran to the bed and closed her eyes and buried her face in his chest, feeling his wiry hairs against her cheek, the hairs all tangled with his sticky blood. Oh dear God, what had she done to deserve this? To see the two men she'd loved killed in front of her, one by her enemies, one by her countrymen? Was God punishing her for her sin? Harry was still warm; she could almost believe he was alive, that his soul hadn't left his body yet. She was glad she'd told him she loved him. She squeezed him tighter as if that would bring him back to life, lifting his body off the bed. But then when she released him he fell back lifeless. Still she wouldn't let him go. She whispered to him, telling him again and again how much she loved him, how happy he'd made her.

She heard shouts from the street, and boots coming up the stairs. Would it be Rory, back with some pals to finish the job? She blessed herself, took a deep breath and got ready to die.

Two Auxies ran into the room, rifles pointed, breathless, eyes flicking this way and that. Aisling felt strangely relieved to see them; at least she was no longer alone.

'Jesus!' said one. 'Look at what the bastards have done.'

'Fuck me,' said the other. 'Are they still here?'

'No,' said Aisling. 'They're long gone.'

'Are you his wife?' asked the first Auxie.

'No. I'm not his wife.'

'You're Irish, aren't you?'

'Yes. I'm Irish all right.'

'So are you one of them or are you one of us?' asked the second Auxie, cradling his rifle close. He pointed it at Aisling and drew a circle in the air with it as if he was measuring her up. Aisling stood up slowly. Harry's blood was all down the front of her dress. She didn't know what to say. But she thought that if Rory had killed her and had told Mick that she'd been caught in the crossfire, he wouldn't have been far wrong. Not far wrong at all, at the end of it.

CHAPTER THIRTY-THREE

The goose was thin as an arrow and its wings were blown back by the wind into a sharp V shape. By its face it looked as if it was desperate to get somewhere, but it didn't know where. This was the place all right, thought Aisling, looking up at the picture on the sign as she stood amongst the deserted wooden benches and empty ashtrays of the pub's terrace. She didn't expect anyone to be sitting outside on a sharp February afternoon like this one; but she couldn't see anyone inside, either, and that worried her. The wind off the Thames behind her bit into her face and made her skin feel raw. London seemed colder than Dublin, though she had to admit it rained less. She looked up at the top windows. He'd have a nice view of the river if that was his room. She rattled at the door of the Public Bar and found it locked. Of course; pubs had had to close every afternoon ever since the war with Germany. At home there would have been a back door open, but in England, she'd noticed, people seemed to think that laws were for keeping.

Normally, on a Sunday, Aisling went across the road to Regent's Park with a few of the girls after eleven mass and lunch in the servants' hall, but this week she'd told them she was meeting a friend, and had taken the tram down to Hammersmith. It had been good to make the journey on her own and have some time to think.

She'd been lucky so far, she knew. After they'd found her, the Auxies had taken her to their barracks, where a nervous little man with captain's pips and a twitching eye had questioned her. She'd been able to get away without saying a word of a lie: she was his maid, she'd been in the house when the gunmen had come, she'd seen it all happen, she couldn't stop them, naturally she was distressed, he was a good man, he'd been good to her. After three hours they'd let her go. She'd not even gone back to the house, heading, instead, straight for the docks where she got on the two o'clock boat, hiding the blood down her dress with her tightly wrapped shawl. She had to get out, now; both the English and the Irish had reason to finish her off. The boat was the only way. After the killings across the city that morning, the trains had been stopped and no motor traffic was allowed. As well as seeing her on to the boat to Liverpool, Harry's money had put her on a train to London, and had left her enough for a new set of clothes and a few days in a boarding house. She'd found the position in the big house in Albany Street within a week, helped by the reference Harry had tucked into the envelope. Mercifully, she'd been the only Irish girl there. She'd been able to tell an almost true story about having lost a sweetheart in the 'troubles',which explained away her crying jags in the middle of the night. The other girls were kind to her; several of them had lost sweethearts or even husbands in the war with Germany, and they knew the story, knew what came after. The hours were long and didn't leave her too much time to think. She began to believe that she might yet make a life in London.

But all that was coming to an end now. At first she'd prayed that it wouldn't be true, that it was a false alarm, but that time had passed; there was no more doubt. She was able to forget about it during the day because she was so busy, but it came back to her when she woke early in the morning. Now she had to face it. In a matter of weeks – no, days - she would lose her job and would be alone on the streets of London. There was still some of Harry's money left over, but when that ran out she would be finished.

She wondered if it was God's judgement on her. She'd made her confession soon after she'd arrived in London. She'd gone to the brand new Catholic cathedral in Westminster, with all its mosaics shining like you'd been carried off to another country, in the hope of finding a priest who wasn't Irish. After queuing a long time she ended up with a smooth, womanly man who sounded a deal posher than Harry. He'd been nice and all, let her stay in for a little cry, and said that he could tell that she was a good and loving soul, only that she'd put her love in the wrong place. When she'd finished her cry, he'd spoken of a new start and putting the past behind her. She'd knelt and said the Hail Marys he'd given her for her penance gratefully enough, but as she'd walked out of the Cathedral into a crowd of office workers pouring into Victoria Station, she'd realised that she couldn't put Harry in the past like packing away a winter dress in spring. He was with her still. His shattered face reared up at her in nightmares, leering at her, crying out to her for help. As she went through her daily duties, polishing silverware, ironing tablecloths, sweeping out grates, she felt Harry's touch and heard his voice; he was more real to her than the people around her. Sometimes she wanted to sing with joy when she thought of him, and sometimes she wanted to scream with rage. She and Rose had been polishing spoons together one day, and Rose had said, 'It's been three years since I got the telegram about Edward, and it's like he's sitting in that chair now, telling me I should be using my thumb for this bit. But it must be worse for you, Aisling.' Yes, she'd told Rose, it was worse for her, and they'd stopped for five minutes while she wept and Rose held her, until Mrs Smithson came in and told them to pull themselves together and get on. If Harry was here now, she thought, hourly. If he'd lived. Or if she'd died with him. But he wasn't. She hadn't. And anyways, even if he had lived, it could never have been. Irish Catholic girls from Connemara couldn't marry English Protestant soldiers from Norfolk. That was just the way the world was. That story about his friend Quinn – it could never have been, even if the German bullet hadn't got Quinn. The posh girl would never have done it.

She rattled at the door of the Public Bar again. Nothing. She didn't have long. She had to be back in Albany Street in time for supper. She'd have to come back next week, make sure to come earlier. But even one more week might be too late. She banged on the door. She called his name: once, twice. Then a third time, a desperate screech. Above her, a window was flung open, and a tousle haired man stuck his head out.

'What is it you're wanting now?'

For all her determination to avoid them in London, it was good to hear an Irish voice.

'It's Patrick Kelly I'm after,' she said.

'Well he's after having his sleep. That's what four pints of stout for lunch does for you. Who are you, miss, when you're at home?'

'Just tell him Aisling.'

'Are you his fancy woman?'

'Just tell him I'm here, will you.'

'Sure he needs a good woman. He needs looking after. It's only a good woman will be getting him off the drink. I'd have slung him out myself by now if he wasn't family.'

The man shook his head as if in despair, and disappeared inside. Aisling stepped back. She'd wait. She had to. She had nowhere else to go; nothing else she could do. She looked down the river, and saw the dizzying towers and sweeping cables of Hammersmith Bridge dwarf the people walking across it. A woman was leaning against the rail, looking down at the river. No. That was no way out. Whatever had happened, she wasn't Emily Lovegrove.

There was a fumbling and a clunking of locks and bolts, and the door to the bar opened. Patrick stood there, blinking in the winter sunlight, trousers and shirt and sweater all pulled on in haste, his curly hair springing up from his head as if it wanted to escape. She felt an immense relief at the sight of him. He'd lost weight; he'd gone from being slim to being skinny. His face looked beaten and tired, and she could see the remains of the drink in him. But that contained energy, like a tightly wrapped coiled spring, was still there. He was still a good looking fella all right. And it might not be too late to get him off the drink. At the end of it all, he was Aisling's only hope.

'Jesus,' he said. 'Aisling. If it isn't yourself.'

'If it isn't yourself, Patrick.'

'How did you find me?'

'You told me. You told me in the note your friend pushed under the door that you'd be working at your cousin's pub, The Wild Goose, in Hammersmith. London's big, but it's not that big.'

'But what are you doing in London?'

'It's a tale that takes some telling, and there's a sting in the end of it. Get your coat and we'll go for a walk by the river so and I'll tell you.'

Patrick still had his trenchcoat, but it no longer bulged with a gun. Aisling thought it looked a bit thin against the London cold. They walked towards Hammersmith Bridge, under its arches, past the warehouses on the other side. The sun blinked at them off the wide stretch of the river, while a car going over the bridge broke the silence and then was gone. It was quiet; London was quiet on a Sunday, quieter than Dublin, that was all full of people coming and going from Mass. Aisling remembered their walk by the Liffey, when she'd given Patrick what she'd copied from Harry's notebook. It seemed a lifetime away, and yet she felt right to be walking with him again, felt comfortable, as if she could tell him things. That was a good sign. She might be safe yet.

'You have work here?' he said.

'I've a place in a big house up in town. Albany Street.'

'Grand. Good on you.'

He walked on for a bit. He's still angry, thought Aisling.

'I thought you'd given up on me, you know,' he said. 'When you didn't get on the boat.'

'I did, then. But now I'm here.'

'They killed Lovegrove, didn't they? I read about it in the London papers. Him and fourteen others. Mick did a good job.'

Aisling swallowed hard, and blinked back the tears. She mustn't show him what she felt. Not now.

'They did.'

'And you were with him. So I read.'

'They killed him right in front of me. His blood down my dress.'

'After I got you out.'

The anger in his voice was sharp like a knife.

'I know, Patrick. Thank you for getting me out. I'm glad you did.'

'You went back to him.'

'They were after killing me, you know.'

'Rory, was it?'

'Himself.'

'The mad bastard. What stopped him?'

'Auxies.'

'Did they get you, the Auxies?'

'Yes. But they let me go. So I came here. Half of Dublin had reason to plug me, so I wasn't going to hang around.'

He was looking ahead, not at her. He wasn't after touching her. She wished he would at least look back at her, or make some sign he cared. But then she couldn't blame him, after what she'd done. He had no reason to help her now. Still less in the way she needed.

'You know the English evened the score?' he said. 'You heard about Croke Park?'

'The football match?'

'The same. That very afternoon. Fourteen killed by Tans and Auxies both. Men, women and children. One of them a girl a week from her wedding. Another a boy of ten years of age.'

'Are you still after fighting that war, Patrick? I thought you'd come here to get away from it.'

He sighed deeply, and thrust his hands into his coat pockets. The warehouse they were walking past blocked out the sun and threw a chill over them. A tugboat chugged up the river, pushing determinedly against the tide like an eager child. They walked without saying anything for a while, the rough gravel of the towpath crunching under their feet.

'You loved him, didn't you?' said Patrick at last.

Well, she saw now, she was going to have to tell him the truth. It wasn't like he was stupid. And it was the only way if this was going to work.

'Yes, Patrick. I did.'

'After what he did to Seamus and Colm? After what he did to a dozen other boys? After what his lot did to your Da?'

'After all that.'

He cursed under his breath, and then he fell silent again. He took out a cigarette and lit it as he walked. He turned away from her, blowing the smoke out at the river. The terraces of the football ground loomed up at them ahead, empty and silent. Maybe she should just give up now. It would save her from being humiliated at least. But give up and do what?

'Why did you come and find me?' he asked.

'To see... to see if you still felt the same way about me. The same way you said you did.'

'Haven't I thought about you every day? And every night?'

Her heart gave a little leap of hope. She felt it, physically, in her chest.

'You have?'

'Only, I've thought, why should I be bothering with a woman who prefers an English murderer to me?'

He took a last drag on his cigarette and flicked it in the river. She had to be bold now. What did she have to lose?

'Patrick,' she said. 'I loved him all right. I won't try to deny it. And I won't try to deny it was wrong. He was married, and he was English, and he was all you say. But... oh, we can't help the people we love.'

'You're right in that. I couldn't help loving my brother for all he was a bastard and a traitor. And for all you did what you did, and for all the man you did it with, I can't help loving you, Aisling O'Flaherty. And I think I will till the day I die. There. There, you've got it out of me now.'

She wanted to jump on him and kiss him then, just out of the relief of it. But she had to be patient. She wasn't done yet.

'Would you think of giving me another chance?' she said.

'I wouldn't think of it,' he said. 'I'd do it.'

'Grand. That's grand, Patrick. Only...'

'Only what, Aisling?'

'Only it wouldn't just be me you'd be taking on.'

He stopped dead at that. He turned to look at her. His look was like he was holding a gun at her.

'What's that you're saying, Aisling?'

'I'm saying that Harry Lovegrove's dead, and that I've left him behind in Dublin. But that he left a part of himself with me. And that if you took me on you'd have to take that part on as well, as if it were your own. Do you understand what I'm saying now, Patrick?'

Patrick stared at her a bit longer. He looked as if he'd been hit in the stomach. Then he turned his back on her and put his hands in his pockets and looked down the river, his eyes following it as it curved round and disappeared into the distance.

'Jesus,' he said softly. 'Jesus, Mary and Joseph. Would you believe it now?'

She'd said it at last. She'd said what she'd come to say. There was nothing more to do now than to wait, like a guilty man in the dock about to receive his sentence, wondering if he would be reprieved or if he would be shot.

HISTORICAL NOTE

'Bloody Sunday', as the events of November 21st 1920 became known, was a significant turning point in the Irish struggle for independence. As Patrick tells us, the killing of fourteen British Army officers by the IRA in the morning was matched in the afternoon by the shooting by the British of fourteen civilians at a football match at Croke Park. During the Queen's state visit to Ireland in 2011, she made a point of visiting Croke Park. This was a courageous act on Her Majesty's part, and rightly seen as a hugely significant gesture of reconciliation; the troops who had opened fire on that day had acted in the name of her grandfather.

The IRA action did serious damage to British intelligence, while the retaliation against civilians only strengthened popular support for the cause of independence. In July 1921 the British were forced to agree to a truce. However, Irish euphoria was short lived. Michael Collins was sent to London by his arch rival Eammon De Valera to negotiate with the wily British Prime Minister Lloyd George (thereby blowing his cover). Inevitably, he was forced to compromise on many of the Irish demands. The treaty he brought back split Ireland. De Valera refused to accept it and led his supporters out of the government; the country soon slid into a vicious and brutal civil war. What this war meant for Patrick, Molly, Aisling, and Harry and Aisling's child will become clear in *My Enemy's Enemy*, the sequel to *Whatever You Say, Say Nothing*.

ACKNOWLEDGEMENTS

I'm grateful to the authors of a number of books that have helped me to write *Whatever You Say, Say Nothing*. Anyone with an interest in the history of Ireland in the twentieth century owes a huge debt to Tim Pat Coogan. His books are gossipy and partial but unfailingly entertaining and informative. *Easter 1916*, *Ireland in the Twentieth Century* and *Michael Collins* can all be recommended. Peter Hart's *Mick* provides a healthy counterbalance to Coogan's somewhat hagiographical approach to Collins. Clair Wills's *Dublin 1916: the Siege of the GPO* is wonderfully evocative, as is Annie Ryan's *Witnesses*. Michael T. Foy's *Michael Collins's Intelligence War* was a treasure trove of information, while Joseph E.A. Connell's encyclopaedic *Dublin In Rebellion* was never off my desk. In film, Neil Jordan's *Michael Collins* is sentimental and highly inaccurate, but at least had the merit of putting the other side of the Irish question to a British audience; Ken Loach's *The Wind That Shakes the Barley* is more honest, and better drama. Sebastian Barry's *A Long Long Way Down* and Roddy Doyle's *A Star Called Henry* are both superb fictional recreations of the period. I here confess to bringing forward two dates: Aisling's home town of Clifden was burnt down by the Black and Tans, but not until the summer of 1921; similarly, Patrick's squad of gunmen did not move into their premises above the carpenter's shop until early 1921.

Thanks to the immensely talented Hafsa Bell for the beautiful cover. Thanks to Mike Willdridge, artist, former British Army officer and cousin of the Big Fella himself, for taking me to Collins's home town of Clonakilty, thereby igniting my enduring love for all things Irish. Thanks to Sarah Bower and all at TLC for making *Whatever You Say* a better book. Thanks to Annette Crosland and Bill Goodall at A for Authors for tireless and loyal support and encouragement. Thanks to Tara Hanley, Claire Vickers, Lucy Wallace and dozens of sixth formers for accompanying me on annual school trips to Dublin, thereby helping to imprint the streets and the history of that magnificent city on my brain. Thanks, above all, before all, and at the end of it all, to Jean and Alice, for letting me plaster the walls of the spare room with maps of Dublin and photos of IRA gunmen, for putting up with the tapping of the keyboard before dawn, and for being the very rock and stone of my life. 'War's annals will cloud into night / Ere their story die.'

Julian Bell
London
October 2015

6817211R00210

Printed in Germany
by Amazon Distribution
GmbH, Leipzig